"So you are leav

"I'm apologizing to you—belatedly—over jumping to the conclusion that you upset Melanie the other night."

Ben turned back toward Emily then, his brow furrowed as if he'd forgotten what she was talking about.

"I thought you made her cry," she reminded him.

"Why?" he asked.

She sighed. "Because I've seen you make other girls cry."

He sucked in a breath with alarm. "Who? Who did I make cry?"

She shook her head. "I can't break confidences..." Emily realized now that she was the one who hadn't moved on, who wouldn't let herself forget Ben's reputation and how he'd hurt her friends. She wished that was just out of loyalty to them, but she knew there was more to it—just as there was more to Ben Haven than she'd realized.

Her breath caught, trapped in her lungs, and as she gazed up at him, her pulse quickened then raced.

And just like that, Emily could feel herself falling...

Dear Reader,

Welcome back to Willow Creek, Wyoming! I hope you enjoyed your first trip here in *A Rancher's Promise*. But it's okay if you haven't read that first book in my new Heartwarming series, Bachelor Cowboys. You can quickly catch up with everything that's been happening in Willow Creek.

More tragedy befell the Haven family, leaving three little boys orphaned. Don't worry, their great-grandmother, Sadie Haven, has a plan to help those boys, and her whole family, recover from their loss. She's doing some matchmaking, and as you'll soon find out, Sadie is a force to be reckoned with—but if anyone's up to the task of taking on Sadie, it's her grandson Ben Haven, the current cowboy mayor of Willow Creek.

Ben's onto Sadie's matchmaking plan, and he intends to turn the tables on her. It's more likely that his widowed grandmother would fall in love with her old nemesis than his nephews' beautiful teacher, Emily Trent, would ever fall for him. Emily's already given her heart to the little boys and has no intention of risking it on him. But Sadie's still a force to be reckoned with, even if her plans don't always go the way she intended...

Happy reading!

Lisa Childs

HEARTWARMING

The Cowboy's Unlikely Match

Lisa Childs

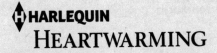

HARLEQUIN®

HEARTWARMING™

ISBN-13: 978-1-335-42666-6

The Cowboy's Unlikely Match

Recycling programs
for this product may
not exist in your area.

For questions and comments about the quality of this book,
please contact us at CustomerService@Harlequin.com.

Harlequin Enterprises ULC
22 Adelaide St. West, 41st Floor
Toronto, Ontario M5H 4E3, Canada
www.Harlequin.com

Printed in U.S.A.

Ever since **Lisa Childs** read her first romance novel (a Harlequin story, of course) at age eleven, all she wanted was to be a romance writer. With over seventy novels published with Harlequin, Lisa is living her dream. She is an award-winning, bestselling romance author. She loves to hear from readers, who can contact her on Facebook or through her website, lisachilds.com.

Books by Lisa Childs

Harlequin Heartwarming

Bachelor Cowboys

A Rancher's Promise

Harlequin Romantic Suspense

Bachelor Bodyguards

His Christmas Assignment
Bodyguard Daddy
Bodyguard's Baby Surprise
Beauty and the Bodyguard
Nanny Bodyguard
Single Mom's Bodyguard
In the Bodyguard's Arms
Soldier Bodyguard
Guarding His Witness
Evidence of Attraction
Boyfriend Bodyguard
Close Quarters with the Bodyguard

Visit the Author Profile page
at Harlequin.com for more titles.

For the strongest woman I know and admire and love, my mother-in-law, Sharon Ahearne, who deals with all things—even the loss of the love of her life—with grace and more concern for everyone else than herself. She's a truly selfless and special person.

CHAPTER ONE

SUNLIGHT STREAMED THROUGH the stained-glass windows, casting brightly colored shadows over the guests gathered inside the church, and over the groom standing at the altar, waiting for his bride to appear.

Ben Haven couldn't see his older brother's face from where he stood at the back of the church, but he imagined Jake was getting impatient. He'd waited twelve years to make Katie O'Brien his bride.

Ben couldn't imagine making anyone his bride. He didn't ever want to walk down the aisle. He hesitated now to make that trek just to join his brother. But his hesitation had less to do with the wedding than the memory of the last time he'd walked down this church aisle six weeks ago, when he'd helped carry out his brother Dale's casket.

The grief and pain of that day gripped him with such intensity that he froze for a moment...until the hand on his arm tightened and tugged. He turned his head toward the bridesmaid he was supposed to be escorting down the aisle. With her pale golden-blond hair and bright blue eyes, Emily Trent was definitely a head turner—especially in the blue dress she was wearing that left her shoulders bare. Her beauty distracted him for a moment from his pain, and he managed to flash her a smile.

She glared at him and, in an urgent whisper, hissed, "Get moving…" Then she turned her head away from him to focus on the front of the church.

And the groom?

Ben suspected, from the couple of times he'd overheard her singing Jake's praises, that the young teacher had a thing for his brother, so this day probably wasn't any easier for her than it was for him.

It was difficult for him because of where they were and what they'd done here last. Said goodbye to his brother and his brother's wife much too soon…

Ben drew in a shaky breath, pasted on a fake smile and started down the aisle with Emily. They didn't make it halfway down the white runner before a little boy darted out of the first pew and ran up to her. The dark-haired toddler lifted his arms toward her. As well as teaching his older nephews, Emily had become a nanny to the youngest one since Grandma had moved her and a few other women out to the ranch after Dale and Jenny's deaths.

Emily dropped Ben's arm and reached for the little boy, picking him up. The church guests chuckled and smiled as the three of them continued moving. Ben moved his hand to the small of Emily's back, but instead of guiding her, it seemed to make her walk faster, because she surged ahead and his hand slipped away. As he pulled it back to his side, his fingers tingled a bit, and he curled them into his palm.

Emily took her place on the bride's side with the little boy in her arms while Ben moved over to stand behind his brother's best man—Katie's son, five-year-old Caleb Morris.

If Dale had been alive, Ben was sure that Jake would have picked him to stand up with him. But Dale and his wife were gone, leaving behind three little boys. The toddler, Little Jake, had wrapped his arms tightly around Emily's neck, clinging to her. The other two, five-year-old Ian and seven-year-old Miller, waved at them from the front pew, where they were sitting with their great grandmother, Sadie Haven. All of the boys wore suits with little white Stetson hats except for Little Jake, who must have left his on his seat.

The maid of honor—or was it matron, since there was some speculation about whether or not Miller's physical therapist, Melanie Shepard, was married?—stood next to Emily. She, like everyone else, was turned toward the back of the church, where the next bridesmaid and groomsman started down the aisle—Ben's youngest brother, Baker, and the cook Grandma had hired, Taye Cooper.

Jake shifted and peered around them, obviously anxious to see his bride.

"No cold feet?" Ben whispered to him.

Like the little boys and Ben, Jake also wore a white Stetson. But the hat barely moved when Jake shook his head and grinned.

How could he have no doubts? No fears?

Because he was Big Jake Haven and just as fierce and fearless as their grandfather had been, the right person to have been named after him.

Caleb, Jake's soon-to-be stepson, turned toward Ben and peered up at him. "Are your feet cold?" he asked. A lock of blond hair slipped out beneath his white hat and fell across his blue eyes.

He looked more like Emily's kid than he did red-haired Katie's. But apparently he looked exactly like his father, another man who'd died too soon.

Ben nodded at the little boy. "Always..."

His feet would always be too cold to carry him to the altar to marry. After all the losses he'd endured, and the losses he'd watched others suffer, he had no desire to risk that kind of heartache.

But then the music changed, and everyone stood and peered down the aisle, where the bride had just appeared, holding her father's arm. Ben turned his attention from her to his brother, and the look he saw on his face...

Ben had never seen Jake look as happy as he did right then. Ever. Maybe the risk of heartache was worth it for Jake, for that kind of happiness.

It wasn't for Ben. He had vowed long ago to stay single forever.

It wasn't fair. But Emily had learned at a young age that life wasn't fair. So she shouldn't have been surprised that the best of the Haven brothers was the first to get married. What wasn't fair was that it was to someone else, but she couldn't be jealous of Katie. She'd been through so much herself that nobody deserved happiness more than she and Jake deserved it.

The people of Willow Creek laughed and smiled now as they enjoyed cake and ice cream in the community room off the church—not just with happiness for Jake and Katie, but with relief that something good was happening in a place that had last held a funeral. To Emily—and to Dale and Jenny's boys, the youngest of whom sat in her lap—it wasn't enough good. Losing the loving young couple so soon *really* wasn't fair—not at all.

That wasn't the only reason Emily wasn't laughing and smiling like everyone else, though. She was also too stricken with the injustice of how good Ben Haven looked in a suit.

Especially when Emily felt so frumpy in her hastily purchased dress.

After having waited twelve years to marry, Jake and Katie hadn't wanted to wait a moment longer. Since there was no waiting period for marriages in Wyoming, they'd obtained their license right away and had thrown together their ceremony within two days.

Katie's wedding party—which consisted of the latest hires at Ranch Haven: Emily; the physical therapist, Melanie Shepard and the cook, Taye Cooper—had had to find whatever dresses they could off the rack. And it showed…

Taye's was too tight and Emily's was too big—so big that it kept falling off her shoulders like a peasant blouse. If not for the fitted bodice above the empire waist, she might have lost the whole thing on her fast trek down the aisle with Ben. Well, it had been fast once he'd put his hand on her back. Then she hadn't been able to get away from him fast enough… From his touch, which had felt like a hot brand through the thin material of her dress.

Even though he'd grown up on the ranch, he wasn't a real cowboy like his brothers. He wasn't one to brand the cows or calves or whatever ranchers branded. He was a politician—though he often wore a cowboy hat with his suit, like today.

But his clothes fit him perfectly, had probably been tailor-made just for him, so that he looked more like a model for *GQ* magazine or a movie star than a small-town mayor. With his dark hair and eyes, chiseled features and long, lean build, he was *that* perfect—like he wasn't even real.

Emily suspected that he wasn't, that he was just as fake as some other people she'd known growing up, such as the ones who'd befriended her in school because they'd felt sorry for her—not because they'd actually respected or liked her. She'd known Ben too back then; she'd been a couple grades behind him. Ben Haven—all the Havens—had been popular because of their good looks and charm and intelligence and humor. But Ben had been notorious because of all the hearts he'd broken.

Emily herself had mopped up tears shed over him. Not her own tears. She wouldn't have been so stupid as to ever go out with him. But some of her friends had dated him for the one or two times he'd gone out with anyone before he lost interest in them.

A bowl of ice cream appeared on the table in front of her. She glanced up with a smile, expecting that it was probably nurturing Taye who'd brought it for her. But when she saw who stood beside her, her smile slipped away.

"What are you doing?" she asked Ben.

"Bringing you ice cream." He glanced at

the toddler asleep on her lap. "Doesn't look like you can move right now."

It would have been a sweet gesture if anyone else had done it. But from him…

He had to have an ulterior motive. She narrowed her eyes and studied his handsome face. "Why would you think to bring me anything?" she asked. "We just walked down the aisle together. We're not on a date."

He chuckled, although it had a bit of a nervous sound to it, and he reached for his tie, tugging at it slightly as if the blue silk was suddenly choking him. "'Walked down the aisle together.' You make it sound like we got married."

She laughed then—at the thought of the two of them ever getting together. "That would *never* happen."

"Oh, no, you've made it clear that I'm not the Haven brother you're interested in," he said, but from the slight grin on his face, he didn't seem too bothered about her lack of interest. "I figured since that brother just got married, you might want to drown your sorrows in a pint of ice cream." He picked up the bowl in his palm, acting as if it was a scale. "Might not be quite a pint…"

She glared at him now. "I don't have any

sorrows to drown," she assured him. "I'm very happy for Katie and Jake." She turned her attention to where the newly married couple stood near the decimated cake. Taye had made it, so Emily wasn't surprised there was barely any of the buttercream-frosted marble cake left. Katie and Jake hugged each other closely, their faces lit up with bright smiles. And she smiled herself.

Ben's breath audibly caught. And she glanced back to see if he was staring at the happy couple too. But he was staring at her, and with an expression so intense that she shivered.

"What?" she asked.

He shook his head. "Just... Now I get it..."

"What?" she asked again.

"You," he said. "I get you..."

She shook her head now and made clear what she thought she had earlier. "That's *never* going to happen."

"I'm not proposing," Ben said, and again there was a nervousness in his voice, in the smile he forced. "I just see what the boys see in you."

Being blonde and petite, she was used to men noticing her. But he hadn't said *men*. "Boys?"

He gestured at the toddler asleep on her lap. "The little guys. I see it…"

"Kid whisperer is what Taye calls me," she admitted.

He nodded. "I've heard that."

He would have seen it, had he spent much time at the ranch since she'd moved in, but he'd only visited his nephews a few times over the last six weeks, since the funeral. So much for helping out with the recently orphaned kids…

Emily shouldn't have been surprised, though. She'd known families who had acted like Ben Haven had, families who abandoned instead of helping. She'd had a family like that herself. After her mother died when Emily was six, she'd lived with her maternal grandparents. Soon after, they'd claimed they weren't young enough to raise a child and so they'd passed her on to an aunt, who'd passed her on to a cousin, until Emily had wound up in foster care. So that *family* wasn't her family anymore. She snorted softly with derision.

"What?" Ben asked. "What have I done that makes you dislike me so much? Have I offended or hurt you?"

She shook her head. "Not me personally…"

He narrowed his dark eyes and studied her face. "Someone you know..."

"A few someones back in high school," she admitted. "A few other ones more recently..."

Just a couple of years ago, she had listened to the sobs of a friend who had fallen hard for the politician when she'd been helping out on his campaign. Poor Maggie...

Maggie Standish desperately wanted a lasting relationship and the kind of love her parents had for each other. Because that was all she'd known, that love and security—the young woman was much too trusting.

Being too trusting would never be an issue for Emily. Maybe that was why, even though she had a lot of friends, none were particularly close to her. She was the one in whom other people confided, but she rarely confided in anyone.

"We went to high school together?" he asked, his eyes narrowing as if he doubted it.

She sucked in a breath at the fact he didn't even remember her. Willow Creek hadn't been that big a school, and she'd thought everyone had heard her sad story. About how nobody had wanted her, so she'd wound up living with one of her teachers.

"Wow," she said, "you are self-involved."

And he sucked in a breath now. "And you're self-righteous and judgmental."

He was lucky that Little Jake had fallen asleep on her lap, or she might have jumped up and dumped that bowl of melting ice cream over Ben Haven's handsome head.

Little Jake chose that moment, however, to jerk awake, and his chubby little hand upset the bowl, knocking it onto the floor next to Emily. The melted dessert splashed up and over her leg, sliding down her calf to pool in her shoe. It was cold against her skin, so cold that she yelped and jumped up with the sleepy toddler clasped in her arms. Her foot slid inside her wet pump, making her so unsteady that she might have fallen had strong arms not caught her and Little Jake.

If not for holding on to the toddler, she would have *rather* fallen on the floor than where she was now—in Ben's arms, pressed close to his long, lean, muscular body. Her pulse was racing, her heart pounding furiously, her skin tingling.

No.

Life wasn't fair at all.

CHAPTER TWO

"MISS TRENT, MISS TRENT!" Caleb Morris called out with alarm as he squeezed between Ben and Emily. "Are you all right?"

Ben eased his grip on the blonde teacher, and she tugged free of his hold on her bare shoulders. The five-year-old best man's concern reminded Ben of why he'd grabbed her. Because she'd been slipping...

But once he'd grabbed her, his mind had slipped; he hadn't been able to think, only to feel—so many emotions and so much attraction. Like when she'd smiled earlier...

He'd realized the first time he'd met her that she was pretty; he hadn't realized how beautiful she was until that moment, until she'd looked at him with something other than her usual disdain. Apparently he must have met her before the day she'd moved into the ranch, though.

She'd gone to school with him?

He couldn't remember her, and that must

have been insulting. He felt a flash of regret over that, and over what he'd said to her about her self-righteousness. He usually didn't get so defensive, but something about her…

Unsettled him.

"Are you all right, Miss Trent?" Caleb asked again.

She nodded and uttered a shaky breath. "Yes, ice cream spilled on my leg and got into my shoe and I started slipping in it."

"Then it was good Mr. Ben was here to stop you from falling," the little boy said.

"Yes…" Emily murmured, but she didn't sound as convinced as Caleb was.

Then the little boy giggled and shot a look at Ben. "Now Miss Trent has cold feet too, like you."

Ben chuckled. "She certainly does. At least one."

He'd watched the glob of melting ice cream hit her leg and slide down the toned muscle of her calf and into her shoe. And for a moment he'd been envious of the ice cream.

Her brow lowered as she stared at the two of them laughing at her. Then a giggle spilled out of Little Jake too, and her lips curved into a smile.

If she felt at all like Ben did, then any

sound the toddler made was welcome. He used to babble all the time before the car accident that had claimed his parents' lives and injured his brothers.

"I need to go clean up," Emily said, and she handed the toddler to Ben.

The little boy slung one arm around his shoulder and grasped his tie with the other, tugging on it hard enough that it tightened. And Ben gasped for breath.

Emily laughed then before turning and walking away from them, leaving them all to stare after her.

Caleb murmured with puppy-love adoration, "She's so pretty..."

While Little Jake's grasp on Ben's tie slipped, and Ben was able to loosen it again, he wasn't able yet to draw a deep breath—not until Emily disappeared into the ladies' restroom. Then he managed to pull enough oxygen into his lungs that he no longer felt so light-headed, so unsteady—nearly as unsteady as she'd been with ice cream in her shoe.

"Don't you think she's pretty?" Caleb asked him.

He could not lie; he could only nod and murmur, "Very..."

Had she always been pretty or had she had

an awkward phase in her teens? Was that why he couldn't remember her? Or had he been—and still was—as self-involved as she'd accused him of being?

Ben shrugged off the thought and focused on the boys. "So, little men, did you get enough cake?"

Caleb shook his head. "I can never get enough of Miss Taye's baked stuff, but the cake's pretty much all gone now. I came over here to get you, Mr. Ben."

"Uncle Ben," Ben automatically reminded him. Caleb Morris was more than Big Jake's best man; he was his son now and Ben's nephew.

The little boy smiled broadly, revealing a couple of missing teeth. "Uncle Ben..."

"Why did you come over here to get me?" Ben asked with surprise. He'd figured the kid had just wanted to hang around the teacher he adored.

"Grandma Sadie wants you," Caleb said.

Ben groaned. So the old lady had enlisted her new grandson in her mission. She was going to be even more insufferable than usual since the first phase of her not-so-secret match-making mission had proved successful—Jake and Katie had just gotten hitched.

"I heard that," Grandma admonished him.

She must not have trusted Caleb to carry out her mission, or Ben hadn't reacted fast enough, because she'd already joined them at the table.

"What do you want, Grandma?" he asked, although he could have guessed. For him to spend more time at the ranch…

She seemed to forget that he had a whole town depending on him. And, better than most people, she should know how busy he was, since her father had served of mayor of Willow Creek longer than anyone else ever had, including the former mayor whom everybody called Old Man Lemmon. Well, everybody but Ben, who respected his deputy too much to call him that.

"Caleb and I need your help," she said.

Ben gave the kid a pitying look. She really had embraced the boy as one of her own, which meant that she was going to manipulate and manage his life as much as Caleb would let her. "What do *you* need?" he asked his nephew while ignoring his grandmother.

"Me and Grandma got Mommy and Daddy Jake a wedding present, but they—they don't want it," he said, his voice and his bottom lip trembling a bit.

Little Jake's bottom lip began to quiver too, and he murmured, "Cab…" The first word he'd spoken since the accident; the first time he'd said it had been a week ago. Ben hadn't heard it then, just been told that the toddler had talked. Ben was happy to hear it himself now. Little Jake's grasp on Ben's tie tightened.

He choked again before loosening the knot once more. After clearing his suddenly strained throat, he asked, "Why won't they take it?" Ben knew how much Katie and Jake loved the little boy; he couldn't imagine that they would do anything that would hurt his feelings.

"They say they can't leave us," Caleb replied.

Ben's brow furrowed with confusion. "Why would they leave you?"

"To go on a trip for their honeymoon," Caleb said.

Knowing the little boy wouldn't have thought of gifting his mom and stepdad with a honeymoon, Ben turned back to his conniving grandmother and studied her with narrowed eyes. She widened her dark eyes in her slightly wrinkled face and managed to look innocent—or maybe that was the pure white of the hair that framed her face. She must have worn heels today because her dark eyes were level with his, and he was six-three.

"What are you scheming now?" he asked. The same question he and his brothers had been asking her and each other for the last six weeks—ever since she'd hired beautiful single women to help care for her great grandsons.

"Jake and Katie never had the chance to live out the plans they made together back in high school," Sadie said. "They never got to travel. So Caleb and I gifted them with a trip for their honeymoon."

"But they don't want to leave me and the other boys and the ranch," Caleb said.

Ben turned back toward the boy and studied his little face as intently as he'd studied his grandmother's. That bottom lip was trembling again, but was that because they wouldn't accept the gift, or the fear that they actually would? "You would really be okay with them leaving?" he asked.

Caleb had lost his dad a year ago; Ben's nephews had lost their parents two months ago. More parental figures leaving these kids probably wouldn't be healthy for any of them.

"It's only for two weeks," Caleb said, "and I know that they'll be back."

Sadie uttered a hopeless-sounding sigh. "They can't come back if they won't go…"

Ben had a pretty good idea why they'd refused, but he asked, anyway. "Why won't they go?"

"The boys, the ranch…" She lowered her shoulders as if she was carrying the burden. "It's all been Jake's responsibility—his and his alone…"

Ben flinched, but he couldn't deny it. It had been, and for so many years Jake had sacrificed his happiness—and his love for Katie—because of all those responsibilities. When their grandfather had died twelve years ago, Jake had quit college and broken up with Katie. Just as he had insisted that Ben stay at the college he'd just started attending on scholarship, Jake hadn't wanted Katie to give up anything to help him with the ranch and his younger brothers. Ben and his brothers had grown up, but now Jake had assumed the primary responsibility for their nephews.

Ben handed the toddler to his grandmother, and assured her and his new nephew, "I'll take care of this."

He didn't know exactly how he was going to convince his big brother to accept the honeymoon trip, but he was going to make sure

Jake didn't make any more sacrifices, even if Ben had to make some himself.

"YOU'RE SUPPOSED TO put the ice cream in a bowl," Taye Cooper remarked with a teasing smile. "Or better yet, your mouth."

Emily glanced up from the bathroom sink, where she was washing out her shoe, and met Taye's gaze in the mirror. "Funny…"

"Maybe that's how you stay so thin," Taye remarked. "You put all your food in your shoe."

"I wouldn't waste your food like that," Emily assured the talented chef/baker. But she glanced at Taye again with concern that she might have heard a tinge of vulnerability. Taye was tall and curvy, and with her pale blue eyes and thick golden hair, the younger woman was also drop-dead gorgeous.

Ben Haven hadn't remembered Emily when they'd gone to school together—maybe she'd been unremarkable back then.

She used to feel like everyone was staring at her in high school—with pity, knowing she was the poor little orphan that Mrs. Rademacher was letting live with her. She'd hated then that everyone had known her private business and had spread around her sad story.

But maybe thinking that everybody in

school had to have known who she was made her as self-involved as she'd accused Ben of being. He'd been a couple of grades ahead of her, and they hadn't had any classes together. So she'd actually only seen him in the halls, flirting with her friends. But she remembered him.

Ben Haven was one of those people who was impossible not to notice or remember. He was that good-looking.

"It's not fair," Emily murmured again.

"It's just a shoe," Taye told her. "Though I think you've destroyed it with all that water."

Emily groaned as she shut off the faucet. Now the silver pump wasn't just sticky but saturated as well. "I wasn't talking about the shoe."

She was talking—thinking—about Ben Haven entirely too often. Probably just because he irritated her so much. That had to be the only reason.

"So then you heard," Taye remarked.

"Heard what?"

"About the honeymoon."

"Katie and Jake are taking a honeymoon?" Maybe she shouldn't have been surprised, with as fast as they'd managed to plan a wedding, that they had planned a trip as well.

"No," Taye said with a sigh. "Sadie and Caleb gifted them with a two-week trip to San Francisco and the Hawaiian Islands, but Jake and Katie told them they couldn't accept it."

Emily wasn't surprised—not with how busy Jake was at the ranch and with the boys. "I understand why they had to turn it down." But she felt badly for them and for Caleb, who'd probably been disappointed.

Or maybe not. Given how much the boy loved his mother and new stepfather, he might not have been happy at the thought of them leaving him even if it was just for two weeks.

"They deserve to spend some time alone together," Taye persisted, "some time to connect as a newly married couple."

Emily knew their story even better than Taye did, since she was older and had been in school with them for a couple of years. She remembered how besotted they'd been with each other in high school, and how they'd split during college when Jake took over the ranch.

Emily wasn't happy that Katie and Jake couldn't honeymoon, but she couldn't help but think it was for the best for the youngest Haven boys. Almost reluctantly she admitted, "I'm not sure how the little guys would handle it if Big Jake wasn't around."

"As long as you're around, I think they'd be fine," Taye said. "You're the kid whisperer."

Emily's shoulders slumped slightly with the weight of that title. Sure, she was helping the boys, but she wasn't certain she was doing enough. Since the accident, Little Jake still had nightmares and barely spoke, and Ian's short-term memory loss from the concussion wasn't improving much. And Miller, the seven-year-old, was so unhappy, and nobody knew if it was because of the heavy cast on his broken leg or the loss of his parents. Probably both.

Emily also didn't know how much longer she could stay at the ranch. She had a life of her own, a job that she might lose if she didn't return to it.

It was going to be as hard on her to leave the kids as it would be on them when she left. But she—and her boss—had only agreed to a temporary leave from the school in town. When teachers had to report back later this summer to plan for the upcoming school year, she would need to be there as well. That wasn't that many weeks away.

"Are you okay?" Taye asked with concern.

Emily nodded. "Of course. I just feel badly for Katie and Jake. It would have been nice for them to have that honeymoon."

"Maybe if you assure them that we'll take care of the boys for them," Taye suggested.

"Of course we would take care of the boys for them," Emily said. "But it's not just the boys that Jake is responsible for…"

"It's the ranch too," another woman finished when Emily trailed off. Melanie Shepard pushed open the door to a stall and joined them at the sink. She washed her hands thoroughly before drying them on one of the folded towels.

"I can't help with the ranch," Emily said. Despite growing up in Wyoming, she'd never learned to ride. She'd never actually been on a ranch until Sadie Haven had asked her to move to hers to help with the boys.

Taye shook her head. "Me neither."

Melanie's teeth nipped her bottom lip briefly before she murmured, "I know someone who could…"

"Who?" Emily asked.

"It doesn't matter." She shook her head. "He obviously has no intention of helping."

And Emily wondered what and whom the physical therapist was talking about.

Before she could ask, Taye addressed her again. "I'm surprised you're not going off like you usually do over how Ben could help but doesn't."

Emily shrugged. "What good would it do? Like Melanie said, if someone hasn't stepped up to help yet, they're probably never going to…"

Melanie's pretty face paled and she grabbed the edge of the sink.

Concern shot through Emily and must have Taye too, because she cupped the physical therapist's shoulder and urgently asked, "Are you okay?"

Melanie nodded. "Yes, just feeling bad for Katie and Jake."

And maybe a little bit for herself as well, Emily suspected. Melanie was shy and hadn't shared much with her and Taye, but she and Katie had gotten close—close enough that the bride had chosen her as matron of honor.

Melanie didn't wear a ring, but she'd made a few remarks about being married. Obviously, it wasn't a happy marriage since she never spoke about her husband and hadn't seen him since arriving at the ranch, so this day had probably brought back all kinds of feelings for her.

Strangely enough, it had brought out feelings in Emily she hadn't let herself feel for a while either.

When Ben had held her, to stop her from falling, she'd felt something she'd thought she was too smart to ever feel for him. Her pulse had pounded with it, her skin had tingled with it...

Attraction.

And after comforting the teenage girls all those years ago, and a woman who'd cried over him, Emily knew all too well where an attraction to Ben Haven led.

To heartbreak...

CHAPTER THREE

BEFORE TALKING TO Jake and Katie, Ben sought out his youngest brother, Baker. He found Baker standing alone outside the church. Ever since Dale and Jenny's deaths, Baker had been nearly as quiet as Little Jake and as unhappy as Miller. Baker didn't talk as often as he used to, and Ben had rarely seen him smile over the past several weeks. In his dual role as a paramedic and a firefighter, Baker had been the first on the scene of their brother's accident, and he didn't seem to have fully recovered from what he'd seen.

Ben couldn't imagine, and never wanted to imagine, what that had been. But right now he couldn't coddle his baby brother like he probably should; he needed Baker's help. "Come with me," he said, snagging his arm to drag him back into the community room.

"What...? Why?" Baker murmured, but he stumbled along behind Ben.

Focused on finding the bride and groom,

Ben scanned the guests. The only one he really noticed was Emily as she stepped out of the restroom. Other women were with her, but she was the one he noticed. How had he missed her in high school?

He shook his head, disgusted that once again, by ruminating on his past, he was proving her accusation true of being self-involved. Right now he intended to be the exact opposite of that, so he dragged his attention from Emily and sought out Katie and Jake instead.

Like Baker, Jake was the kind of man who preferred the quiet of solitude over company and the noise of crowds. But that wasn't new for Jake; he'd been that way the last dozen years. Since he'd given up Katie...

He wasn't giving her up now. Even while she chatted to their guests, his arm was looped around her waist, holding the beautiful redhead with flawless skin and deep green eyes close to his side. That was where she'd always belonged.

"What's going on?" Baker asked. "Have you sold me out to Grandma like you did Jake? Are you dragging me off to meet some woman?"

Ben snorted. He doubted that after recently

appearing in a firefighter calendar for charity, Baker needed any help finding women. He'd probably been outside the church hiding from them. "Don't worry about that now," Ben assured him. "I think she's still focused on Jake and Katie."

"Why?" Baker asked. "She got what she wanted. They're married now."

"But they're not going to celebrate it," Ben said.

Baker tugged free of him and gestured at the room still filled with people. "What's all this then?"

"This isn't enough," Ben insisted. "Grandma and Caleb are trying to give them a honeymoon trip as a gift—"

"Caleb?" Baker snorted now. "Yeah, right, like a five-year-old thinks about honeymoons."

Ben shrugged. "It doesn't matter if it was his idea or not to start with, but he's fully embraced it now." Remembering how the kid's bottom lip had quivered with the threat of tears brought back Ben's sense of urgency. "He wants to do this for his mommy and Daddy Jake."

Baker smiled—just slightly—but it was

more than he'd done in a while. "That's sweet. So what's the problem?"

"Jake and Katie won't go," Ben said. "*We* have to convince them."

He grabbed Baker's arm again and dragged him the last few steps to the couple's side. Predictably, Baker stayed quiet and Ben did all the talking. But when it mattered, when it counted, to reinforce Ben's promises, Baker nodded in agreement.

"You two deserve this," Ben said. "And it means so much to Caleb to give this to you—"

Jake chuckled. "Yeah, right. You know who's behind all of this." He glanced across the room to where their grandmother stood with the little boys. "And you know she probably has ulterior motives for doing this—likely for the two of you."

Baker paled, as if he was afraid of her.

But Ben shrugged. "Who cares what her motives are? I'm not going to be stupid enough to fall in with her plans like you did," he teased his older brother.

Instead of being offended, Jake laughed and tugged his new bride a little closer against his side. Katie smiled up at him, her eyes shining with love for her new husband.

"When Sadie's right, she's right," Jake said of their meddling grandmother.

"Shh…" Ben said. "Don't let her hear you say that. And if you repeat this, I'll deny it, but she is right about this, about the honeymoon. You need to go."

Jake shook his head. "I'd love to, but there's too much going on at the ranch."

"We'll handle it," Ben assured him again. "Between the two of us…"

"Neither of you can handle that bronco Dusty shipped here," Jake said, reminding them of the temperamental stallion their other brother had sent to the ranch.

"Dusty should be here," Baker agreed. "Being the rodeo rider, he could handle the ranch better than we can."

"I'll call him," Ben said. "I'll get Dusty to come back."

Dusty, Dale's twin, had taken off immediately following the funeral six weeks ago. He hadn't even joined the others in the community room for the luncheon afterward. Just like their mother. She'd taken off right after their father's funeral almost twenty years ago. Dusty had probably left for the same reason she had—to return to the rodeo. He hadn't stuck around long enough to give any of them an actual reason for leaving, just as their mother hadn't. And they hadn't seen her since. Ben figured that was because she hadn't really loved them.

Jake shook his head. "Dusty isn't coming home."

"He will. And in the meantime, we can handle the ranch. We grew up working on it too," Ben insisted. Even after growing up and moving away, they spent a lot of time helping out around the ranch. They weren't totally clueless. "And you've already looked at hiring a new ranch foreman. We can follow up on the candidates for you."

"I've narrowed down my search to a couple of viable options," Jake admitted.

"Give me the applications," Ben said. "And we'll try them out."

"What about Midnight?" Jake asked.

"I can take care of Midnight." It wasn't Ben or Baker who said that, but little Caleb, who'd walked up behind them.

Jake groaned. "That's the problem, Caleb. You think you can ride him, and you're going to get hurt if you try."

Katie was biting her bottom lip as if to hold in her tears and fears.

Jake continued, "He's been trained to not let anyone ride him."

But Dusty had; that was how he'd won the bronco off its owner. Instead of taking care of the animal himself, though, he'd shipped Midnight home to Jake. Yeah, Ben was totally calling Dusty when he got the chance, but that could wait until after he'd convinced Jake to go.

Ben guided Caleb to stand in front of him, and he put both his hands on his new nephew's small shoulders, then spoke for him. "Caleb will promise to stay out of harm's way the entire time you're gone. He won't get hurt. And he'll show me how to deal with the devil horse."

Caleb tipped back his head to stare up at Ben and nearly lost his white hat. "He's not a devil," he protested, but he was smiling. "And, yes, Mommy and Daddy Jake, I will be extra careful and not get a scratch on me the whole time you're gone."

The boy's parents looked highly skeptical. So Ben added, "And if something happened and he did, Uncle Paramedic Baker will patch him all up for you. We've got this, guys, really. We can handle the place for two weeks."

"Two weeks is a long time," Jake murmured, but he was clearly tempted.

Ben could hear the longing in his voice and see it in his face when his oldest brother looked down at his new bride. "If it seems too long or something happens, you can head back early," he pointed out.

"But nothing will happen," Caleb said. "We'll all be extra good while you're gone."

"What about when we get back?" Katie asked with a smile.

"We'll be extra, extra good then," Caleb promised.

The kid was a character. Ben was glad he was part of their family now; he'd already cheered up the other little boys—except maybe for Miller—so much. "See, everything will work out. No problem."

Then he realized that the kid wasn't the only one who'd snuck up behind him and Baker, when Grandma said, "So you'll move into Jake's room in the main house while they're gone."

Ben froze for a moment as panic gripped him. He hadn't actually considered, when trying to convince Jake and Katie to leave, that he would have to stay at the ranch. He figured he'd have to take some time away from city hall, but that he would be able to drive back and forth to the ranch every day.

"It's the only way," Jake told him. "Little Jake still gets up with nightmares, and even though Miller's getting his cast off in a couple of days, he still needs help getting around. And Ian…"

Pain gripped Ben's heart as he considered Ian's biggest problem, the concussion from the accident that had left him with short-term memory loss. So the five-year-old kept forgetting that his parents were dead and had to be reminded…over and over again. Ben swallowed the groan threatening to escape and forced himself to nod. "Then, yeah, of course, I'll move in. It's only two weeks. The deputy mayor can handle the town, and I'm sure the fire chief will give Baker some time off to help run the ranch."

"I'm not staying…" Baker murmured in protest.

Ben shot him a threatening look. Baker could not blow this now, when they were so close to convincing Jake and Katie. "I'm staying, so you can too," he told his younger brother before turning back to his oldest. "So it's all covered. You crazy newlyweds can go on your honeymoon."

Jake and Katie stared at each other for a long moment in which they must have somehow silently communicated, because then they both grinned and said, "Yes!"

Ben should have been relieved; this was what he'd wanted. For them to make up for some of the time together that all Jake's sacrifices had denied them.

But now that they'd agreed to leave, Ben's heart was beating fast and hard with anxiety. He couldn't help but wonder, despite his assurances that it wouldn't be a problem, that it would be a big problem—for him.

THE ROOM ERUPTED with applause, and Emily found herself clapping even though she had no idea what it was about. Jake's brothers, grandmother and new stepson had gathered around him and Katie. All of them were beaming, especially Caleb, so it must have been something good, maybe a toast to their future. Caleb turned then and ran across the room, weaving around the other guests, to get to her.

"Miss Trent! Miss Trent! They're taking it!" he exclaimed.

"What?"

"The gift me and Grandma Sadie got them. They're taking the honeymoon!"

Happy for him and for them, she smiled. "That's wonderful!" Even though doubts nagged at her.

Those doubts must have nagged at Taye too, because she asked, "Who's going to take care of the ranch?"

"Uncle Ben and Uncle Baker," Caleb said. "And they're going to try to get Uncle Dusty to come home to help out with Midnight."

A gasp slipped out of Melanie, who was beside Taye, and all the color drained from her face. "Dusty's coming home?"

Emily snorted. "I doubt that's going to happen. Dusty barely stayed away from the rodeo long enough to bury his twin, and he didn't even bother to return for his oldest brother's wedding. There's no way he's going to come back for Jake's honeymoon."

"I can take care of Midnight then," Caleb said.

Emily shook her head. "No, you can't. You will stay away from that bronco."

Usually Caleb obeyed her, but this time he shook his head. "No, Uncle Ben said he needs my help with it. And guess what, Miss Trent?"

Her heart pounded a little faster. Maybe it was just because she could see how much more was going to fall on her shoulders when Jake was gone. Or maybe it was because she had an inkling what Caleb was going to say even before she asked… "What?"

"You're not going to guess?" he asked, his mouth tugging into a slight frown of disappointment.

She closed her eyes as if she was searching her mind for answers and replied, "You've really been eating all those carrots you bring out to the barn…"

He giggled. "No. It's not about me."

"Then who's it about?" she asked.

"Uncle Ben."

That had been her inkling, the one that had produced a strange fluttering feeling in the pit of her stomach. "What about him?"

"He's moving into the ranch with us!" Caleb exclaimed. "Isn't that cool?"

The little boy was obviously excited to get to know his new uncle better. But Emily already knew Ben Haven better than she wanted to; she knew he wasn't to be trusted around anyone's heart. Big or little…

SOMETIMES SADIE HAVEN's family treated her like she was the Grinch who stole Christmas, so maybe it was no coincidence that her heart felt as if it was swelling now to more than its regular size. So much love filled it…

Filled her. For her family…

That was why she did everything she did, and this wedding was the culmination and celebration of the first phase of her plan. She gazed around the community room at her grandsons and great-grandsons, and the women she'd hired to help out who had become the girls she'd never had. Well, she'd had one, but for far too short a time.

Jenny. Sweet Jenny…

Sadie blinked against the sudden sting of tears. Her granddaughter-in-law would have loved this even more than Sadie did; she would have loved seeing Katie and Jake reunited and married.

"You getting choked up?" a deep voice asked skeptically. "I'm surprised you're not doing that whole evil-laugh thing at how well your scheme worked out."

Her tears dried as a smile tugged at her lips. She turned toward her eldest grandson. "You should be thanking me."

He nodded. "I should. And I am very grateful to you for bringing Katie and Caleb out to the ranch. I can't imagine my life without them now. A future that doesn't include them.

I do thank you for that, Grandma." He leaned down and kissed her cheek.

Big Jake was the only one of her grandsons who had to lean down to kiss her when she was wearing her boots. He was as big as his grandfather had been, and as strong and stubborn. Fortunately, in this case, with Katie and Caleb, his heart had overruled his stubbornness and propensity for self-sacrifice. He'd finally claimed what he wanted—a life and family of his own.

She narrowed her eyes as she peered up into eyes as dark as her own. "Why do I sense a *but* in there somewhere?"

He grinned now. "Because I'm not sure you know what you're doing, sending me and Katie off on this honeymoon." He gestured at his brothers. Baker was already heading back outside while Ben was standing on the other side of the church community room in a deep conversation with that old fool Lemmon. "They've promised to help out before."

She felt a little pang of uncertainty that they would follow through on their promise, but she pushed aside the doubt. "They will step up this time," she said. "Because you won't be here like you always were, they won't have a choice."

"And if you're wrong?" Jake asked. "You're sending me and Katie across the country. We won't be able to return that fast."

"I know." That was what she was counting on; that the couple would get the time alone they needed and that her other grandsons would have to spend more time at the ranch.

"It might all fall on you, you know," he warned her.

In the crowd, she focused on those special young women in their mismatched blue dresses. "No, it won't," she said. "Not anymore. Emily and Taye and Melanie will take care of the boys."

"That is the first priority," Jake agreed. "But what about the ranch?"

"Your grandfather and I helped build that ranch into what it is today," Sadie reminded him. "I won't let anything happen to it while you're gone."

It was Jake's baby as much as it was hers. He'd given up so much for it. Too much. And so had she…

A husband.

A son.

And more. But, as she always did, she stopped herself from thinking about what else she'd lost. So much more than her grandsons even knew…

She blinked against the sudden sting of tears and focused on her oldest grandson again, reaching up to pat his cheek. "Don't worry. You know the ranch is in their blood too." No matter how much Baker might deny it. "They'll step up. They'll take care of it."

"That's not your only plan for them, though," Jake said knowingly. "They might not disappoint you with the ranch, but none of my brothers is ready to do what I just did."

"Were you ready a month and a half ago?" she asked Jake. "Did you think then that you would be getting married now?"

He released a shaky breath. "No. I thought it was impossible."

"So there you go…" She smiled in anticipation of the next wedding. "Nothing's impossible."

"But you only have two weeks," Jake said. "Two weeks before we're back from our honeymoon. If we're not called back sooner than that…"

"You won't be," she said with certainty… except for that one little annoying seed of doubt. But surely if the stubbornest of her grandsons had fallen in with her master plan, the others would not need as much time. "And you don't know—they might even stay after you return."

Jake shook his head. "Their jobs are in town, Grandma. Ben's the mayor. Baker has to be close to the fire station. You might pull off two weeks, but that's all the time you're going to have."

She drew in a deep breath, bracing herself, before she nodded and said, "Then it will have to be enough."

CHAPTER FOUR

ONCE THE SOUND of applause died down, Baker had slipped out of the community room again and Ben had sought out his deputy mayor. Ben had been surprised to see his former boss and the current deputy mayor at the wedding. Lemar "Lem" Lemmon wasn't Grandma's favorite person. They'd been rivals since they were in elementary school together, competing for grades and other achievements. Katie had probably invited him. Lem's son, Bob, had recently joined her accounting practice in town and was going to help with the ranch bookkeeping. Fortunately, that was one thing that Ben wouldn't have to deal with while she and Jake were gone.

He would have helped out earlier, after the accident, but Grandma had insisted that he had enough on his plate with being mayor and handling his grandmother's properties in town. Of course, it had been her plan to bring in Katie, who'd already been doing the ranch taxes, to handle the daily ranch accounting of expenses and billing and payroll, so that she and Jake would reconnect and fall in love.

"Hey, Lem," Ben greeted the older man, who had scraped the spatula of all that was left of the decadently delicious cake Taye had baked.

Everybody had called the former mayor Old Man Lemmon for as long as Ben could remember, probably because for as long as Ben could remember the guy's hair—including his bushy mustache and beard—had been white. Cake crumbs and frosting littered the beard, and when the short man looked up at him, there was a smudge of yellow frosting on the tip of his long nose. "Hey, Ben. It's wonderful to have a happy occasion here again."

"Yes, it is," Ben heartily agreed. Then he pointed to the frosting and added, "You got a little something there."

Lem swiped his finger over the end of his nose. Instead of being embarrassed, he chuckled. "Good stuff. Good stuff. Your grandma knew what she was doing hiring that Cooper gal away from the bakery—though Mrs. Campbell will probably never forgive her for it. I'm not sure I will either. I miss the blueberry muffins she used to make."

"Me too," Ben said. At least that was one

perk of staying at the ranch for the next two weeks—Taye's cooking. And the other...

His gaze traveled from the deputy mayor in his wrinkled suit over to Emily Trent, who was tugging up one sleeve of her dress to cover a bare shoulder. Little Jake covered the other one with his head as he clung to her. The toddler had stopped talking, but that in no way reflected on his intelligence. The little boy was incredibly smart. He knew to hang on to the prettiest woman in the room.

"Uh, Lem, I probably should have asked you first about this," Ben admitted. "But I just agreed to help out at the ranch while Jake and Katie are gone on their honeymoon for the next two weeks."

Lem's pale blue eyes widened with surprise. "Jake's taking a honeymoon? I'm surprised that he would leave the ranch so soon after losing Dale and Jenny."

"It wasn't exactly his idea," Ben said. "Grandma came up with it and enlisted her new great-grandson, Caleb, to make sure that Katie and Jake accepted their wedding gift of a trip."

Lem's eyes widened even more. "A gift? From your grandmother? What strings are attached?"

Strings…

Ben sometimes wondered if Grandma had attached strings to all of them at birth and played them like marionettes. But then Jake would never have broken up with Katie twelve years ago, and Dusty would still be at the ranch. And Dale and Jenny…

He flinched at the pang in his heart and almost wished that she did control them. If so, she would have made certain that tragedy had never happened. Even she couldn't control the cruel twists of fate that had affected the Haven family.

"There are no strings for Jake and Katie," Ben said. "The strings are for me and Baker. We have to take Jake's place at the ranch. I have to stay in the house." And if he had to, he was going to make certain that Baker stayed too, despite that he was already protesting.

Lem chuckled.

"What?" Ben asked, wondering at the older man's amusement.

"Sadie's up to something, huh?" Lem remarked.

Ben sighed. "Probably." He glanced over at her, and she was smiling broadly, looking very pleased with herself. With good reason in this case. Jake and Katie were finally married. "But if it's matchmaking me or Dusty or Baker with anyone—" like those young women she'd hired "—she's going to be disappointed."

Lem laughed. "I don't know, Ben. I'd be careful if I were you. Sadie March Haven usually gets what Sadie March Haven wants."

Not everything she wanted, or she wouldn't have lost her son and her husband and now her grandson and granddaughter-in-law. No. Even Sadie March Haven didn't get everything she wanted.

"It doesn't matter," Ben said. "Jake and Katie deserve this, so I offered to stay out at the ranch for the time they're going to be gone. Is that okay with you?"

"You're the boss now, Ben," Lem reminded him. "I work for you. Heck, I think I was working for you back when you were my deputy mayor. You're a lot like your grandmother."

Ben grimaced. Jake had recently said the same thing to him, had called him a manipulator, just as Sadie had. While he had occasionally talked people into doing things he wanted, like convincing Lem to serve as deputy mayor to quell the townspeople's concerns that Ben didn't have enough experience, he always had the best of intentions. He'd known what he could achieve for the town, how his vision could revitalize it and help it thrive for the local business owners, how it could attract new businesses and industries and even tourists.

He had so many new projects in the works for sprucing up the park, for fixing the roads, for adding a shopping center; now was not the best time for him to be away from city hall. Not when he was so close to bringing the town back to its full potential. Not when he was so close to fulfilling the promises his great-grandfather had made to his constituents. They were the same promises Ben had made to his. "So you don't mind picking up my slack for a couple of weeks?" he asked his deputy.

"You don't leave any slack," Lemmon assured him. "You're a good mayor, Ben."

He hoped to be the kind of mayor his great-grandfather had been, the man for whom he'd been named. Benjamin March had been legendary for how the town had grown and prospered under his leadership; because of his success, he had served the longest as mayor of Willow Creek, Wyoming. But he'd had so many more plans for the town, like the shopping centers and factories, that Ben intended to see come to fruition.

"I might be a good mayor, but I haven't always been a good brother or uncle," Ben admitted ruefully. "Especially when they've needed me most."

He'd always thought Dusty was the most like their mother, but now he was worried that he might be more like her than he'd realized. Ben had only been eleven when his dad died in a ranching accident and his mother had taken off right after, so he didn't remember either of them that well. He glanced across the room at his nephews, who were gathered around Emily Trent like flies to honey.

Miller, Ian and Little Jake were all younger than he'd been. Would they remember Dale and Jenny? He and his brothers had to make certain that they did, that the boys knew how special their parents had been. Tears stung his eyes, but he blinked them back.

Lem reached out and squeezed Ben's arm. "Give yourself a break. It's not easy to lose people you love."

Like the Havens, the Lemmons had suffered some recent losses. Late last year Lem's daughter-in-law had died, and a few years before that Lem had lost his own wife to Alzheimer's. Ben had been his deputy mayor during her illness and had talked Lem out of resigning his office. Then he'd talked him into coming back as his deputy the next election cycle. Lem was like Sadie, which might be why they didn't get along. Like Grandma, Lem needed to be needed, and had to stay busy and involved to be happy and feel fulfilled.

Lem continued, "And everybody handles loss differently."

People like Ben's grandmother and Jake stepped up and assumed responsibility to fill the void, while people like Ben's mother and Dusty ran away from the responsibility and the grief. Had Ben been running these last several weeks? Had he been hiding out in town, using his mayoral responsibilities as an excuse not to grieve his brother and sister-in-law and help his nephews?

With Lem stepping in to help him, Ben had no excuse anymore. And with living at the ranch, he wouldn't be able to avoid his grief any longer.

He also wouldn't be able to avoid Emily Trent. Not that he wanted to...

He doubted she was happy that he was going to be around more because he felt her glare and glanced back at her to meet it. What had he done now? She'd made remarks before about Jake being the only responsible one of the Haven brothers. Albeit a little late, Ben was finally stepping up for the family.

Why was she still annoyed with him?

HE WON'T REALLY DO IT.

Emily was certain that Ben Haven would find a way to back out, just as he had backed out of every promise he'd made over the last several weeks to help out with the ranch and his nephews. Mayor Ben Haven wasn't moving away from his adoring constituents in Willow Creek. The town was the excuse he'd been using—that he was too busy to come by more often, and right now he was talking to the deputy mayor, probably getting the man to back up that excuse.

She would have been relieved if he got out of his promise to Jake…if Caleb and his parents didn't seem so excited about this honeymoon.

Melanie was hugging Katie now. "I'm so happy for you."

"Me too," Katie said with a wide smile.

Her happiness had Emily's lips curving into a smile as well—one that Ben must have interpreted as meant for him because he grinned at her. She scowled at him before looking away from him to focus on her friends. Before moving into the ranch with them, Emily hadn't known these women well—she hadn't known

Melanie at all—but they had become very important to her over the last several weeks. Bonded by the recent tragedy and their role in helping the survivors in the aftermath of it, Melanie, Katie and Taye had become Emily's very best friends. They hadn't become her friends because they pitied her, like her old high-school friends had. They'd become her friends because they all respected each other and had so many things in common, like the boys and their concern for them. And loss…

Emily suspected that she, Katie and the little boys weren't the only ones who'd lost someone that mattered to them. Melanie and Taye identified with the Haven orphans on some level too, for their own reasons. Emily knew why she did—because she'd been almost Miller's age when her single mom had died. And Katie…

Katie had lost her husband a year ago in a car accident. She really did deserve Jake Haven and that vacation with him.

When Melanie pulled back, Emily and Little Jake, who was usually attached to her, hugged Katie next. "Congratulations," she said.

"You told me that already," Katie reminded her.

"I really mean it," Emily said. "You just married a great guy."

Katie grinned. "I know. I'm so very lucky. I've had two awesome husbands."

Melanie blanched then. If she was married, apparently her husband was not in the "awesome" category. She seemed to confirm it when she murmured, "You are lucky. Some of us don't even get one."

"Some of us aren't looking for husbands," Taye Cooper remarked and bumped her shoulder against Emily's—the one that Little Jake was not clinging to. "Right?"

"Not now," Emily agreed. Not when she was so busy with the boys and worried about losing her job at the school. But someday she would like to have a family of her own...if she could ever find a man she could trust to keep his promises. One who wouldn't let her down, like the family members who'd promised Social Services that they would care for her, only to pass her along to another relative.

"Save yourself some heartache and don't ever get married," Melanie murmured. Then her face flushed and she told Katie, "I don't mean that you shouldn't have gotten married. Jake's a great guy."

"Maybe the last one," Emily said.

Katie laughed. "I'd like to think so, but I'm

sure there are at least a few more great men out there yet. One for each of you."

Emily groaned. "You're not going to start matchmaking now like your new grandmother-in-law, are you?"

Katie shrugged good-naturedly. "I have no complaints about Sadie's meddling."

"You wouldn't," Emily agreed. "Because you got the best of the Haven cowboy bachelors."

Katie laughed again, and she looked so very happy. "That I did. But Ben and Baker are great guys too. And Dusty…"

"What about Dusty?" Melanie was the one who asked… And yet she wasn't from Willow Creek and hadn't met the family before becoming Miller's physical therapist. Maybe she was curious about the absent brother who came up frequently in the Haven household.

Katie smiled with affection for the brother-in-law who hadn't even shown up for her wedding. Of course, they hadn't given him much notice, with just a couple of days passing between the proposal and the ceremony. "Well, Dusty always made it clear that the rodeo would be his only love," Katie said. "Too bad their mother hadn't done the same…"

Emily's brow furrowed then. "What about their mother? She loved the rodeo too?"

Katie nodded. "You don't know about her? About how she went back to the rodeo after their dad died?"

Shocked by the revelation, Emily sucked in a breath. "No. I didn't know about that."

She'd known Sadie's son died a while ago, and she'd just assumed the mom must have died with him in the accident, like how Dale and Jenny had died together. Now she felt a flash of shame over the hypocrisy of her accusing Ben of being self-involved when she'd clearly been the same.

"When did that happen?" Melanie asked before Emily could.

"Their dad died when Jake was thirteen, so nineteen years ago," Katie replied. Then she turned toward Emily and added, "But I think it might still affect them. So don't judge Ben too harshly."

Her displeasure over Ben's absence on the ranch lately was no secret among these women. He had accused her of being judgmental. Maybe he hadn't been wrong about her. But had she been wrong about him?

Katie glanced at her son, who was playing with Ian and Miller. They were swatting deflating balloons back and forth between them like beach balls. "Caleb's so excited about giving us this present."

Emily gestured toward Sadie, who was speaking with Jake. "She's the one who would have been the most disappointed if you hadn't agreed to go."

Katie smiled. "Probably."

"So you know that she has an ulterior motive for getting rid of you and Jake?" Emily asked.

Katie nodded. "Of course. She wants to get her grandsons to move back to the ranch."

"They're not going to do it," Emily insisted.

"Of course not," Katie agreed. "I doubt they'll get Dusty to come back at all. And once the two weeks are over, Ben will need to move back to town. He's the mayor, after all. And Baker, as a firefighter, has to live in town too."

"You really think they'll come through?" Emily asked.

Katie's mouth slid down into a slight frown of uncertainty. And Emily felt a pang of regret. But it was better that Katie face the facts now than be disappointed when the honeymoon plans fell apart later.

Emily herself had been let down so many

times when she was growing up. With people who'd promised to be there for her, but hadn't…

Hadn't claimed her.

Hadn't given her a permanent place to live or a home to call her own. And most of them had been family.

Now she knew that family wasn't about DNA; it was about who loved you, whom you could trust…

Even after learning more about Ben's childhood, Emily didn't trust him. Or maybe that was because of what she'd learned. Apparently it was in his genes to run from responsibility. Knowing it was in hers had made Emily even more determined to keep her promises and her commitments, like her commitment to the school where she taught, where the teacher who'd given her a permanent home had taught.

"They'll show up," Taye said with certainty, and she reached out to squeeze Katie's shoulder. "Don't worry. They won't disappoint you and Jake." The younger woman cast a pointed glance in Emily's direction. "They will be at the ranch the next two weeks. Katie and Jake have nothing to worry about."

Maybe not. Maybe the other Havens would finally start helping.

Emily nodded. "Sure, of course…"

Katie smiled at her. "Are you hoping that they don't show up?"

"Of course not," she replied. "I want them to fill in for you and Jake, and I don't care if they're around the ranch more." But she did. She cared about the little boys, and she didn't want anyone disappointing them.

Making promises that they shouldn't have made in the first place…

"Maybe you should," Katie said with a teasing smile. "Maybe you're the next one Sadie wants to make her granddaughter-in-law."

Emily gasped. "Don't even joke about that."

Taye laughed. "Why? Are you worried that if we talk about it, it might happen?"

"No," Emily said. "There's no chance of that."

CHAPTER FIVE

SUNDAY MORNING BEN was running late. After leaving the church Saturday evening, he'd gone into his office at City Hall and made a list of all his ongoing projects, which Lem would have to manage for him while Ben was at the ranch. But even after he'd left the office and headed back to his condo, he'd kept thinking of additional items to add. Poor Lem…

That to-do list had gotten longer and longer.

After going for a quick run, showering and packing a bag, Ben stopped at city hall again to put the two lists together. And to take care of a few more things he'd noticed on his desk.

He hadn't been stalling. Really.

But he hadn't been eager to head out to the ranch. So he stopped at Baker's apartment near the firehouse on his way out of town. His brother's truck was parked in the back lot. He hadn't left either, and when Baker opened the door to Ben's knock, he looked like he hadn't slept. Dark circles rimmed his topaz-colored eyes.

"Why are you still here?" Ben asked.

"Why are you here at all?" Baker responded.

Ben groaned. "C'mon, if I have to stay at the ranch for the next two weeks, so do you."

"It's not as easy for me to get time off work as it is for you," Baker pointed out. "I'm not the boss."

"No, I am," Ben agreed. "I'm kind of the boss of your boss, so do you want me to give him a call?" Ben pulled out his cell phone. "Because at the last budget meeting between city council, my office and the fire department, Captain Thomas brought up how he's been trying to get you to take some time off. I'm sure he'll have no problem giving you these next two weeks—"

Baker reached for Ben's cell and clasped his hand around it. Ben wouldn't release it, though. He didn't give up his phone for anyone—not even someone younger and a bit stronger than he was. Maybe he needed to work out more. But no matter if the firefighter had more muscles than he did, Ben held on tightly to his cell phone.

"You don't need to call him," Baker said.

"I stopped by the fire station after I left the wedding."

"You asked for the time off?"

Baker sighed and nodded. "And like you said, Cap was happy to give me the vacation." Clearly, that made one of them.

"Then why aren't you at the ranch yet?" Ben asked.

"Why aren't you?" Baker shot back at him.

Ben flinched. "I had to wrap up a couple of things at city hall."

Baker snorted. "Yeah, right…"

"Hey, Willow Creek doesn't run itself."

"No," Baker agreed. "Old Man Lemmon runs it with a lot of interference from Grandma."

Ben glared at his brother. Baker clearly had no idea how much Ben had had to step up when he'd been deputy mayor. But it had been necessary so that Lem could spend time with his wife before the Alzheimer's that had taken her memory had eventually claimed her life.

It was past time for Ben to step up again, to help out his family now, like Jake had always done. "Speaking of Grandma's interference, we need to get out to the ranch before she—"

The cell they were both still holding began to vibrate and ring with an incoming call.

Baker jerked his hand away from it. "That's probably her now. You jinxed us."

"You brought her up first." Ben held out the ringing phone to his younger brother.

Baker shook his head. "That's your cell. She's not calling *me*."

"That's just because she has me on speed dial," Ben grumbled.

Baker wasn't wrong about Grandma's meddling in running the town. From the time she was a little girl, she'd interfered with her dad's long tenure as mayor, then with Lem's and now his. She had an opinion on everything even though she was rarely affected, since the ranch was so far from town.

He groaned and accepted the call, putting her on speaker. "Yes, Grandma?"

"Where are you?" she asked. "You should have been at the ranch over an hour ago."

"We're on our way," Ben said with a pointed look at his younger brother.

"Our way?" she repeated incredulously. "Baker didn't back out."

Had she expected just Baker to back out, or for Ben to back out as well? Was that why she was calling?

"No," Ben said. "He didn't."

Baker groaned then and reached inside the

open door of his apartment. He lifted out a loaded-down duffel bag and pulled the door shut behind himself.

"Good," she said. "Katie and Jake are going to miss their flight if they don't leave soon for the airport."

"They haven't left yet?" Ben asked.

"No. Jake wanted to make sure the two of you actually showed up, and he has some things he wants to go over with you before they leave."

Ben groaned now. "The candidates for Dale's job…"

Baker's face paled.

"Jake and Katie need to leave soon, or they're going to miss their flight," Grandma said again.

"I'll call him on my way there," Ben offered. "They can take off right now."

Sadie pitched her voice lower and murmured, "He's not leaving until you get here."

Ben cursed and headed toward his black SUV, which he'd parked next to Baker's pickup. His big brother really didn't trust him to follow through. Maybe that was because Ben had promised before to help out with the boys and the ranch, but it was so hard.

It was so hard to be at the ranch, to be

around his nephews, without Dale and Jenny there. Without them laughing and teasing their kids and each other and Ben...

His heart ached from missing them, and when he was at Ranch Haven or around his nephews, that ache intensified. He sucked in a breath and braced himself. It was going to be a long two weeks.

It was a long drive to the ranch from town as well. Ben passed the time with a phone call to Jake and constant glances in his rearview mirror to make sure Baker didn't turn around and head back to Willow Creek.

Once he parked in front of the big two-story, cedar-sided house with the covered porch spanning the front of it, Baker's truck pulled up behind his SUV.

"I thought you were on the phone with him. You couldn't talk him into leaving?" the firefighter asked Ben when Jake and Katie stepped onto the porch to meet them. Jake held his namesake, Little Jake, in one arm, while Ian and Miller leaned against either side of him.

Ben shook his head. "You didn't have to wait for us," he told his older brother and new sister-in-law. "We're keeping our word."

Katie smiled at him. "Of course you are. I knew you would."

And he almost believed her. "Then why are you still here?"

"It's just hard to leave," she said, and she had one arm around her son, who was clinging to her side, while the other boys stuck close to Jake.

"Have you changed your mind?" Ben asked Caleb, almost hopefully. He'd worried that the kid would have second thoughts about his mother and new stepfather leaving him. Clearly, his nephews weren't that eager to let Uncle Jake go; he had been the adult they'd seen the most their entire lives, besides their parents and Sadie. Jake used to live in the foreman's cottage, though, until the accident. Then he'd moved into the main house to be closer and more available to the kids.

Unlike Ben and Baker, who'd stayed on the ranch for a couple of weeks and then moved back to town when Grandma had hired the women to live and work at the house. Jake had become the one Haven that Dale and Jenny's kids could count on, and now he was leaving them.

Ben felt a twinge of guilt that he'd let the ache of his own grief affect his ability to help the little Havens over the loss of their parents. "Baker and I are here now. We'll take care of everything."

His nephews didn't look that certain. They still clung to Jake, but Caleb pulled away from his mother and ran down the steps toward Ben. Feisty, Sadie's little Chihuahua, followed him, jumping around the boy's ankles and then around Ben's. "Uncle Ben, I knew you would come!"

Clearly, Caleb was the only one. His grandmother and Jake hadn't seemed to believe it. And now Emily Trent stepped onto the porch with the physical therapist and the cook, and her blue eyes were wide with surprise too.

"Of course I'm here," Ben said, as he ruffled the little boy's blond hair with one hand. "I told you I would be." He turned toward Jake and Katie again. "So you two can head to the airport."

"I'll drive you," Baker offered.

"In the pickup?" Jake asked. "You don't have a back seat and just buckets in the front." Then Jake grinned and said, "We can take Ben's SUV." He knew Ben didn't like anyone else driving his expensive vehicle. It had been a splurge for him.

Ben narrowed his eyes. "What? The honeymoon over already? You don't want to share a seat with your new bride?"

Jake chuckled. "We'll be more comfortable in the Lincoln," he said. "But are you sure you can handle this…?"

"Baker driving my car?" Ben asked.

Jake gestured around him, at the boys, at the ranch. "All of this?"

Emotions rushed up on Ben, the primary one being panic, but he shoved it down with a gulp of air and nodded. The little boys—except for Caleb—looked like they were choking back tears. His heart swelled for them, for all the tears they'd already cried. He didn't want them crying more. So, keeping one arm around Caleb, he headed toward the porch and reached out for Little Jake, then grinned at Ian and Miller. "It's only two weeks, guys," Ben told them. "They'll be back before you know it. And while they're gone, we're all going to have a lot of fun. We'll stay up too late and eat junk food and play video games."

"Ben," Katie said, with a sudden sternness to her voice that reminded him of his grandmother. She didn't have to raise her voice, just use that particular tone.

Her son must not have noticed it, though, or he didn't care, because he didn't hesitate to challenge it. "It's summertime, Mommy," Caleb said. "We can stay up later. We don't have school in the morning." Then he grimaced and gave Ian a sympathetic glance. "Well, you still do."

"I do?" Ian asked. Of course he would have forgotten. His concussion was the reason he needed extra help with school, the reason Grandma had hired his teacher, Miss Trent, for the last five weeks of term. But that had ended a week ago and she was still here. For those one-on-one lessons with Ian? Or for Little Jake, who was obviously attached to her?

"We'll still have plenty of time for video games and junk food," Ben assured Ian.

The little boy smiled at him. Only Miller didn't smile. But then, he rarely smiled anymore.

"You can go now, Mommy and Daddy Jake," Caleb said, dismissing his parents. "Uncle Ben and Uncle Baker are here. They'll take care of us and the ranch."

Ben ran a town, sure, but suddenly that seemed like a lot less work than being Big Jake Haven.

A lot less work than dealing with all these kids and the ranch and…

He glanced up and met Emily's gaze. She

was staring at him again, like she had yesterday at the church's community room. It wasn't the way women usually stared at him—there was no interest or attraction in her gaze, just disdain.

Clearly, she didn't think he could handle it.

EMILY HADN'T BEEN certain that she would have to say goodbye to Jake and Katie this morning. She really hadn't thought Ben would keep his promise to help out. But here he and his younger brother were. She'd barely glanced at Baker, who'd said very little.

It was Ben who'd been running his mouth since he'd arrived. Late.

"Staying up all night and eating junk food," Emily murmured. She wasn't a bit surprised that was how he would take care of the kids.

She and the other women gathered around the passenger side of Ben's Lincoln SUV to say goodbye for real this time. Jake and Katie were leaving.

"Don't worry," she told Katie, who had opened the back door to slide in next to her husband. "I will make sure the kids get their rest."

"And I'll make sure they eat well," Taye assured her.

"And I'll make sure everyone stays well," Melanie added.

"I know you will," Katie said.

"So don't worry," Emily said. "We'll take good care of them while you're gone."

"Yes, we will," a deep voice agreed as Ben joined them beside his SUV. He stepped closer to that open door, closer to Emily. While he brushed against her, he seemed totally focused on his new sister-in-law.

"I know you will," Katie repeated.

Emily opened her mouth to offer one more assurance, but Ben interrupted her before she could utter it. "They have to leave or they're going to miss their flight," he said, and he leaned over her, his face close to hers, to speak to his brother in the front seat. "Don't drive too fast, though. If you get a ticket with my ride, you're paying it."

"Then let me get them to the airport," Baker said, and he started the engine.

Ben reached around Emily again and closed the door on Katie, shutting her inside the back seat with her new husband—shutting Emily outside with him.

Where had Melanie and Taye and the boys gone? She could see only Ben when she turned around, his chest too close to her face. His body too close to hers.

He was so big. But then all the Haven men were. There was just something about Ben Haven that unsettled her more than the others did. Probably because she knew he couldn't be trusted.

"If they miss that flight," she said, "it'll be your fault. Nobody really believed you'd show up or they would have left already."

Ben winced, and regret unfurled within her. Instead of arguing with her in his defense, he just sighed. "I know. But we're here."

Actually, just he was, as his brother drove off with Katie and Jake. He gazed after his SUV as if he wondered, like she did, if Baker was coming back or if he would keep driving.

"Em, I have your picnic basket ready," Taye called out from the porch.

"Picnic?" Ben asked.

"That's the plan," Emily murmured. "The contingency plan we made in case you actually showed up and Katie and Jake left."

"Good to know you had a little faith in me," he remarked with a trace of humor and sarcasm.

"This isn't about you," she said, and she

turned away from him to head to the porch, where four subdued boys and one subdued Chihuahua had gathered around Taye and Melanie. Where had Sadie gone? Emily had figured that she'd be here gloating since her plan had worked, but she hadn't come outside when Ben and Baker had driven up a short while ago.

"Hey, guys," Emily greeted the boys. Their sudden quietness concerned her, making her heart ache for all the losses they'd already endured. She understood them so well, understood that pain and that fear they had to be feeling. That helplessness…

They were just kids, and the people they'd relied on the most were gone. Emily knew all too well how that felt—the panic over the uncertainty of a future you had no control over. She'd felt that way even before her mother had died because they hadn't often had a place to live or food to eat. Her mother had struggled so hard to support them with no help from any of her family. So Emily shouldn't have been surprised that none of them had been willing to help her daughter either.

The boys had family that were supporting them, though. And they had her. For now…

She clapped her hands together and forced

a bright smile for them. "We're going off on an expedition!"

"Expedition?" Ian queried. "What's that?"

"An adventure," she said.

"Adventure?" Caleb asked, his blue eyes brightening with interest. She could always count on Caleb. "What kind of adventure?"

"We're going hunting," Emily said.

Behind her, Ben chuckled deeply. "Hunting? You hunt?" he asked skeptically.

Emily stiffened, offended that he obviously didn't think she could. "Yes, we're hunting."

"Hunting?" Miller asked, perking up a bit. Then he started forward with his crutches and groaned. "I can't go. I can't ride with this cast."

"It comes off tomorrow," Melanie reminded him.

"But I want to go hunting today," Miller said, his voice slipping into a slightly petulant whine. The poor kid had been through so much, he was entitled to some self-pity.

Especially now... Jake had had Miller up on a horse even with the cast, but Jake was gone. And it was clear that Miller was very aware of that. She could have asked Ben to help his nephew, but she needed some distance from him. He kept standing entirely too close to her, so that she was aware of his warmth, of his scent…

He wasn't wearing a suit today. But he looked just as *GQ* in jeans, a checkered shirt, a black hat and boots. Too good…

"I'll help you," Ben offered.

She turned toward him, then glared at him. "We don't need your help. We're not going riding."

"We're not?" Caleb asked, and now that slightly petulant whine was in his voice. He loved horseback riding.

Emily had never done it herself, so she had no intention of taking them. "No, we need our hands free for the gear we're bringing and the picnic basket," she said brightly. "Once we've collected our hunting trophies, we'll have our picnic lunch."

"Trophies!" Caleb exclaimed with excitement. "We're going to get trophies?"

"We have to see how good we are," she said.

"I'll be very good," Ben said.

She pinned him with her gaze. "You have to take care of the ranch."

He shook his head. "Jake cleaned out Midnight's stall already, and since it's Sunday, he doesn't have the hands doing any big projects, just checking the animals. So there's nothing for me to do today but hang out with my nephews."

She wouldn't have minded that if he'd been spending time with them all along. She might have even believed he'd changed and grown up and become less self-involved than he'd been as a teenager. But he hadn't been around much these last several weeks. He hadn't been there for the kids since the accident, like he should have been.

"And eat junk food and play video games?" Miller asked. Now he sounded excited.

"The video games will have to wait," Emily said. "We all need some fresh air." They'd been at the wedding the entire previous day; the boys needed to expend some of their energy. That had been her plan, although it was beginning to crumble, especially when Taye handed the picnic basket to Ben.

"There's no junk food in here."

"No cookies?" Caleb asked, his mouth turning down with disappointment.

"Cookies aren't junk food," Taye said. "At least not my cookies. I use all-natural ingredients in my baking—no preservatives."

Emily could have used some preservatives about now—she needed something to preserve her patience since Ben had invited himself along on her picnic with the boys. And she couldn't very well refuse to let him go. These were his nephews, his family ranch, so she couldn't tell him what to do, like she did the younger Haven males. If she could, she would certainly tell him where to go, and it would be far away from her—far enough that she couldn't see his ridiculously handsome face, that she couldn't hear his deep voice, that she couldn't smell his rich cologne…

Far enough away that she wouldn't be tempted to forget how unreliable he was.

JAKE HAVEN PACED the airport terminal. They hadn't missed their flight. In fact, it had been delayed, so they'd had plenty of time to make it, which was good since Baker hadn't driven very fast to the airport. It was almost as if he'd wanted them to miss their flight, like he didn't want them to go.

Jake wondered the same about Katie, who was sitting in one of the uncomfortable chairs, her hands knotted together in her lap. "Are you okay?" he asked his bride. "If you don't want to do this…"

"I want to," she said, and she met his gaze

with a look that had his pulse racing. "I really want this honeymoon, but I'm worried…"

"About the boys," he finished for her.

She nodded. "As much as I want to be alone with you, I really hate leaving them."

He sighed at the ache in his own chest. "I know. Me too."

"And the ranch," she said. "You must hate leaving it too."

It had been his total focus for so many years: his legacy, his baby, his life…

But now he knew there was more to life than work and responsibility. There was love. His heart full of it, he kneeled in front of her chair, unknotted her hands and took them in his. "Let's do this," he said. "Let's go, and if it sounds like they need us—for any reason—we'll come back."

She drew in a shaky breath and nodded. "Yes, yes…"

"She said yes," someone called out.

And Jake turned his head to see that they had attracted onlookers. He grinned. "She said yes a couple days ago and 'I do' yesterday," he shared with pride and gratitude. He couldn't believe how lucky he was, especially after all the misfortune that had befallen his family.

It was time for their fortunes to change. He'd been first—the first to find his happily-ever-after—but he knew that if his grandmother had her way, he would not be the last.

"The newlyweds have been upgraded to first class," the attendant at the gate announced over the speaker. "You may board now."

Katie drew in another shaky-sounding breath and stood up. "Let's do this," she said back to him, and she smiled brightly, albeit a bit nervously. "Are you sure, though, that your brothers can do this? That they can really take care of the ranch and the boys?"

"No," Jake admitted. "But they have help. Emily and Taye and Melanie and Grandmother. Those women can handle anything." Even his brothers...

He was actually more worried about his brothers being able to handle them and whatever plan Grandma had put into motion.

CHAPTER SIX

"THESE ARE NOT TROPHIES," Ben grumbled as he held up a jar of bugs. Sunshine shimmered off the glass. He regretted now that he'd crashed Emily's expedition with the boys. "And this is not hunting. It's exterminating."

Emily's lips curved into a slight smile before she pulled her mouth into a frown again. She was still not happy that he'd invited himself along on the outing.

Emily grabbed the jar from Ben's hand and examined the top. "They're not supposed to die. I punched air holes in all the lids." She gently tipped the jar back and forth until the butterfly opened its silvery blue wings. "You must have scared it."

"I think that if the mob of little boys chasing it with nets hadn't already scared it, then *you* must have when you shoved it into the jar," he pointed out.

"I had to," she said. "You wouldn't touch it."

Ben repressed a shudder at the thought. He

did *not* like bugs…of any kind. They were creepy and crawly. "This hunting trip was your idea," he reminded her.

"And you invited yourself along," she said. "So you need to make yourself useful." She held on to the jar but thrust the handle of one of the butterfly nets into his hand. "Help Little Jake add to his trophies."

"I don't think he needs any help," Ben replied. His nephew had had no problem using his pudgy hands to pull the bugs out of the netting.

"The bugs do," Emily said, "if they're going to survive. I don't know if that grasshopper will make it." She bit her bottom lip, expressing more sympathy for it than she had for Ben's aversion to bugs.

"I think he's forgotten all about trophies." Little Jake was now sitting on the blanket next to the picnic basket. His eyes were beginning to drift shut, as he must have been exhausted from running around with the net. Because of Miller's cast, they hadn't walked far from the house, just into the field behind it, which was rife with wildflowers and butterflies and assorted other winged and multiple-legged creatures.

Emily's lips curved into a smile again as

she followed Ben's pointing finger to the little boy. He was cute. With his dark hair and big dark eyes, the toddler looked like the spitting image of his namesake—Big Jake—or like Ben. The other boys, Ian and Miller, looked like their father, with Dale's light brown hair and hazel eyes. Jenny had been a brunette with curly brown hair and enormous doelike eyes that had always glowed with love—love for her husband, love for her family...

Ben sucked in a breath as that ache of loss intensified for a moment. This was why he'd struggled to be as present for the boys as he should have been. It was just so hard to see them and not think of all that they'd lost...

All the love. All the goodness...

"You really hate bugs," Emily remarked.

He released a shaky sigh and nodded. "Yeah, not a fan..."

"But you grew up on a ranch," she said. "You must have been around bugs a lot."

"Even more when my brothers figured out how much I don't like bugs," he admitted. "Then bugs showed up everywhere. In my bed. In my dresser drawers..." He grimaced with disgust.

And she chuckled.

"I should have known better than to expect

any sympathy out of you," he said. Clearly, she didn't like him, and he wasn't certain why. Was it because of something he'd done or not done in high school?

Or because of something he'd done or not done since she'd moved to the ranch...

Because he'd not been around enough? He couldn't blame her for judging him over that. He was judging himself pretty hard right now over that too.

"Hmm..." she murmured and took the net from his hands. "Maybe I'll catch some more for another project..."

Ben narrowed his eyes. "If I find any in my bedroom, I will know how they got there."

"Yes, but you will be too afraid to reciprocate," she replied. Her smile widened, making her face glow, her eyes shine brighter. She really was incredibly beautiful.

Ben felt a strange twinge in his chest. It was close to the feeling he'd had when he'd realized her hunting was for bugs. Fear...

BEN HAVEN WASN'T perfect after all. He had a weakness. A phobia...

Emily probably shouldn't have been so amused by it, but she welcomed the humor as a release from the tension that usually gripped her in his presence. Not that she was at all attracted to him…

She knew better. Sure, he was incredibly good-looking and charming. But she was in no danger of succumbing to that charm. She knew it was only superficial, just like all the promises Ben made.

To her friends. To his family…

He'd promised to help out before, but she'd seen very little of him over the six weeks that she'd lived at the ranch. Her heart ached for his young nephews, who probably felt as she had all those years ago, when she'd waited for her grandparents to pick her up from the foster home where her mom's cousin had dropped her. "We just need a break, Emmy," they'd told her when she'd had her case worker call them. "We'll pick you up soon." They'd never come for her. None of her family had. Only Mrs. Rademacher… At least Ben had come back to the ranch. She'd probably seen more of him today than she had the entire month and a half she'd lived there. The "hunt" and the picnic were taking longer than she'd thought, but the boys seemed reluctant to return to the house.

She couldn't blame them. The early June sunshine warmed her skin and brightened

her mood. Or maybe that was her amusement over the grimace of distaste on Ben's
face as he pulled a butterfly from Ian's net.
He opened his hand too soon, and the silvery
blue insect flew off.

"You let it go!" Caleb exclaimed, and he
swung his net at it even though it was far beyond his reach already.

"It's good that it's free," Ben said. "It's too
beautiful to keep, anyway." He turned toward Emily and pointedly added, "In fact,
we should release all the *trophies* before we
head back to the house."

"Of course you would think that," Emily
said. Clearly, he didn't want the insects anywhere nearby.

"I agree," Melanie remarked, startling
Emily with her sudden appearance in the
field. "I don't think those bugs should get
into the house." She glanced at the full jars
the boys had left lying on the ground and
shook her head in revulsion.

Obviously, the physical therapist was not
a fan of insects either, which was probably
why Melanie had bowed out of the outing
Emily had planned. For a moment, when she
and Taye had backed out of participating in
the *expedition* after Ben had invited himself

along, Emily had wondered if Sadie had enlisted the two of them in her matchmaking scheme. She wouldn't have been surprised if Taye was in on it; she and Sadie were extremely close. But Melanie...

Just yesterday, she'd made the comment that Emily shouldn't go looking for a husband. Ever...

Which was probably good advice. She would be smarter to protect her heart, rather than risk it on someone who didn't deserve it.

"I have everything arranged for tomorrow," Melanie said. She walked up to Miller, who was balancing on one crutch while he waved the net around with his free hand. "That cast will be off soon."

"Good!" Miller exclaimed. "Can we come back out when it's off, Miss Trent? Can we go hunting then, so I can get more trophies than those guys?"

He was referring to Ian and Caleb, who'd become Ian's instant best friend in Emily's kindergarten classroom last year. Ian and Caleb were running through the wildflowers and weeds, waving their nets wildly around their heads. She was surprised that they'd caught anything. But they seemed to have a system. Ian caught most of them, and Caleb gently plucked them from the nets and put them in the jars. Or if Caleb was busy, Ian had Ben take them out of his net. With their system, they had filled quite a few jars.

Ben was probably right. They really needed to set all the creatures free.

"I caught something!" Ian exclaimed. He held his net toward Caleb, but he was working on collecting something from his own net. And Ben hadn't chased after them when they'd run off.

"You can get it," Caleb assured him. "You know how."

Ian's brow furrowed. "I do?"

"Just reach inside," Caleb instructed with a patience most five-year-old boys didn't possess. He'd been so great with his friend, so gentle with Ian's memory lapses. He had more patience than Miller had for his younger brother.

And sometimes more patience than Emily. It was so hard to work with Ian and have him forget everything she'd taught him just a few moments after the lesson ended. How was he ever going to advance to the first grade?

She needed to work with him the whole summer to make certain that he could. But surely, Principal Kellerman would be calling her soon, wanting her to participate in the summer planning sessions, if Emily intended to go back.

She wasn't sure that she could yet. Not with the boys needing her so much.

But if she didn't return, the principal couldn't keep filling her position with substitutes, so Emily risked losing her job. Sadie was paying her well right now, but the boys wouldn't need her forever. And then where would she go?

Jobs at the school in Willow Creek seldom opened up. Many teachers worked long past retirement age because they loved their students and the job so much. Like Mrs. Rademacher had, so much that she'd welcomed Emily into her home when none of Emily's family had taken her and when no foster parents had kept her either. Mrs. Rademacher had already been past retirement age then, but she'd stayed working even after Emily's high-school graduation and had helped with her college tuition.

Still overwhelmed by that sweet woman's kindness, Emily blinked against the threat of tears. Mrs. Rademacher had finally retired, at the urging of her adult children, a few years ago to move closer to where they and her grandchildren had settled. Even though they talked often on the phone, Emily still missed her.

"I would help him with that net, but I'd probably just let it go again," Ben warned Emily, "so maybe you should help him."

Ian was clearly struggling, because he peered into the net with great caution before reaching tentatively inside it. Maybe Ian shared his uncle's aversion to insects; maybe that was why he'd been having Caleb or Ben take them out for him.

"Ian, don't worry about it," she called out to the little boy. "I'll help you—"

But before she could reach him, he let out a scream and dropped the net. "It bit me!" Then he screamed again, and his body dropped to the ground, disappearing into the tall weeds and wildflowers around him.

Emily's heart slammed against her ribs with fear, and she ran and kneeled down next to him. Curled up in a ball, he rolled around, screaming and crying. "Are you okay, Ian?" she asked with concern. "Where did you get bit?"

But he didn't answer her. He just kept panicking until he was nearly struggling to breathe.

"Slow down, buddy," Ben murmured as he joined them. "It's okay. It's okay. Deep breaths. Deep breaths…"

The kid was still hysterical. Emily touched his arms and lifted his hands to search them for the bug bite.

"Where is it?" Melanie asked as she leaned over Emily. "Was it a bee sting? He could be allergic."

Her question brought another scream from Ian's lips.

"Shh…" Ben murmured. "It's okay, buddy."

"I don't see anything," Emily said with a glance back at the physical therapist. "I don't see any red marks on his hands or arms."

"It's gone," Ben assured his nephew. "The bug is gone. It's okay…"

A sharp pang of regret passed through Emily's heart. She hadn't realized that one of the boys could have shared Ben's phobia. Usually the little boys and girls she taught in kindergarten loved insects.

Ben lifted Ian's trembling body from the weeds. "We can go back to the house, buddy. You're fine. You're fine."

Ian drew in a shaky breath, released it in a hiccup and then stared up at his uncle with a bleary-eyed gaze. "What are you doing here, Uncle Ben?"

Ben flinched then, as if he'd felt something too. Guilt? "I'm going to be staying at the ranch while Uncle Jake and Aunt Katie are on their honeymoon."

"Aunt Katie?"

"My mom married your uncle, Big Jake," Caleb informed him.

"Sheesh, we were just at the wedding yesterday," Miller said and then groaned in frustration. "How could you forget already?"

"Forget what?" Ian asked.

Miller groaned again. "Forget it!" Using his one crutch, he hobbled off toward the house.

"Are you okay?" Ben asked Ian.

The little boy nodded, but his brow was still furrowed with confusion. "Where's Mommy and Daddy?"

And Emily felt the question like a punch to the gut. "Ian, they're gone."

"Where?" he asked.

She opened her mouth to tell him the terrible story that was news to him every time she'd had to tell it, which had been so very many times. Her shoulders slumped with the burden of having to tell it again.

But before she could, Ben was speaking.

"They've been gone for two months, Ian. They passed away in a car accident. You were in it—with Little Jake and Miller and your parents."

"But we didn't die," Ian said, and he stared after his brother, who was hobbling toward the house.

"No, you didn't," Ben said. "And we're so grateful for that, that we have you here with us."

"But Mommy and Daddy..." Fresh tears trailed down his face now.

Ben gently wiped them away. "They're with you all the time," he said. "Watching over us all from heaven. They're together there."

"With my daddy," Caleb added.

The little blond boy leaned against Ben's side, and Ben reached down and affectionately squeezed his shoulder. "Yes."

And something squeezed Emily's heart so sharply that she let out a little gasp. She wouldn't have thought Ben capable of such empathy and kindness, but then she really didn't know him. She just knew *of* his reputation of charm but little substance.

"Are you okay, Miss Trent?" Caleb asked her. "Did you get bit too?"

She shook her head. "No, I'm fine." But those tears were stinging her eyes again. She drew in a shaky breath and added, "We should all head back to the house and get cleaned up."

"We need to let all the trophies go first," Ben told her, but his mouth twisted into a grimace of distaste.

"I'll handle that," she offered. "Since you handled this…" She gestured at Ian.

Ben helped the kid to his feet and said to him, "Why don't you and Caleb help out by getting all the picnic stuff back into the basket?"

"There might be some cookies left!" Caleb exclaimed, and he headed off toward the blanket where Little Jake had fallen sound asleep.

"Wow," Ben murmured once the kids were farther away. "I can't imagine how hard that must be to deal with, having to remind him…" He trailed off as if he couldn't repeat what he'd just said.

She should have been grateful and impressed with how well he'd handled his nephew, and part of her had been—too impressed. Instead of expressing that gratitude or complimenting him, she found herself remarking, "You wouldn't have to imagine it if you'd been around more often these past several weeks."

Ben jerked his head back as if she'd slapped him, but he just nodded as if he agreed with her. "Well, I'll leave you to the jars, then, and help the boys carry that basket back."

"Wow," Melanie murmured after he'd walked away. "You're being pretty hard on him."

Startled, Emily jumped and turned toward the dark-haired physical therapist, who was standing behind her. She'd thought Melanie had left with Miller. "I—I didn't know you were here."

"Would it have stopped you from saying that to him?" Melanie asked, and she arched a dark eyebrow.

Heat rushed to Emily's face with embarrassment and shame that she'd been overheard being so snippy with Ben. Taking him to task was almost a defense mechanism with her now, as if she needed to protect herself from him or from what she might feel for him...if she let herself. She could *not* let herself.

"What's your issue with him, anyway?" Melanie asked. "He showed up today with a bag bigger than for just overnight. He clearly intends to stay at the ranch. I really think he's trying to help out."

Maybe he was. Or maybe he was just faking it, like so many people had for Emily... until the case worker had left, until it was just her and her caretakers. Then she'd been treated as a burden, an inconvenience, and she was worried that the Haven boys might begin to feel that way themselves—if everyone around them didn't show them love and appreciation. Emily shrugged. "I just don't know if Ben's genuine."

Melanie sighed. "It's hard to know what to believe sometimes." She ran a hand over her belly.

Emily followed the movement of that hand, watched the material of the other woman's big shirt mold over a slight swelling. Was Melanie pregnant?

Morning sickness would explain what Emily had previously suspected was a long-lasting stomach bug Melanie had been suffering from. Every morning...

How had she not figured it out before now? Emily wanted to ask if Melanie was expecting, but if the physical therapist had wanted her to know, she would have already shared her news.

Melanie had probably told Katie. But she hadn't said anything to Emily yet. Didn't she trust her?

Difficulty trusting was something else she and Melanie shared, something that could bond them just as they'd bonded over the boys. Clearly, Melanie wasn't ready yet to open up fully to Emily.

Just as Emily wasn't ready yet to trust Ben. She suspected she never would be ready for that, or for him.

SADIE BARELY RESISTED the urge to rub her hands together to express her glee. Or utter that laugh Jake had accused her of having to contain at his wedding...

An evil laugh.

Sadie wasn't evil, though. She was just very determined. Too many bad things had happened to the Haven family. It was past time for some good.

For a lot of good...

She sat at the head of the long table in the big farmhouse-style kitchen. The hearth was at her back, but there was no fire in it. It was getting warm outside now. Too warm for a fire to be needed.

It also seemed to be getting warm inside

with the way that Ben and Emily kept stealing glances at each other. Emily could have managed to look a little more interested than irritated, though, and Ben could have looked a little less...

Affronted.

What had happened during their excursion earlier today?

So nobody would accuse of her meddling, Sadie had laid low in her suite after saying goodbye to Katie and Jake. She figured the less she was around, the more that Ben and Baker would have to interact with the women.

But only Ben had stayed at the ranch.

"Where's Baker?" she asked. He hadn't joined them for dinner.

Ben shrugged. "My SUV is back in the driveway, and his truck is still here. He has to be somewhere on the ranch."

Dinner was over now and the table had been cleared, but everybody had lingered in the kitchen. Sadie was glad that when they'd renovated the house and added on those wings a few years ago, they'd also expanded the size of the kitchen; it truly was the heart of the home. At least now it was that way, with Taye here cooking for all of them, with everyone gravitating toward her just like they gravitated toward Emily. Melanie was the only one who held herself back, except with Miller.

Those two were kindred spirits, wounded and unwilling to open up fully with the others. Sadie had offered to go with them tomorrow to the specialist who was removing Miller's cast, but he'd insisted he only needed Melanie.

Instead of being stung, Sadie had been relieved. She knew they would be all right on their own; she wasn't so certain about the ranch with only Ben and Baker running it even if just for a day.

Ben stood up from the table. "Want to go hunting with me, boys?" he asked.

Emily quirked one of her blond brows. "*You* want to go hunting?" she asked with skepticism.

"We're not going hunting for bugs," Ben said. "We're going hunting for Uncle Baker."

"Do we bring the nets?" Caleb asked, his eyes bright with excitement. He was always up for anything. Such a sweet and resilient little boy.

Ben chuckled. "Yes, let's."

"Don't be gone too long," Taye said. "Dessert will be ready in less than an hour." The smells of cinnamon and apples emanated from the oven.

"We'll be back," Ben said in a poor imitation of that muscular movie star. But the boys laughed and so did Taye and Melanie.

Emily's lips just twitched, but if she'd been tempted to smile, she suppressed it. She just stared after him as he and the boys—even Little Jake—hurried out of the house through the French doors that opened onto the patio.

"He's good with the kids," Melanie said as she got up from the table and joined Taye at the sink in the long kitchen island.

"He is," Sadie agreed with satisfaction. She turned to Emily, whose pretty face was twisted into a slight grimace, as if she objected to the idea that Ben was good at anything. "You don't think so?"

Emily shrugged. "He is good with them when he's here. But the boys need someone they can count on."

The boys weren't the only ones who needed that. Sadie suspected that Emily needed that just as much, if not more. She'd gone most of her childhood with nobody she could count on until Mrs. Rademacher had opened her home and her heart to the young orphan.

"He stuck it out today," Sadie said. "And

bugs are really not his thing. For your next outing, you'll have to plan something a little less disgusting to go with the picnic." And more romantic. "Like a horseback ride or a moonlit stroll…"

Sadie smiled wistfully as she recalled all of the many, many times she and her husband had taken late-night rides around the ranch. She pressed her hand over her heart, to the hollow ache she'd had inside for the past twelve years that the original Big Jake Haven had been gone.

"There won't be a next time," Emily said with a pointed stare at her.

The young woman was nobody's fool; she'd figured out early on what Sadie's intentions had been.

But that didn't mean that Emily Trent didn't have her weaknesses. So she asked the young teacher, "You trust him alone with the boys?"

Emily's eyes narrowed as she continued to study Sadie's face. "You just said he's good with them," she reminded her.

Sadie shrugged. "Good with them and good *for* them are two different things."

Emily wasn't biting yet. "What are you saying? He's your grandson. Their uncle…"

"That's why I wouldn't trust him alone

with them," Sadie confided. "Because I know him so well, and I know he doesn't have much experience with kids. He's not been around them very often." Somehow she managed not to choke on that last lie; Ben had been around the boys and the ranch much more often before Dale and Jenny had died. So had Baker. It was probably just too hard for them to be here now…when that special young couple wasn't. It was hard for Sadie too, which was why she preferred to focus on putting together some other couples. Like Katie and Jake, and…

"If you don't trust him, why did you just let him walk out of here with all of them?" Emily asked, her voice getting high and slightly screechy with panic.

Sadie managed a ragged-sounding sigh. "I'll just hope for the best, that nothing happens to them."

Emily jumped up from the table, pushed open the French doors and rushed off in the direction Ben and his little male entourage had disappeared moments ago.

While Melanie closed the doors behind her, Taye laughed and admonished Sadie, "You're bad."

Thinking of the wedding the day before, of

how happy Jake and Katie were, she shook her head. "No, I'm good. I'm very, very good."

Melanie sighed and murmured, "Poor Emily…"

Sadie cringed, glad the teacher had to be out of earshot by now. Emily hated hearing that phrase; Mrs. Rademacher had confided in Sadie years ago about the special child she'd fostered.

How proud, even as a young girl, Emily Trent had been. How she hadn't wanted to ask for help and how she'd never wanted anyone to pity her. She preferred to take care of others rather than have anyone take care of her.

She was as strong as she was beautiful. Just like Ben…

They would make a perfect match…if they'd just give each other a chance. Sadie had two weeks to somehow compel them to take that chance to get to know each other—to get to know each other so well that they fell in love.

CHAPTER SEVEN

SINCE BEN HAD no idea where else to look for his brother, he led the little boys to the barn. Baker had made it pretty clear that he only wanted to work the ranch. Was that why he hadn't come around for dinner?

His loss, since the meat loaf and smashed red potatoes was the best meal that Ben had had in a long while, if not ever. Taye Cooper was one talented chef.

"If we find Uncle Baker, he won't fit in the jar," Caleb said. "So how do we make him a trophy?"

Ben's lips twitched with the urge to grin, but the little boy was very serious. "We can use my phone to take a picture of him," Ben offered. "Prove that we caught him that way. That can be the trophy."

He would have rather done that with the bugs instead of physically handling them. He had to suppress a shudder of revulsion over the memory of all the wings and legs he'd touched, all the squirmy insect bodies…

"Why would we put Uncle Baker in a jar?" Ian asked.

"Because that's what we did with the bugs," Caleb explained patiently.

"What bugs?" Ian asked.

Miller sighed. "Don't you remember? You started crying just because one of them touched you."

Ian grimaced. "One of them touched me?"

"Why are you such a baby?" Miller asked.

"I'm not!" Ian protested.

"Yes, you are. Only babies are afraid of bugs!"

"I am not a baby!" Ian yelled, and he shoved Miller, who stumbled back on his crutches and might have fallen had Emily not rushed up behind him.

"What's going on?" she asked.

"They're fighting," Ben said, and their argument was giving him flashbacks from his childhood and how his brothers had picked on him for his fears. "Miller, Ian is not a baby just because he doesn't like bugs." Then he confided, "I don't like bugs either."

He expected Emily to make some sarcastic comment about that, about him. Instead her face flushed, and she said, "Boys, everybody has something they don't like, and we shouldn't judge each other over our personal aversions."

"What are personal aversions?" Caleb asked.

"Things you don't like," Emily explained. "Like you don't like carrots." She turned toward Miller. "And you don't like your cast."

"That's because it's heavy and it itches," the seven-year-old grumbled.

"It'll be off tomorrow, buddy," Ben reminded him. Then he turned to Caleb. "And if you don't like carrots, why are you carrying a bunch of them?"

Caleb looked at the carrots and scrunched up his nose with distaste. "These aren't for me. These are for Midnight."

The horse, the black bronco that Dusty had won in some bet, stuck his head over the door of his stall and whinnied, as if he knew Caleb was talking about him. Or, since his nostrils were flaring, maybe he'd just smelled the carrots. He pawed at the ground as if he was impatient for them.

And Caleb chuckled. "I'm coming. I'm coming."

But a frisson of uneasiness raced down Ben's spine and he reached out to hold the little boy back from the bronco. "I'm not sure that's a good idea, buddy."

"It's not," Emily agreed. Perhaps for the first time with him. "You can't go near that thing, Caleb."

"But, Miss Trent, Midnight is my friend now. He won't hurt me. I help Daddy Jake take care of him, and now I have to help Uncle Ben do it."

"I'm sure Uncle Ben can handle it on his own," Emily assured Caleb.

But Ben suspected she had her doubts; he certainly did. While he'd grown up riding, he was not a horse whisperer like Dusty and Jake were, and like Dale had been. Dale could have effortlessly handled the thing. Ben turned toward the horse, studying it uneasily. It seemed to return the sentiment as it pawed at the floor of its stall.

"Midnight's really hungry," Caleb said. "I need to give him his carrots."

"Why don't you let me do that?" Ben asked. "That way I can get him to be my friend too."

Caleb nodded. "Good idea." He passed the carrots to Ben. "Just so you know, it tickles when his lips touch your fingers."

Ben hoped that his teeth only tickled. He glanced down at his hand. "I'm kind of attached to my fingers. I hope I don't lose them…" he murmured.

Emily chuckled now.

Ben drew in a deep breath and stepped closer to the door of that stall. And Midnight raised his front legs off the ground and emitted a guttural sound. Not a whinny at all… more like a warning cry.

Emily gasped. "Maybe you shouldn't do that…"

"Somebody has to take care of Midnight," Caleb said. "I'll do it."

"No, no, I got this…" Ben insisted, but he was even less certain than before that he could handle this beast.

"Uh, boys, we need to get back to the house before Miss Taye's dessert gets cold," Emily said.

Obviously, she didn't want the kids to witness him losing his hand. He turned back toward her with his eyes narrowed. "Are you afraid of the sight of blood?" he asked.

"Who's bleeding?" Ian asked.

"Nobody," he assured him, but he turned back toward the horse and murmured, "Yet…"

"Come on, guys," Emily said. "We need to head back, eat our dessert and then I'll help you bathe before bedtime."

Unable to resist teasing her, Ben turned back with a grin. "Will you help me too?"

She narrowed her eyes. "No, you're on your own."

"I'll help you, Uncle Ben," Caleb offered. But he must have thought Ben was talking about the horse because he stepped closer and covered Ben's hand that held the carrots. "I'll help you feed Midnight."

He really didn't want the kid getting hurt. "No, I need to start making friends with him on my own. You can help me tomorrow with cleaning out his stall and feeding him."

Caleb gave an eager nod as somewhere behind him Emily huffed in disapproval.

"Now go and get that dessert," Ben said. "But leave me some..." And maybe some bandages for when this horse took a bite out of him as well as the carrots.

Emily shepherded the boys out of the barn without another glance in his direction. Obviously, she didn't approve of his enlisting Caleb to help him with the bronco, but she must not have had a problem when he'd helped Jake with it. So her only problem seemed to be with Ben.

"Wow, you're already falling into Grandma's

trap," Baker remarked pityingly as he stepped out of the shadows.

His sudden appearance startled both the horse, who reared up again in his stall, and Ben, who huffed out a breath. "Where were you?" he asked.

"Tack room," Baker replied.

"Didn't you hear us out here?" Ben asked.

His younger brother shrugged, so he probably had. Was that why he'd stayed in the tack room? He hadn't wanted to see all of them?

"And what do you mean I'm falling into Grandma's trap?" he asked.

"The way you were just staring after the schoolteacher, you look like you're already falling for her, and you know Jake's been warning us that Grandma probably intends to marry off all of us. You're going to be next."

Ben snorted. "Yeah, that's not happening."

Baker nodded. "Yeah, I agree. Miss Trent doesn't seem at all interested in you."

"Is that why you didn't join us for dinner?" he asked. "You're trying to avoid Grandma's matchmaking?"

Baker shook his head. "I'm too smart to fall in with that."

"And yet you're here."

"And so are you," Baker pointed out. "And

for the same reason—for Jake…because we owe him. He's always stepped up, every time he was needed." His throat moved as if he was struggling to swallow something, and he added, "And we owe it to Dale and Jenny…"

Ben's heart felt heavy with missing them. Clearly, he wasn't the only one. "So why were you hiding in the tack room?"

"I was getting everything ready to ride out tomorrow and check the stock," he said.

Ben shook his head now. "No, you should go with Melanie on the trip to Sheridan tomorrow for Miller's cast coming off. Make sure everything's good for the kid."

"I'm a paramedic," Baker said. "I'm not a doctor."

"Yeah," Ben said. "You have more medical knowledge than I do."

"Everybody has more medical knowledge than you do," Baker said. "Especially Melanie. She's the physical therapist—she can handle it."

"It's a long drive, and they're probably going to have to spend the night," Ben pointed out. "She shouldn't have all that responsibility on her own."

"Are you a double agent for Grandma?"

Baker asked. "And you're trying to set me up with Melanie?"

Ben chuckled. "I think she's the safest one for you to be with—she's already married, or so somebody said…" He wasn't entirely certain the rumor was true since she didn't wear a ring.

"It doesn't matter if she is or isn't," Baker said. "And since she brought Miller home from the hospital on her own, I think she'll manage just fine bringing him back for his cast coming off."

That had been because they'd just held the funeral for Dale and Jenny, two weeks after their deaths. They'd waited for Miller to be recovered enough from his surgeries to attend, but in the end, he hadn't wanted to come back to the ranch until after the funeral.

"I still think it would be nice for one of the family to go with the kid," Ben insisted.

"Then you go," Baker replied. "I'm going to work the ranch tomorrow. You're the one who's acting like a nanny, playing with the boys all day."

Ben grimaced over Baker acting like Ben had spent the day goofing off. Obviously, the paramedic had no idea how hard it was to be a nanny to kids who'd suffered so great a loss, who continued to suffer from that loss, like poor Ian...

Ben couldn't imagine how many times Emily had had to tell the child where his parents were, and his heart ached with the kid's pain. He'd had to do it before today, back when he'd stayed those two weeks at the ranch right after the accident, but it never got easier to tell him.

Ben didn't want to put that burden entirely on Emily anymore, so he couldn't leave right now. "I'm supposed to be helping with the ranch too," he reminded his younger brother.

"You handle that beast," Baker said, gesturing back toward the bronco's stall. "I don't want anything to do with him. And come out to the pastures when you get the chance."

Ben glanced uneasily back at the horse. The thing was restless and edgy. Because of him and Baker? Or because he wanted his treat?

Ben tossed the bundle of carrots over the stall door. The horse dipped its head down and plucked them up from the ground, his teeth biting cleanly through the hard vegetables. Ben shuddered at the thought of feeding that thing by hand.

"We'll have more help with the ranch,"

Ben informed his brother. "Jake has a couple of those foreman candidates starting tomorrow." That was some of what his oldest brother had covered on the call they'd been on while Ben had driven out to the ranch earlier that day. He couldn't believe it had just been a day since he'd been here, with the boys, with Emily...

"Where will they stay?" Baker asked.

Ben shrugged. "Probably the bunkhouse for now since he hasn't given either of them the actual position yet." He had a feeling that Jake was holding out for someone else to take that job, for Dusty to come home and assume his late twin's responsibilities on the ranch. Ben had a feeling that Jake and Sadie would be waiting a long time for that to actually happen, though.

"Good," Baker remarked.

"Why do you care where they'll be staying?" Ben wondered.

"Because I'm going to be using the foreman's cottage for the next two weeks."

"That's Jake's place."

Baker shook his head. "Not anymore. He's moved into the main house now."

"Just to help out until the boys get better," Ben reminded him.

"How are they going to get better?" Baker asked. "How are they ever going to get over the loss of both their parents?"

Ben realized that the kids weren't the only ones struggling to handle that loss. Baker was struggling as well. Ben uttered a ragged sigh. *He* was struggling too. "I don't know," he admitted.

"Someone has to fill that void," Baker continued. "And Jake and Katie are the logical choices."

"Because Jake always steps up," Ben said. "He always does the right thing. You and I need to do that now. And so does Dusty."

"How are you going to convince him to come home?" Baker asked.

"The same way I convinced you," Ben said.

Baker snorted. "I'm just staying these two weeks. I'm not staying permanently. Are you?"

Ben shook his head. "I can't. The ranch is too far from town, and I have responsibilities there." He had too many projects started that he needed to supervise, to make certain his vision for the town became a reality. That it became more prosperous than it had ever been…even under his namesake, his great-grandfather.

Baker nodded. "Me too." He dragged in a deep breath and murmured, "It's just two weeks…"

Like he was trying to convince himself…

Like he was scared of being here any longer than that.

"I'm going to head up to the house for dessert," Ben said. "Coming? That's one reason I have no problem staying at the main house—the meals Taye makes."

Baker shook his head. "I don't need dessert."

"Are you worried you'll enjoy it so much you'll want to have dessert with us all the time?" Ben teased him.

Baker glared back. "Like I said, you're the one who should be worried…" He turned then and walked out of the barn.

Ben faced the bronco for a moment. The horse had gone curiously quiet; maybe the carrots had done the trick. Or maybe he was just more relaxed since there were fewer people around him. He stared at Ben over the door of his stall, his eyes big and unblinking, and almost expressive. Like he was pitying Ben.

"It's only two weeks," he told the horse, just like Baker had just told him. And one of those days was nearly done, though it had seemed to last forever. On his way back to the main house, he stopped at the old schoolhouse that served as the business office for the ranch. When he pushed open the door, the scent of honeysuckle enveloped him. Katie.

She'd made the place her own now. She intended to keep working primarily at the ranch while her new hire, Bob, handled clients at her office in town. He was also going to remotely handle the ranch business for Katie while she and Jake were off on their honeymoon.

After the accident, Ben could have stepped in and helped out with the books that Dale and Jenny used to do. As well as his political-science degree, Ben had completed a master's in business. But Grandma had told him she had it handled…because she'd obviously wanted to bring Katie back into Jake's orbit.

Her plan had worked. What was her plan where he and his fellow bachelor brothers were concerned? Who did she have picked out for him—Emily Trent?

Like Baker had said, that wasn't going to happen and not just because she clearly wasn't interested. Ben had no interest in ever getting married or even in having a serious relationship. Given his family history, Ben wasn't going to risk his heart, not when so many people he'd already loved had left him. Either because of death, or because the person must not have really loved him. Why else would his mother have just taken off like she had—leaving him and his siblings—if she'd actually loved them? And if his own mother hadn't loved him enough to stay with him, Ben doubted anyone else could.

He expelled a shaky breath and shook off his maudlin thoughts. Then he walked over to Jake's desk; it was a heavy oak desk with very few papers on top of it. Jake would rather ride a horse than a desk. Ben was the opposite of his older brother. And because he would prefer not to spend the next two weeks on a horse, Ben picked up the applications. On the two résumés, Jake had scribbled down the start date for each candidate's trial period. But on top of one of those, Jake had affixed a sticky note with the name of another candidate: Dusty.

Who else could take Dale's place except his twin? No one. Not even Dusty could take Dale's place. Not on the ranch and not with his kids.

Ben's heart ached so much that he pressed

his hand to his chest. But just because he knew he couldn't be a father to Dale's boys didn't excuse him from trying harder, from being there for them—from being just Uncle Ben. Despite Baker goading him about playing nanny, Ben didn't regret spending the entire day with the boys…or with Emily.

Thinking of them, he left the office and hurried up to the house. But he was too late. He'd missed dessert and the kids had already showered and headed up to bed. Even Grandma and Feisty had retired to her main-floor master suite.

So Ben headed up to the room that Jake had been using, was probably going to still use when he and Katie returned. For now Jake had cleared out his things so that Ben could take his place.

But just as he couldn't take Dale's place, Ben sure wasn't going to be able to take Jake's either. Nobody could fill Big Jake Haven's shoes. And Ben didn't want to; he just wanted to be himself, but a better version, one who was more present for his family. Right now, that family was asleep while he was lying in bed staring up at the ceiling.

The high ceiling in his condo had rafters above, like the rest of the old industrial warehouse that had been converted into living spaces. The renaissance of abandoned buildings in Willow Creek was one of the projects he'd spearheaded as deputy mayor.

Since he'd done that with old properties, he had to be able to do that with his family... and with himself. He had to figure out a way to revitalize his personal life too.

Thinking about that—about how to help the boys—was better than thinking about Emily Trent...

Even when she was looking at him with disdain, she was beautiful. Her eyes so blue, her hair such a pale blond that it shimmered in the sunshine, and when she smiled at the boys, her whole face lit up with such a glow of warmth and loveliness from the inside out.

What the...?

Was Baker right? Had Ben been mooning over her like one of the little boys? He was not about to join that prepubescent fan club of hers, because she so clearly was not a fan of his. And even if she was...

He wasn't looking for commitment.

He recoiled at the thought of ever risking his heart that way, of ever trusting anyone enough not to break it. Then he pushed thoughts of all those things from his mind and focused only on sleeping. He must have finally drifted off because he jerked awake at a sound—the earsplitting sound of a blood-curdling scream.

But it wasn't his. He'd actually been having a sweet dream about a certain blond-haired teacher. The scream repeated, jolting him fully awake and out of bed. He rushed out of his room and down the hall to the nursery.

Little Jake's nightmares—that must have been what had awakened the toddler. Nightmares that he never spoke of, just awoke from, screaming. That was partly why Ben had only stayed at the ranch those first two weeks after the accident...

It had been so hard to comfort the kids. No. It had been impossible to comfort the kids. But suddenly the screaming stopped even before he pushed open the door, and when he did, he saw why...and now he wondered if he was fully awake or if he was still dreaming.

Because Emily, with her blond hair tousled, looked like a dream. Like an angel...

UNDER THE INTENSITY of Ben Haven's unblinking stare, Emily shivered. Although her oversize T-shirt and pajama bottoms were not the least bit provocative or revealing, she wished she'd taken the time to pull on a robe. But Little Jake's scream had been so loud, had sounded so full of terror, that she'd rushed to the nursery to pull him from his nightmare and into her arms. He clung to her, his hands fisted in her already messed-up hair, as sobs racked his small body.

"It's okay," she said. "I've got you. You're fine. It was just a dream. Just a bad dream…"

But she didn't believe that any more than he probably did. She figured it was memories— of the accident that had taken his parents from him—that plagued Little Jake's dreams and gave him these night terrors.

"I didn't know he was still having these," Ben murmured as he joined her in the room.

How was it that she got out of bed feeling so frumpy and sweaty and disgusting, while he woke up looking so sexy? His T-shirt molded to his chest, his pajama bottoms hung low on his lean hips and his hair looked as if it had been styled in a salon to look as effortlessly tousled as it did.

He was just too good-looking, which for some reason irritated her so much that she couldn't stop another pithy remark from slipping out of her lips. "How *would* you know?" she asked. "You haven't been around."

He flinched then, like he had in the field when she'd admonished him for not being around more.

And she felt a twinge of guilt, especially when she turned and noticed that they were no longer alone. Little Jake's screams had awakened everyone, at least on this floor of the house. The other boys, Taye and Melanie stood in the hall outside the open door to the nursery. Miller had come out without his crutches, and he leaned heavily against Melanie, who had big dark circles beneath her big dark eyes, as if she was exhausted. The two of them had the long trip tomorrow; they needed their sleep.

"You can all go back to bed," she told them. "I've got him…"

"Looks like he has you," Ben remarked as he slid one of his fingers over his nephew's pudgy hand, which was locked tightly around the tresses of her hair. "It's okay, little guy. We're all here. You're safe. You're fine…"

And as if he'd needed the reassurance of a deep, male voice, Little Jake's cries stopped, and a ragged sigh escaped his lips.

Ben's words must have reassured him. But Emily did not feel reassured. In fact, she felt just the opposite. She felt that she was not safe. She was not fine.

Not with Ben staying at the ranch, not with him looking as effortlessly handsome as he looked, and especially not with him being so sweet with the little boys who meant so much to her.

He was getting to her in a way that she'd sworn he never would. She could not be attracted to him—such an attraction would only lead to emotional pain…for her. Just as it had for those girls in high school, the ones who'd thought he would fall for them just like Jake had fallen for Katie, and Dale for Jenny. But as a teenager, and even as an adult, Ben had never given his heart to anyone, just heartbreak. And Emily had had more than enough of that in her life.

CHAPTER EIGHT

BEN KNEW WHEN he wasn't wanted, and clearly Emily did not want him anywhere near her. She actually seemed to resent his mere presence in the nursery. But at least he wasn't the only one she was trying to get rid of; she'd directed everybody else to go back to bed too.

The only one who actually seemed to be listening to her, though, was Little Jake, who'd gone limp in her arms.

"He fell back to sleep that quickly?" Ben asked with surprise.

"I'm not sure he was actually ever awake," she said.

Despite his body being limp, the little boy's hands were still clenching her hair. "Do you want me to help you with him?" Ben asked, but he could have guessed her response before she even uttered it.

"No. I've got him," she said. But then she arched her neck toward the hall. "Can you get the rest of them back to bed, though?"

He didn't know if she actually wanted or needed the help, or if she was just using it as an excuse to get rid of him. Either way, the other kids had to go back to sleep, especially Miller, who was leaving in the morning.

"Back to bed for all of us," Ben murmured as he approached the open door.

"You said we were going to stay up all night," Caleb reminded him. "And play video games and eat junk food."

Ben suppressed a groan over having his own words tossed back at him, especially when he was getting tired himself, so tired that his eyes felt gritty from lack of sleep.

"You did?" Ian asked him with surprise. "What are you even doing here, Uncle Ben?"

"We're kind of having a sleepover," he replied. He did not want to go where late-night conversations with Ian had headed those two weeks Ben had stayed at the ranch. He didn't want to tell the little boy why his parents weren't home. "And tonight that means to actually sleep, so let's get you all back to bed."

Miller didn't bother suppressing his groan of disappointment.

"You're leaving in the morning, bud," Ben reminded him. "You need your sleep."

"Yes," Melanie agreed with a smile of gratitude at Ben. It lit up her dark eyes with warmth, and he felt a pang of recognition in that she looked very much like Jenny—very maternal and loving. "We're going to have a long day tomorrow, so we need to get back to bed." She slipped her arm around the boy and helped steady him as they turned in the hall.

"Do you need help?" Ben asked her. "I can carry him."

"I'm not a baby, Uncle Ben," Miller said, his pride obviously injured at Ben's offer. "I don't need anybody to carry me." He pulled away from Melanie and hobbled off down the hall to his room.

Ben sighed and murmured, "I can't do anything right…" Not with Emily and not with his nephews.

Melanie reached out and sympathetically squeezed Ben's arm. "He's always grumpy when Little Jake wakes us up like this. And I think he's nervous about tomorrow. I'll go talk to him." She headed off down the hall after the seven-year-old.

Taye took Ian's hand. "I'll bring this one back to bed," she offered.

Maybe she'd suspected how badly Ben did

not want to deal with the question Ian always asked. *Where's Mommy and Daddy?*

Taye wasn't giving him the chance to ask, though, as she quizzed the little boy on what his favorite cookies were and if he preferred cake over pie.

"Cake," he replied. "Because of the frosting…"

"He's right," Caleb murmured as his friend disappeared down the hallway. "Cake is better."

"Guess that leaves you and me," Ben said to his new nephew as they stood alone in the hall. Behind him, Emily was whispering something to Little Jake, something soft and sweet that made tension curl in the pit of Ben's stomach.

"We're going to stay up all night and play video games?" Caleb asked hopefully.

Ben smiled until he noticed the faint sheen of tears in Caleb's eyes. He wasn't sure if the boy really wanted to stay up all night, or if he just didn't want to be alone.

"What's wrong, buddy?" Ben asked him. "Are you okay?"

Caleb nodded and blinked furiously against the tears that continued to pool in his blue eyes. But he didn't say anything, as if he didn't trust himself to speak.

Ben slid his arm around his shoulders and steered the little boy down the hall toward his room. Once they were inside and Ben saw the neatly made bed, he could tell that Caleb hadn't even been in it yet despite how late it was. "Didn't anybody tuck you in earlier?" he asked as he tried to lead the child toward the bed.

But Caleb resisted and shook his head. "I didn't want anybody to…" And those tears filled his eyes again. "I don't wanna go to sleep."

"You can talk to me," Ben told the boy. "You can tell me what's going on."

Caleb drew in a shaky breath before replying. "I wanna play video games instead. Or we could watch a movie…"

The five-year-old clearly didn't want to be alone.

"You don't want to talk?" Ben asked. "You don't want to tell me what's bothering you?"

Caleb shook his head again. "Nothing's bothering me. I'm a big boy. I don't need my mommy. Like Miller, I'm not a baby either."

"Just because you need your mom doesn't make you a baby," Ben assured him, his heart aching for the little boy and aching over his own loss. He'd been eleven when his dad had died, and he'd never needed his mother more than he had then. But she'd taken off, rejoining the rodeo she'd always regretted giving up for his father, for them.

Ben hadn't been able to count on Darlene. Caleb could count on Katie.

"But Mommy's not here," Caleb said, his voice cracking as the tears finally overwhelmed him.

Ben picked up the little boy and held him close. "She's coming back, hon. She's only gone for her honeymoon, and she wouldn't have left you if she didn't think you were really okay with her being gone for a couple of weeks. Your mommy will never leave you."

"But my daddy left," Caleb said between sobs.

And pain clutched Ben's heart. "He didn't choose to do that," Ben said, defending the man he'd never met. Matt Morris must have been a very good man from how much his son and his widow loved and still missed him. "That was an accident, and it wasn't his fault. He loved you very much."

Caleb sniffled. "I know. He wouldn't want me to cry. He would want me to be happy."

But clearly the boy was miserable instead, and he was second-guessing that he'd urged his mother to leave him for two weeks. Ben considered carrying the child down to his grandmother, since Sadie was the one who'd orchestrated this whole honeymoon thing.

"If you would be happier to have your mother home, we can call her," Ben offered. "We can tell her that you need her to come back."

"I'm not a baby," Caleb said again. "I'll be okay." But he was still sniffling, trying to suck up the tears that streaked down his little face.

And broke Ben's heart.

"You're not a baby," Ben agreed. But five was so young, so young to have already lost his father, so young to have had all the changes in his life that he'd had. "You're going to help me with that bronco tomorrow. Teach me how to handle it."

He'd thought mentioning Midnight would get the little boy's mind off his mother, but Caleb was too tired and too emotional to do anything but cry.

As his tears were soaking Ben's T-shirt, they were also wearing Ben down, making his heart ache even more. "I have your mom's cell-phone number. I can call them and tell them to come home," he offered. "They'll be on the next plane back to Willow Creek."

Caleb blinked back the tears and stared up at him almost hopefully. He didn't want to be the one to ask them to come back, but he clearly wanted them home. Poor kid...

"What are you doing?" a female voice asked, and Ben turned to find Emily standing in the doorway, her blue eyes wide.

He was trying to comfort a little boy, but Caleb must not have wanted Miss Trent to see him crying because he quickly brushed away his tears and wriggled down from Ben's arms to jump onto his bed.

"I'm going to sleep," he told the teacher, as if he expected her to reprimand him for being up yet.

But from the scowl she focused on Ben, he was the one who was about to get reprimanded.

She confirmed it when she asked, "Can I see you in the hall for a moment?"

Ben drew in a breath to brace himself before nodding. Then he turned back to Caleb and offered him a slight smile and a wink. "Sounds like we should both be in bed already, buddy. But if you need me for anything, you come get me."

Caleb nodded. "I love you, Uncle Ben."

Those words flooded Ben's previously aching heart with warmth and had tears stinging his eyes. He leaned over the bed to kiss the little boy's forehead. "I love you too."

EMILY BACKED UP into the hall to wait for him to step out of Caleb's room, and because she needed a moment to compose herself.

How had he done it already? How had he enthralled Caleb Morris so quickly? Just as he'd charmed so many of the teenage girls in their high school and, more recently, enough of the town to get elected in what had been called a landslide victory.

Of course, she had to begrudgingly admit, he'd done some good for the town. He'd improved areas of it that had been neglected, like the empty buildings and some roads and parks. And he'd introduced a lot of new projects and even encouraged more support for the public school system.

Yet she still didn't trust him. So after putting Little Jake back to bed, she'd followed the sound of his voice to Caleb's room, and she'd overheard what he'd been trying to talk the little boy into—into calling Katie and Ben back from their honeymoon already.

Ben finally stepped out of Caleb's room and pulled the door shut behind him, as if he knew how angry she was with him.

"How dare you!" she exclaimed, but she had to keep her voice down so she wouldn't disturb everybody else, as they'd probably just gotten back to sleep.

"How dare I what?" Ben asked, and he sounded surprisingly innocent.

"I heard you trying to coerce Caleb into asking his mother to come home," she said. "You couldn't even make it twenty-four hours? Is being with your family, taking care of these kids, too much for responsibility for you?"

Ben sucked in a breath and shook his head. "You don't understand—"

"No, I don't," she agreed. "I don't understand people who shirk their responsibilities, who turn their backs on family." Like her family had turned theirs on her after her mother died. By then they had already abandoned her mother. If they had ever supported the young single mom, she might not have been so desperate for attention that she'd hung out with the wrong people and gotten into bad things, things that had led to her untimely death from a drug overdose.

Ben looked like he had in the nursery, when she'd criticized him for not being around more. "I don't understand people like that either," he murmured.

And she remembered what Katie had told her about his mother. About how she'd taken off when his dad had died…

Katie had probably shared that story so that Emily would cut him some slack, but it had only made her more wary of him. Because now she knew he had that behavior as an example, that shirking of responsibility…

"You *are* people like that," she said, and maybe she was reminding herself of that as much as she was pointing it out to him. "You've not been present for these kids. And now you're trying to get out of the two weeks you committed to staying here with them by getting Caleb to call his mom to come home already. That's low."

He arched a dark brow. "Even for me?" he asked. "Isn't that what you meant to say? Why do you dislike me so much?"

"I—I…" She couldn't explain why he irritated her. Maybe it was because he didn't seem to appreciate the wonderful family that he had—with the boys and Jake and even Sadie, despite her meddling. Or maybe she couldn't get over how he'd made so many of her friends cry over him.

Or maybe…

No. She refused to admit to any attraction to him. While she could acknowledge that he was ridiculously handsome, she was not like her friends—she was not besotted with him. She looked for more than good looks; she looked for substance.

"Miss Trent," a little voice called out from behind the closed door.

She reached for the knob, and that put her hand near his side since Ben had not moved out of the doorway. He stood between her and the little boy. "Caleb needs me," she said.

But he still didn't step aside. "Caleb needs his mother," he said.

"You better not call her," Emily warned him. "Katie and Jake deserve this honeymoon. And even if you can't last twenty-four hours, Taye and Melanie and I will take care of the boys the next two weeks."

He sighed and moved aside, letting her open the door for Caleb's room. She turned back to warn him again not to call Katie, but he was already walking away from her.

"Miss Trent," Caleb called out from within the room, his voice querulous with tears.

"Oh, sweetheart," she murmured as she hurried to his bedside. "Are you all right?"

Caleb was always upbeat and happy; she'd never seen him like this, though she knew Jake had mopped up his tears a couple of times when he'd been missing his late father. Caleb nodded even as more tears streaked down his face. "Don't be mad at Uncle Ben," he said. "He was only trying to make me feel better."

"What?" Maybe she hadn't lowered her voice as much as she'd thought she had, since it seemed that the little boy had overheard the conversation in the hall. Not that Ben had said much…but she certainly had.

And she felt a flash of regret over that. Was she judging him too harshly again?

"Uncle Ben knows I'm missing Mommy, and he was saying that she'll come home if I call her."

That regret sharpened to the pain of remorse. "You're missing Mommy?" she asked.

He nodded, and the tears streaking down his face dripped off his pointed little chin.

"I thought you wanted her to go on this honeymoon," she said.

"I did," he said. "I do. But I still miss her. I never even spent the night away from her before."

And since his father had died, he was probably even closer and more dependent on his mother. Emily had been so worried about the other boys that she hadn't given enough attention to Caleb. He'd acted so unconcerned earlier, had even refused her tucking him in for the night.

"I'm so sorry, sweetheart," she said. "I had no idea you were missing her this much. Uncle Ben is right." And she was surprised she could admit that. "You can absolutely call her, and she would come home right away."

He released a shaky little breath and nodded.

"You want to call her?" she asked.

He shook his head now. "No. I want her and Daddy Jake to take the honeymoon me and Grandma gave them. I just…"

He needed reassurance, and Ben had given him that…until she'd blown it when Caleb must have overheard her yelling at the man— albeit quietly—out in the hall.

"Your mother loves you so much," Emily said. "And if you want her to come home, she certainly will. She'll get back to the ranch just as fast as she can." She had no doubt that Katie would move heaven and earth to reach her child if Caleb really needed her.

The tension eased from Caleb's little body, and he relaxed into his pillows. "I know. That's good. I'm good. She and Daddy Jake don't need to come home now, not as long as..."

"As long as what?" she asked when he trailed off.

"As long as Uncle Ben stays," he finished.

Alarm rushed over her now. Had she chased him off with what she'd said to him, with the conclusions she'd jumped to? With as rude as she'd been to the man who'd been trying all day to help with the kids...

Even as her stomach churned with all her regrets, she forced a smile for the little boy. "What makes you think he's not staying?"

"You said he couldn't last twenty-four hours."

And from their lessons on telling time, Caleb knew there were twenty-four hours in a day—not in two weeks. She sighed. "I think I was wrong," she admitted. "I misunderstood your conversation with him..."

And she'd misjudged Ben.

"I don't want him to go," Caleb said. "Uncle

Ben wants me to show him how to take care of Midnight. He's the only one who wants to take care of him besides me."

When she'd told Ben that he could leave, and she and Taye and Melanie would take care of the boys, she'd forgotten all about that horse and about the ranch. They did need Ben. Well, not her—she certainly didn't need him. But the ranch and the horse and even the little boys needed him.

She stretched her smile a little wider and assured Caleb, "I'll make sure he's staying."

Ben probably wouldn't listen to her, not now, but maybe he would listen to Sadie. But first Emily owed him an apology.

Caleb must have taken her at her word because he closed his eyes and drifted off to sleep. She slipped quietly out of his room and closed the door.

Ben hadn't stayed by the door. He hadn't eavesdropped on their conversation, so he probably didn't know that she'd realized how wrong she'd been.

She walked down the hall, passing a few doors until she reached the one to his room. She lifted her hand to it and knocked softly, so that she wouldn't wake up anyone else. She doubted he was asleep already, so he should hear even a soft knock. But he didn't open the door. So she lifted her hand and knocked again, a little bit harder. He must not have closed the door tightly because it creaked open, revealing his bed with the blankets tossed back.

His empty bed.

Maybe she hadn't misjudged him at all. Maybe he really hadn't been able to make it twenty-four hours.

CHAPTER NINE

"Wow, you look like something Feisty dragged in after she played with it until it was half-dead," Taye remarked as a bleary-eyed Ben stumbled into the kitchen.

"Ouch," Ben replied. He was used to women complimenting his appearance, not complaining about it, but he had no doubt the cook spoke the truth.

After Little Jake had awakened everyone last night and Ben had had that ugly confrontation with Emily, he'd known he wouldn't be able to fall asleep again. So instead of trying, he'd gone back out to the ranch business office in that old schoolhouse Grandma had had moved to the property. Since Katie and Jake had everything under control in regard to the ranch books, Ben had used one of the computers to go online to pull up his own emails and files and work on some of his ongoing projects in town. He couldn't leave all of his mayoral duties for Lem to do by himself.

He also wanted everybody to know that even though he was staying out at the ranch, he was not neglecting his duties—his *responsibilities*. He wanted to be reelected next year. His job—carrying on his great-grandfather's legacy—was very important to him; sometimes it felt like all he had.

He had his family too, though, and after Emily had berated him, he knew he couldn't neglect them like he had. Remembering what she'd said, how she'd labeled him one of those people who shirked his duty to his family, Ben grimaced as pain gripped his chest again, squeezing his heart. He wasn't like his mother. He couldn't be. He wouldn't be. He had to be here for them. For all of them...

Instead of going out to the old schoolhouse, he'd considered talking to his grandmother or to Baker, but he hadn't wanted to wake them at that hour. He was going to be at the ranch two weeks—unless Caleb called his parents to come home sooner—so he had plenty of time to talk to them both. To Baker about his reluctance to spend time with the kids, and to Grandma...

Oh, it was no use talking to Grandma. She wasn't going to give up on her scheme, but it didn't matter. No woman in this household was interested in him.

"Couldn't you get back to sleep after Little Jake woke everyone up last night?" Taye asked, and she handed him a cup of coffee.

He shook his head then breathed in the scent of the aromatic brew. Even Taye's coffee was special.

"Why not?" she asked. "He settled back down quickly like he usually does."

"Let's say somebody else didn't settle back down like Little Jake did," he replied.

Taye chuckled. "Are you talking about Caleb or Emily?"

"Did you overhear us talking in the hall?" he asked. Caleb must have, because he'd called out for Miss Trent. Hopefully, she'd been able to comfort the little boy more than he had.

"I didn't hear *you* do much talking," Taye admitted.

He shrugged. "Didn't seem to be much point. Emily has her mind made up about me."

Unfortunately, she wasn't entirely wrong. Although he'd stayed at the ranch the first two weeks after the accident that had taken Dale and Jenny, he'd bailed on the boys once Grandma had hired the women to help out.

He'd convinced himself that it was okay to leave then, that Sadie and Jake had everything under control like they always did. But he'd had a twinge of guilt over it over the last six weeks. He'd known the few visits he'd made during that time hadn't been enough, that he should have been doing more.

Emily apparently thought the same way. That he was one of *those* people who flaked out when they were needed most, like his mother. Did Emily know about his mother, about how Darlene had abandoned them?

If she did, then her words had been especially harsh but still justified. He hadn't stepped up like he should have.

"Emily does not like me," Ben said needlessly, since it had to be clear to everyone how much she disliked him.

"She doesn't really know you," Taye said.

He sighed. "According to Emily, she does. We went to school together."

"You sound surprised," Taye said as she filled her own cup. "Don't you remember her?"

He shook his head. "Not like she remembers me." He narrowed his eyes and studied Taye's face. She looked even younger than Emily was. "We didn't go to school together too, did we?"

Taye chuckled and shook her head. "No. We didn't. You had already graduated when I started high school. And I only went to school here in Willow Creek when I was staying with my dad. My stepsisters were closer to your age."

She shared their names with him, but as with Emily, his mind drew a blank. He could remember his close friends, his teammates, his teachers and his family from his school days, but not much else, or many other people who had made an impact on him. Maybe that was because his grandfather dying just as Ben had begun his freshmen year of college had hit him so hard that it had eclipsed his high-school years. He would have done what Jake had; he would have come home, but Jake and his grandmother had convinced him not to throw away the academic scholarship he'd earned. They'd convinced him that everything was under control back at the ranch. That he wasn't needed; his family hadn't needed him. The ranch had thrived with Jake and Dale running it.

But the town…

It had begun to suffer. Lem was a good mayor, but his wife had been sick a long time, longer than anyone had realized. So Lem and the town had needed Ben. And he'd needed to preserve his great-grandfather's legacy; that had become his entire focus.

He shook his head. "Sorry, I don't remember your sisters."

Taye chuckled. "They remember you."

"Did I go out with them?" he asked. He'd never asked girls out in high school because he hadn't wanted any of them to think that he'd fall for them—like Jake had fallen for Katie and Dale for Jenny. He hadn't been looking for anything serious, but he had gone out with girls who'd asked him out—because he hadn't wanted to reject them and hurt their feelings. But he'd been clear that he was focused on school and his future career.

Taye shrugged. "I think you danced with one at prom."

He'd gone stag, but that was about all he remembered about that night. He sighed. "Maybe I was as self-involved in high school as Emily accused me of being." Maybe he still was.

Taye tensed as if Emily had directed the comment at her. While Ben didn't know the younger woman, he doubted anyone had ever accused Taye Cooper of being self-involved. She seemed very caring and loving, the kind of person who was happiest when she was making others happy, whether with the food she prepared for them or the kind words she said to them.

"I hope you don't take anything she says too personally," Taye told him. "Most of the care for the boys falls on Emily, so she's been under a lot of stress."

Thinking of Little Jake's bloodcurdling cries in the night and Ian having to be constantly reminded that his parents were dead, Ben released an unsteady breath and said, "That's a lot of stress."

And it wasn't fair to Emily. She wasn't family. She was just Ian's teacher, whom his grandmother had coerced into helping out with the boys. Sure, Sadie was probably paying her, but it couldn't be enough to deal with the emotional trauma the boys were experiencing right now. Why had she stayed all these weeks? Why hadn't she left, like she'd accused him of wanting to do last night?

Was that why she'd accused him of wanting to leave? Because *she* wanted to leave?

Ben couldn't imagine how the boys would feel if someone else they were attached to—and they were clearly all very attached to Emily Trent—disappeared from their lives.

Sure, Jenny and Dale and Matt Morris hadn't had the choice to stay, but maybe that made the loss of them a little easier to handle. They hadn't left of their own accord, just as Ben's dad hadn't when he'd died in a ranching accident.

Maybe that was why Ben had taken his mother's loss a little harder than he had his dad's, because his mom could have stayed, but she made the choice to leave them.

Eventually—because she wasn't family— Emily would probably choose to do the same, to go back to her job, to her life… And just as his mother had when she'd left, Emily would also leave behind devastated little boys who would forever miss her.

AT THE RUMBLE of Ben's deep voice, Emily had paused midstep on the back stairwell that led down to the kitchen and eavesdropped unabashedly on his conversation with Taye.

He hadn't left.

Her pulse quickened at that thought and the sound of his voice. She didn't know if she was irritated that he was still here or relieved.

She could use some extra help with the boys, especially since Melanie and Miller would be leaving this morning. Even though

Miller was supposed to be Melanie's sole responsibility, the physical therapist helped out with Ian, Caleb and Little Jake as well.

Just like Taye did, even though her realm was the kitchen. But because there were so many people for whom Taye had to cook, the younger woman didn't have a lot of extra time to spare. Neither would Ben if he was working the ranch…

And it would be better if he was working the ranch, if he was off riding horses on the range, or whatever cowboys called the property.

"Miss Trent?" Caleb called out behind her. "Are you all right?"

"What?" Startled by the sudden appearance of the boy on the stairs behind her, she whirled around and nearly tumbled down the rest of the steps. "Yes, of course…"

But she wasn't all right, not after overhearing the conversation between Taye and Ben that had been too much about her. About her being under stress…

Was she lashing out at Ben because of the stress? She almost wished she was because that was an excuse that she could understand. That was a better excuse than that she was at all attracted to him and trying to fight that attraction so hard that she rebelled at the cause of it. At him…

She still owed him an apology for how she'd treated him the day before. She probably owed him more than one.

He had stayed.

"I have to help Uncle Ben with Midnight this morning," Caleb said as he slipped past her on the stairs. "Uncle Ben, are you ready to go to the barn?"

Emily drew in a deep breath before she descended the last few steps and joined them all in the kitchen. Taye and Ben had already turned toward the stairwell, as if they'd been waiting for her. They must have heard Caleb address her and realized she'd been eavesdropping on them. Heat flushed her face with embarrassment.

"Let Uncle Ben have some breakfast before you head out to the barn," Taye told the little boy. "And you need to eat something too."

"Cookies?" he asked hopefully as he widened his blue eyes.

Taye snorted. "You know better than to try that puppy-dog-begging look on me. Cookies are for only after you've eaten nutritional foods."

Caleb grimaced. "Sounds yucky."

"You need some coffee too?" Taye asked Emily as she held out a cup toward her.

Emily gave an eager nod and reached out for the steaming mug. But she couldn't help adding, "Is caffeine good for someone as stressed as I am?"

"I don't think it's the coffee that's making you stressed," Taye said.

And from her tone, it wasn't clear if she thought the boys were either. Or if Ben Haven was the real cause of her stress.

The younger woman was entirely too astute, a lot like Sadie. Maybe too much like her.

Sadie chose that moment to walk into the kitchen. Emily wondered if the older woman might have also been eavesdropping, especially when she sent Emily a slightly sympathetic smile...or as sympathetic as Sadie ever was. The older woman was so incredibly strong, but then she'd had to be with all the losses she'd endured.

And even though Sadie didn't always show it, she *was* sympathetic, or she wouldn't have been so determined to make certain all of her great-grandsons' needs were met.

Emily had to admit that caring for the boys had stressed her out. She really didn't have an excuse for being as rude as she'd been to Ben, though. All she had to offer him was that apology, but it stuck in her throat.

Feisty pranced into the kitchen behind Sadie then ran over to Ben, tugging at the hems on his pajama bottoms. With a fierce growl, the little dog pulled hard on the material.

"You look so much like something she dragged into the house that she must be trying to drag you back out," Sadie remarked—with no compassion—to her grandson.

Ben ran a hand over the stubble on his square jaw. "I haven't had a chance to shave yet."

Sadie wrinkled her nose. "Or shower."

"I don't think Midnight is going to care if I'm shaved and showered," Ben remarked with a glance at Caleb. "Is he?"

Caleb shook his head. "All he cares about is getting his carrots. He really likes carrots."

"And a clean stall," Sadie added.

Ben sighed. "I'm going. I'm going."

While his grandmother didn't betray any concern for him, Emily felt a little for him. If he'd gotten any sleep at all last night, it hadn't been much, and not nearly enough to fuel him for the kind of long days that Jake put in working the ranch and helping out with the boys. The one cup of coffee Ben had had with Taye wasn't going to fuel him either.

Taye must have realized the same thing because she said, "Just wait a couple of minutes. Have another cup of coffee and breakfast will be ready. You need to eat something." She pointed her spatula at Caleb. "And you need to eat more than cookies." She turned that spatula in Emily's direction and asked, "What do you need?"

As if the cooking utensil was a weapon, Emily held up her hand not holding the coffee. "Whatever you're making is good with me."

Taye narrowed her pale blue eyes and studied Emily's face. "Is that all?"

No. And how did Taye always know?

"Will you be able to watch Little Jake and Caleb later this morning while I work on some lessons with Ian one-on-one?" she asked.

"Lessons?" Caleb asked with a grimace. "School is supposed to be done for summer."

"For you, it is," she acknowledged. Caleb had easily passed kindergarten and earned his summer vacation, which was one reason she'd chosen to do her lessons with Ian one-on-one—Caleb didn't need them. The other reason was that Caleb helped out his best friend too much with his memory lapses. Emily needed to know what Ian remembered of the school year curriculum, not what Caleb remembered—which was, undoubtedly, everything because the little boy was incredibly smart.

"Sorry," Taye replied. "I'm going into town to grab some things for the party we're throwing for Miller when he and Melanie get back home tomorrow."

They'd all planned the party days ago. The seven-year-old certainly deserved a celebration after suffering through surgeries to mend his broken bones and with having a cast for so long. Hopefully, he would be happier once the heavy thing was off his leg.

"Of course," Emily said. "I'll just wait to have a lesson with Ian until after Melanie and Miller are back."

"You don't have to wait," Ben said. "Caleb's already going to be with me helping with Midnight, so I can take Little Jake too."

She narrowed her eyes and studied his face. "Aren't you supposed to be working the ranch? Wasn't that your agreement?"

"An agreement you already don't think I'm going to honor," Ben reminded her.

She wanted him out in the pastures, not near her and the boys, especially after his own grandmother had made remarks about not trusting him alone with the kids. She glanced at Sadie, hoping the older woman would intervene or at least offer to watch her great-grandsons.

But, as if she'd heard Emily's unspoken question, she shook her head, which swirled her long white hair around her shoulders. "I'm going to keep an eye on the ranch books. Make sure Old Man Lemmon's kid isn't ripping us off," she said. "I also want to check out these ranch foremen Jake is trying out for the job."

Taye sighed. "I'm sure you two can figure out something between you," she said, and gestured with that spatula again—at Emily and Ben. "You can break up your lessons and let Ben watch Caleb and Little Jake while you're working with Ian. And when you're done, you can relieve him, so he can work the ranch."

Taye's suggestion was a good one, especially because it was so hard for Ian to pay attention for long periods of time. His lessons were easier when broken into small blocks. But Emily was too proud to admit that Taye was right, especially when her suggestion meant that Emily would have to see Ben again, when they handed the kids off to each other, like divorced parents meeting in a neutral location.

But this was Ben's home. There was no neutral place for Emily here. No place where she felt safe and, at the moment, no one with whom she felt safe. Except for the kids. She felt safe with them; maybe because she understood them so well. Or so she'd thought...

A short while later when she was in the playroom, which had been converted into a classroom, with Ian, she wondered if she fully understood him.

"I want to go to the barn with Caleb, Little Jake and Uncle Ben," he said.

She understood that—that the five-year-old would rather play than work—but she didn't understand how he'd remembered where Caleb was and with whom. She narrowed her eyes as she studied him across the table. "Do you know what they're doing out there?" she asked.

He sighed. "Working with the bronco."

She hoped not. She hoped Ben had enough

sense to make sure that the boys stayed far away from that wild horse.

"So you remember that," she mused. "How about this?" She pointed to the math problem on the paper in front of him.

He sighed again. "That's easy. Two plus two is four."

Just as he'd said, that was an easy one; something he'd known before getting the concussion that had affected his short-term memory. Sadie had said that the doctors believed his brain would eventually heal.

Was it healing?

Was he getting better? She ran through some more problems, which he solved as easily as Caleb solved them.

"Can we go out to the barn now?" he asked.

He still remembered where the other boys were.

And she wondered...

Had his memory returned but he didn't want anyone to know? But why? Was something going on with the little boy, something not about his memory but about his emotional state?

CHAPTER TEN

BEING AROUND THE bronco was a lot like being around Emily Trent. Clearly, neither of them trusted Ben and were likely to lash out without provocation and without any warning.

Just as the horse warily eyed Ben, Ben warily eyed the black stallion while he cleaned the soiled wood shavings out of Midnight's stall. With each scrape of the shovel across the ground, the horse tensed and shifted his legs. And Ben braced himself for a kick.

The horse was probably stressed out. Ben had no idea how he'd even arrived at the ranch. Had Dusty had him shipped over land, or had the horse been flown here?

No matter how he'd wound up at Ranch Haven, the bronco had had to leave his familiar surroundings. He'd been plunged into a new place with new people. Maybe that was why Caleb was so attached to the animal—he related to him. A year ago, after his dad had died, Katie had moved her son back to her hometown and away from the house, friends and school that was all Caleb had ever known in Chicago.

The kid had adapted well, at least to life here at the ranch. On the other side of the stall door, Caleb was taking Little Jake for a ride in the barn. Both wearing the small white Stetsons they'd worn at the wedding, they were riding a bale of hay that Ben had saddled for them in the middle of the barn, where he could keep an eye on them, just like Midnight was keeping an eye on Ben.

Just like Emily had last night when she'd followed him and the boys out to the barn after dinner, as if she didn't trust him alone with his own nephews. When he heard boots scraping against the concrete floor of the barn, he glanced over the stall door expecting to see Emily, even though her lesson with Ian shouldn't have ended yet.

"Uncle Baker!" Caleb called out. "Look at me and Little Jake, we're riding a bronco just like Uncle Dusty!" The boy bucked up and down on the saddle, jostling Little Jake and making him giggle.

Ben chuckled at the sound of that laugh and at Caleb's vivid imagination. Not so much about riding the bronco but about Uncle

Dusty. Dusty had cut out of his twin's funeral without taking time to speak to anyone, so there was no way Caleb had even met him yet.

Ignoring the boys, Baker's topaz-colored eyes—wide with horror—met Ben's over the stall door. "You're in there with that thing?"

At the sound of Baker's voice, the bronco shifted inside the stall, pawing at the ground. And, Ben, done with cleaning, quickly slipped out the door to safety. "He was fine until you showed up," Ben said.

Maybe not exactly fine. But the horse hadn't been as edgy as he was now, as those strange guttural warning noises emanated from inside his stall as if Midnight was telling Ben to stay out. Ben wouldn't be able to do that—at least not for the next thirteen days.

"Midnight likes Uncle Ben," Caleb told Baker. "Prolly cuz Uncle Ben looks a lot like Daddy Jake. Midnight really likes Daddy Jake. He's prolly missing him a whole lot right now." Caleb's little mouth slid down at the corners in a slight frown. Midnight was clearly not the only one missing Daddy Jake.

"I bet some carrots would make Midnight feel better," Ben suggested. "You could run up to the house to get some for him, and maybe Miss Taye would let you have a few cookies now since you ate all your nutritional breakfast."

Caleb's mouth turned back up into a big smile. "I did. Okay, I'll go get the cookies—I mean…the carrots." He jumped up from the saddle so quickly that it began to slip off the side of the hay bale, upending Little Jake with it. The toddler hit the concrete floor and the saddle hit him. He screamed—not as loudly as he had the night before—but loud enough that he spooked the bronco, who reared up and kicked at the door of his stall.

While Baker stood closer to Little Jake, he didn't move—it was as if he was frozen in place. Ben rushed over and pulled off the heavy saddle. But then, even though his heart was pounding fast and hard, he froze too, uncertain if he should move the little boy. He didn't want to hurt him, but he ached with the need to comfort the crying toddler. He glanced up at Baker. "You're the paramedic," he said over Jake's cries. "Is it safe? Can I pick him up?"

Baker finally moved, dropping onto his knees beside the little boy. He swept his hands over him, but he didn't lift him either.

Ben drew in a shaky breath and held it,

waiting for Baker's prognosis. Little Jake had to be all right. The child had already been through too much in his young life.

Caleb leaned against Ben, his little body shaking with fear too. "Is he okay? I'm sorry, Uncle Ben. I didn't know the saddle would slide off."

Ben swept his hand over Caleb's blond hair. "It's my fault, buddy." He thought putting the saddle on the bale of hay would keep them entertained and safe.

"Oh, no!" Emily cried out as she ran into the barn, Ian right behind her. "What's wrong? What happened?" She dropped to her knees beside Baker and Little Jake. "Is he okay?"

Baker nodded. "Yeah, he didn't fall far or hit the ground hard enough to break anything. I think he's just scared."

And yet Baker didn't comfort the little boy. He just sat there, staring at him in alarm. What in the world was going on with Ben's baby brother?

He would have to address that later. Right now he was worried about the other baby, Little Jake.

Emily picked him up and the toddler clung to her, rubbing his wet face against her shoulder as he continued to cry. "Shh…it's okay," she said. "I've got you. You're okay." Over the little boy's head, her gaze—full of accusation—met Ben's. She shook her head and murmured with disgust, "I should have known better than to trust you to watch them."

"You didn't trust me," he pointed out. "Or you wouldn't be out here right now." She and Ian couldn't have wrapped up the morning lesson already—not with Ian's short-term memory loss. He couldn't imagine the patience she had to possess to be able to teach the concussed little boy.

If only she had some of that patience left for Ben…

But he couldn't deny that Little Jake getting hurt was all his fault; he'd already admitted it to Caleb. So he just released the breath he'd been holding in a ragged sigh, and he resigned himself to the fact that the pretty schoolteacher would never trust him. And would never like him…

If Sadie had intended to match him with Emily Trent, there was no chance of her plan ever panning out. Not that it would have, anyway, because Ben had decided long ago that he was never going to fall in love. He still remembered the day his mother had walked away from him and his crying brothers without sparing any of them a backward glance. In the beginning she'd called to check on them and had sent letters with promises that she would come back, promises that she hadn't kept. Since he hadn't been able to trust his mother's love, he was never going to trust anyone else's.

EMILY HADN'T COME out to the barn to check up on Ben and the boys. She'd come out for another reason entirely—to offer him the apology she hadn't been able to muster up that morning.

And to thank him for offering to help with the boys.

Her lesson with Ian had continued to go surprisingly well, so much so that she grew even more sure that he was recovering fully from his concussion. But then, when she'd told him that they could finally head out to the barn, he'd asked her why. He'd forgotten that was where Caleb and Little Jake were.

And she'd put off apologizing to Ben long enough. So she'd headed out to the barn with Ian, but before they'd even neared it, they'd heard Little Jake's screams.

Her heart pounded hard with fear, just as the little boy's heart pounded against her now as he clutched her, one hand fisted in her shirt, the other in her hair.

"Are you sure he's okay?" she asked Baker, as she ran her hand over the little boy's back, trying to soothe him.

Baker was a paramedic; surely he had to be able to assess a person's injuries correctly. But the way the toddler was crying…

Baker nodded. "Yes, nothing's broken. He has a scrape on his elbow, and he's going to have some bruises."

"Oh, no," Ben gasped as if his younger brother had punched him. He shoved one of his hands through his thick hair, knocking his hat onto the floor. "We have a first aid kit in the tack room. It must have some bandages and peroxide in it. I'll go get that." But he hesitated and began, "I didn't think…" His throat moved as if he was choking as he tried to swallow.

"No, you didn't think," Emily agreed. And she stood up with the little boy still gripping her. "I'll bring him up to the house."

"It's my fault," Caleb cried out, and tears streaked down his face. "Uncle Ben told me to hang on to him while we were in the saddle. And I forgot. I jumped up and the saddle slid off. It's my fault."

And now Emily felt like she'd been punched. She'd come out to the barn to apologize, and she'd only made the situation worse when she had—once again—jumped to the wrong conclusion about Ben. But she could have sworn she'd heard Ben saying it was his fault.

"It's my fault," Caleb murmured.

"No, no, it's not," Ben assured him, and he lifted the five-year-old into his arms with more ease than she held the two-year-old. He patted the little boy's back. "It was my idea to put the saddle on the bale of hay, and it was a bad idea."

Caleb sniffled. "It was fun…" His voice broke, though, and he dissolved into sobs again.

Now, that was Emily's fault. If she hadn't reacted so strongly to Little Jake getting hurt, Caleb wouldn't be feeling so bad. "I'm sure it was an accident," she said. "Things just happen sometimes…"

Terrible things. All the boys knew that—they'd experienced it personally.

As Caleb's crying increased, Little Jake's subsided. And he released her hair to reach out to Caleb and Ben. "Cab..." he called out softly. "Cab..."

Hearing him speak made Emily's heart swell. For so long he'd been silent except for those screams in the night. But the first word he'd spoken just a week ago, after those long weeks of silence, had been to Caleb.

Caleb wriggled down from Ben's arms and turned toward the toddler. "You're okay?" he asked, his voice tremulous with his tears. "You're really okay?"

Little Jake's head bobbed in a nod.

And Emily sighed in relief. "Okay, then let's all head up to the house now and say goodbye to Miller and Miss Melanie. They're getting ready to leave, and Miss Taye got an early lunch ready for us since she's heading to town soon."

Emily turned then and started toward the doors. But neither Caleb nor Ian followed her.

"Aren't you coming, Uncle Ben?" Caleb asked. "And what about you, Uncle Baker?"

"I have to go check on the stock and those potential new ranch foremen," Baker replied, which was more information than a five-year-old needed. It was obvious even to Emily that he was defensive.

"You should be going to that doctor's appointment with Melanie and Miller," Ben said.

"If you don't want them going alone, you can go," Baker replied.

"No!" Caleb interjected. "Uncle Ben has to stay here."

Emily's stomach muscles tightened with dread. How could Caleb have become so attached to Ben already? And how was he going to handle Uncle Ben leaving when Jake and Katie returned?

"It would just be for a day," Baker said. "He'd be back tomorrow."

"He can't go," Caleb insisted. "He's taking care of Midnight. Midnight doesn't like you."

Baker released a breath. "No, *he* doesn't…"

But Emily wondered if Baker was talking about the horse now or someone else.

What was going on with the paramedic?

And what was going on with her that she'd started eavesdropping on the conversations of others?

She turned around then and called out, "Boys, we need to head up to the house now to say goodbye. We don't want Miss Melanie and Miller to be late for their appointment."

And she also didn't want Caleb getting any more attached to his new uncle than he already was. Or maybe he was just using Ben as a surrogate for his stepfather. The two men looked alike, but their similarities were only on the surface. Jake was a man of substance, one who took his responsibilities seriously.

While Ben...

She wasn't sure what Ben was anymore. She'd been so convinced that he was slick and full of empty promises. That he had no substance at all.

But then he hugged Caleb and assured him, "Despite what some people may think, I'm not going anywhere except up to the house to tell Miller and Melanie goodbye and good luck."

"Good!" Caleb exclaimed and, clasping Ben's big hand in his, he tugged him toward the open barn doors, where Emily stood with Little Jake.

Ian picked up Ben's hat from the ground and followed after them. As Ben and his five-year-old sidekicks passed her, he didn't even spare her a glance.

Then Little Jake wriggled down from her arms to toddle along after them. And something grasped her heart, something like a sharp twist of panic.

That was crazy. She should have been

happy that the boys were bonding with someone besides her. But she was worried that they were getting attached to the wrong person—to someone who would let them down and disappoint them. Like her relatives and all those foster families she'd grown fond of who hurt her when they'd rejected her.

She didn't want the boys to feel the disappointment—the pain—that she'd felt. They'd already experienced too much. And she'd experienced so much of it with them over the past six weeks. From the moment she'd arrived at the ranch, the boys had become connected to her. Maybe it was because she'd already been close to Ian and Caleb, because they'd been in her class, that Little Jake had been so instantly comfortable with her. And when she'd soothed him from his nightmares, they'd grown even closer.

Miller was still a little guarded with her—with everyone but Melanie—but she had fallen for him too. She'd watched him try so hard to be strong, to be more mature than he was. Like she'd tried to be when she'd been a kid—to be stronger, older, wiser. She'd come to learn then to never get attached, but she was beginning to wonder if she'd broken that rule…with the little Haven boys.

If she'd begun to get too close to them...

But she was going to have to leave them. Her boss wouldn't hold her job open forever, and the boys wouldn't need her forever, not with Ian already showing improvement in his memory and Little Jake no longer as dependent on her.

"Are you okay?" a deep voice asked.

She turned to find Baker standing behind her. He held the reins of a saddled horse. Unlike the bronco, this one was calm and stood quietly beside him.

She drew in a breath and nodded. She and Baker had been in the same class in high school, but unlike his brothers, he hadn't attracted much attention to himself. He'd been smart and athletic, but quiet with just a few close friends. She would have preferred that herself—to have just a few close friends, instead of all the people who'd befriended her probably to feel good about themselves.

"It really wasn't Ben's fault, what happened," Baker said, defending his older brother. "Caleb jumped up so fast that the saddle started sliding off, and we didn't have a chance to grab Little Jake before he hit the ground."

Instead of making her feel better, Baker

had made her feel worse. She had overreacted with Ben—*again*—and now she owed him another apology. In addition to the one she had yet to give him.

"He really wouldn't do anything to hurt these kids," Baker said softly. "He loves them."

In a shaky sigh, she expelled the breath she'd drawn in and nodded again. She couldn't deny that Ben treated the children—all the children—with affection. But she'd thought people had cared about her too, and she'd been wrong. So was Ben genuine? Was he capable of feeling that deeply for anyone?

"Or isn't it the boys that you're worried about?" Baker asked, and his lips curved into a slight smile.

"What—what do you mean?" she stammered. "Who else would I be worried about?"

His smile widened. "If you remember his reputation from high school maybe you're worried about yourself..."

She laughed, but it sounded forced even to her. "Ben can't hurt me."

She wasn't like her friends, who'd foolishly fallen for his good looks and his practiced charm. She knew better than to trust a man like him.

"Ben doesn't want to hurt anyone," Baker said. "He never did."

That might have been true, but it didn't make him any less culpable. Just careless…

Like all the people who'd hurt her over the years. Perhaps they hadn't meant to; they'd just been self-involved and unaware of her feelings. That was why Emily had resolved to be especially careful before she trusted anyone with her heart. Maybe that was why she had yet to fall in love…

"ARE YOU SURE you don't want me to come along?" Sadie asked through the open driver-side window of the van. Melanie was about to take Miller to the specialist who'd operated on him so many weeks ago.

Miller answered before Melanie could with a shake of his sandy blond head. "No, Grandma. I'm not a baby. I don't need anybody to hold my hand. They're just taking off the cast. It's no big deal."

But it was an incredibly big deal for him and Sadie knew it. And maybe that was why he wanted to go alone, so if he had an emotional moment, only Melanie would witness it. It was clear he trusted her implicitly, more than he seemed to trust anyone else. He was trying so hard to be independent and tough, but he was still just a little boy.

"Maybe Miss Melanie needs the help," Sadie suggested, and she was quite serious. The young physical therapist had dark circles beneath her eyes; she wasn't getting enough rest. She was working too hard and not just with Miller. She was working hard trying to heal her broken heart.

A sigh swelled in Sadie's chest, making her own heart ache. Poor girl. She was suffering needlessly. Sadie just knew it. She had faith.

But then Ben and the boys joined them at the van. Ben was holding Little Jake, who had blood oozing from a scrape on his elbow and his face was red and swollen from tears.

And her faith began to slip as she gasped and asked, "What happened?"

"Little Jake fell off the hay horse," Caleb replied.

"Hay horse?"

"The one Uncle Ben put the saddle on," the little boy explained.

She glanced again at her grandson, who shook his head. "It was a bad idea," Ben said, his jaw taut as if he was clenching it. "Just ask Emily…"

Emily joined them next, looking just as tense as Ben. "Ask me what?" she asked.

He shook his head. "About my bad ideas, about how I can't be trusted with my own nephews."

Heat rushed up into Sadie's face. Had she overplayed her hand by insinuating that to Emily? She'd just wanted the young woman to spend some time with Ben, but she'd obviously put the wrong idea in the young teacher's head.

The idea that Ben wasn't trustworthy...

Or was that an idea Emily already had for some reason?

"Is Little Jake okay?" Melanie asked with concern. "Does he need anything?"

"Baker checked him out," Ben said. "He's fine. I'll bring him in the house and clean up his elbow. You need to leave so you're not late."

Melanie nodded and turned the key in the ignition to start up the van.

Sadie reached through the open window and touched her shoulder. "Are you sure you don't want me to go with you? You shouldn't be handling this all on your own..." And she wasn't just talking about bringing Miller to the doctor.

She was talking about so much more…

Melanie's lips moved into a faint smile. "I can manage," she said.

But Sadie wasn't so sure.

"I told Baker he should go with you," Ben admitted. "But I can—"

"No!" Caleb said. "You said you were staying. You have to take care of Midnight."

"We're fine," Melanie said. "Miller and I will have no problem with our little drive and a doctor's appointment. We'll see you when we get back."

Sadie withdrew her hand from the window. The young woman was right. She could take care of that. It was everything else that Sadie worried about, just as she was beginning to worry about her grand plan.

Katie and Jake hadn't immediately fallen back in love, so she shouldn't have expected a miracle already. But she had a feeling that it might actually take a miracle for Emily to fall in love with Ben.

CHAPTER ELEVEN

DESPITE WHAT *SOME PEOPLE*—namely Emily Trent—might believe about him, Ben was not one of those politicians who had more trouble telling the truth than lies. So having to lie to his big brother wasn't easy for him, but when Jake—his deep voice emanating from the speaker on Ben's cell phone—asked, "Is everything really going well?" Ben forced himself to lie.

"Yes, it's going really well." He glanced around him then to see if anyone had heard him, but he appeared to be alone in the kitchen.

After every boy had taken his turn talking to Katie and Jake, Emily had ushered them upstairs to get ready for bed. Remembering how, as a kid, he used to fight falling asleep, he figured one of them might come back down at any moment.

"I know you too well and I know those kids too well to accept that as the truth," Jake informed him.

Ben chuckled. "Let's just put it this way," he said. "Everybody is still alive." But they weren't.

At least Dale and Jenny weren't.

And that was the problem. These little boys shouldn't have lost their parents so soon. Ben had been older than they were when he'd lost his, and he still wasn't over it. He doubted the boys would ever be completely okay.

"Little Jake did fall out of the saddle," Ben admitted.

Jake gasped. "You had him on a horse? He's too young."

"He was riding a bale of hay," Ben explained. "And it happened so fast."

"But he's okay?" Jake asked, his already deep voice gruffer with concern for his namesake.

"Yes, he's fine. He's strutting around like a big boy showing off his riding wounds."

Jake puffed out a breath. "He's wounded!"

"He's fine." It wasn't Ben who'd said that, but Emily, who'd suddenly joined him in the kitchen.

Startled, Ben nearly dropped the phone. He wasn't sure if he was more surprised by her sudden appearance, or by the fact that she'd backed him up.

"And he really is strutting around like a big boy," Emily said with a little laugh.

"Caleb sounded funny, though," Katie commented. Jake must have had his cell on speaker too. "Is he really okay?" the nervous mom asked.

"Yes," Emily said. "Of course, he's missing you guys, but he's keeping busy with Uncle Ben."

Ben narrowed his eyes and studied her face, checking to see if she was being sarcastic.

"Ben is handling them all right?" Katie asked.

"I'm still here," Ben warned his new sister-in-law.

"I know," Katie replied. "But I know Emily will tell me the truth even if it hurts your feelings."

"Especially if it hurts my feelings," he said, correcting her.

Emily gave him the side-eye now. But for Katie, she sounded like she had a smile in her voice when she replied, "No, he's doing really well. The boys all love him, but Caleb probably loves him the most."

Katie released a shaky breath then that rattled the speaker on Ben's phone. "Good. I'm happy."

"Yes, you should be," Emily said. "You're on your honeymoon."

"Yes," Ben agreed. "So go enjoy it."

"Good idea," Jake said.

"But you'll call us if they need anything, if they want us to come back?" Katie asked.

"Of course," Ben said in unison with Emily. "Goodbye." He clicked off his cell and focused on her face again. Even with dark circles beneath her eyes from Little Jake interrupting their sleep last night, she was beautiful.

She must have been wondering the same thing he was, because she asked, "We were both lying there, right?"

He sighed. "Is that another dig?" he asked. "About my untrustworthiness? You think I'm a liar too? Because I'm a politician?"

Her face flushed, and she didn't deny it. Instead, she made another admission. "I hope you were lying about calling them. I don't want to have to ask Katie and Jake to cut their honeymoon short."

"Of course I don't want to do that either," he said. "But you obviously don't believe that or anything else I say—"

"Ben—"

He shook his head to cut her off. "I'm too tired to fight with you any more today," he said. "I'm going to bed too." But when he moved to pass her, she reached out and clasped his arm.

"Don't go…"

Through the thin cotton of his work shirt, he could feel the warmth of her fingers. And his skin tingled from it, the muscles in his arm clenching. Tension gripped him as he acknowledged how attractive he found her. Maybe he'd been spending too much time with the little boys, because he was beginning to understand—too well—why they were all besotted with her.

He was afraid that he might be heading in that direction himself, to where he wanted to follow her around and be as close as he could be to her. But he wasn't a trusting little boy; he knew better than to fall for anyone… even someone as beautiful as her. He knew how badly it hurt to have a broken heart—too badly to risk. So if he was smart, he would pull away from her and run up the stairwell. Or, better yet, out of the house…

But he thought of how Caleb had reacted earlier, of how the little boy had just about panicked at the thought of *Uncle Ben* leaving. So Ben had to stay—for the kids, and for Katie and Jake.

Still, he was worried that it was going to cost him. Maybe his career, if the voters bristled about him taking time off. And maybe more than that…

EMILY HAD GRASPED his arm to stop him from leaving, but now that she had… The heat of his skin beneath the cotton of his shirt and the hardness of his muscles distracted her from her thoughts. All she could do at the moment was feel…things that she hadn't felt in a long while.

Attraction…

She could no longer deny his appeal for all those girls in high school who had been so besotted with him. And even now, the ones who'd given their hearts to Ben as adults and should have known better…like Maggie Standish. Emily hadn't seen Maggie for a while, probably because she hadn't been as sympathetic to Maggie's heartache as she should have been. Emily had also been busy teaching, and for the last six weeks that she'd lived at the ranch, she hadn't seen any of her casual friends. But she'd made better friends in Katie, Taye and Melanie. She had much more in common with them than she'd had with her other high-school friends, whom she'd always kept at a distance. Unlike Maggie, who desperately wanted to find love, Emily didn't trust easily and rarely let others in fully. She knew better than to trust a man like Ben Haven. But was he really the kind of man she'd believed he was for all these years?

Or was there more to him besides his handsome surface? Was there more depth to him than she'd realized?

"Why don't you want me to go?" Ben asked with a pointed glance at her hand on his arm. He hadn't pulled away from her. Despite claiming he was too tired to argue with her, he hadn't just walked away. But then he wearily murmured, "Like I said, I don't want to fight anymore…"

"I don't either," she assured him. "I owe you an apology…"

His lips curved into a slight smile. "Really?"

She sighed and admitted, "I probably actually owe you a couple of them now."

"At least a couple," he quipped, his grin widening as he teased her.

She should have been annoyed, but a smile

tugged at the corners of her mouth too. "I'm sorry," she said. "I know I've jumped to conclusions about you and your intentions the last couple of days."

He arched a dark eyebrow. "Intentions?"

She sighed. "Last night I thought you were trying to get Caleb to ask Katie and Jake to come home so that you could leave."

He shook his head. "No, I wasn't trying to do that. But I would have called them if he'd wanted me to. He was so upset," he said, his voice cracking a bit, like Caleb's had the night before.

She sighed. "I almost called them myself last night," she sheepishly admitted as she remembered the little boy's tears. "It killed me to see him so sad when he's usually such a happy, optimistic kid."

He touched his chest, as if his heart hurt thinking about how forlorn Caleb had been the night before. His hand drew her attention to his chest, to the muscles that strained the snaps of his checkered cowboy shirt. He didn't look the part of the slick, suited-up politician now—not in his worn jeans and cowboy hat.

And she realized she was still holding his arm. Instead of releasing it, she tightened her grasp on him and tugged him a little closer. "Are you all right?" she asked.

He nodded. "Are you?"

No, she wasn't. Because if she was, she would have never touched him. Now that she had, she couldn't force herself to let him go, and that strange tingling sensation she felt every time they'd made contact traveled from her fingertips to her heart. She touched it now with her free hand.

His gaze followed that hand to her chest, and he murmured, "Emily..."

Too deep into all these overwhelming sensations, she could only stare up at him as he began to lower his head toward hers. As if he was intending to kiss her...

That should have made her stumble away from him, to push him back, but when he stopped—his handsome face just above hers—she pulled him closer. She reached up and kissed him, brushing her lips across the light stubble on his cheek.

"Sorry," she said as she stepped back before she could do something even stupider, before she could brush her lips across his. Her mouth was already tingling, just like her hand, and now the rest of her body was. But she forced herself to focus on the real reason she'd stopped him. "I'm sorry I've been so rude to you."

He cleared his throat and nodded in acknowledgement, if not acceptance, of her apology. "I know that I haven't been here like I should have for the boys and for Jake and Grandma," he admitted. "But I want to make up for that now."

He was making up for it, and maybe that was the problem Emily had with him. He was making up too well.

His lips curved into a slight smile. "That's why I just lied to Jake and Katie. I won't call them if the boys want them to come home. They deserve this time alone. It's a dozen years overdue."

She forced her gaze from his mouth and focused instead on his words. "Jake really gave up a lot for the ranch, for his family," she mused.

Ben nodded and asked, "Do you still have a thing for my brother?"

She stiffened with defensiveness and insisted, "I never had a thing for your brother." She couldn't deny that Jake Haven was an attractive man, but he wasn't the one who got under her skin…like Ben had.

"Do you have a thing for anyone?" he

asked, and he glanced down at her hand on his arm.

She hadn't realized she'd left it there, or maybe she had and she just hadn't wanted to let go of him yet. She finally jerked it away now. "No."

He nodded again. "That makes sense."

"Why?"

"If you were in a relationship, I doubt you would have been able to move out to the ranch and spend so many weeks here," he said.

She nodded now. "True…"

"So there's no one special in your life?"

She narrowed her eyes and studied his too handsome face. "I hope you didn't get the wrong idea about that kiss… I was just apologizing…"

"I know," he assured her.

She wished she really believed that was why she'd done it, why she'd touched him like that… Why she'd barely been able to resist the urge to really kiss him.

"Why are you asking about my personal life?" she wondered.

He held up his hands as if she'd turned a gun on him. "I'm playing wingman."

"Wingman?" she asked. "For whom?"

Baker had talked to her that afternoon, more

than he ever had when they'd been in school together, but he'd only spoken to her briefly and just to defend Ben.

"For my nephew," he said with a smile. "Caleb has a thing for you."

She smiled. "He's sweet. All of the boys are." Every one of them had come to mean so much to her.

As if he'd read her mind, or maybe the expression on her face, he asked, "How will you leave them?"

"What do you mean?"

"Won't it be hard for you to leave the ranch?" he asked her.

It would be—so much so that she didn't want to think about it. "I'll deal with that when it's time to leave," she said, more to herself than to him.

"Then you *are* leaving?" he asked, and his long, lean body tensed.

"I can't stay here forever," she said. "I have a job in town." At least she hoped she still had that job, that the principal was leaving her position open for her. She needed to touch base with him now that the school year had ended…more than a week ago.

"The boys will be heartbroken when you go," he said. His voice was gruff with emotion, as if he knew how that felt. Given how his mother had left him and his brothers, he probably did know that kind of heartbreak. She never wanted to hurt anyone like that, least of all the Haven boys.

Tears stung her eyes at the thought of leaving them, and especially at the thought of hurting them. She blinked furiously, trying to clear away the tears.

Ben gasped. "I'm sorry. I didn't mean to upset you." He reached out then and clasped her shoulders, as if to pull her in for a comforting hug.

But if she got that close to him again, she knew that she wouldn't stop at kissing just his cheek. Scared of giving in to that temptation, Emily reached out and pressed her hands against his chest to hold herself away from him. She'd thought the muscles in his arm had been hard…until now, as she felt the muscles in his chest ripple beneath her palms.

Ben released her shoulders. "And I'm sorry again. I was just going to…" He shook his head. "I'm sorry. It was inappropriate."

Not more so than her kissing his cheek or putting her hands on his chest. She snatched them back to her sides now and curled her trembling fingers into her palms. "I'm the one who came down here to apologize to you," she said. "You don't owe me one."

"But I upset you just now."

She shook her head. "No, the thought of hurting those little kids is what upset me." Of abandoning them, as so many people had abandoned her. Tears rushed up the back of her throat now, nearly choking her. And she wished now that she hadn't stopped him from hugging her. She could have used some comforting.

Ben reached out again, but he pulled his hands back before he touched her. "I'm sorry," he said again. "I'll try not to hurt them...when I leave."

She sighed. "They're already getting attached to you too."

"I know..."

She was beginning to worry that the boys weren't the only ones. "But you'll leave when Jake and Katie return from their honeymoon?"

He nodded. "I have to. I doubt anyone would reelect a mayor who doesn't spend any time in the town he's supposed to be serving."

"It's just two weeks," she said, and she was reminding herself as much as she was reminding him. She could resist this attraction for that time, especially when she knew he wasn't staying.

She wasn't staying either. Like him, she would have to return to town—to her job and her life there. "Maybe Katie and Jake being married, being that parental unit for the boys…"

He nodded. "Maybe that will fill some of the void of Dale and Jenny's loss."

"Some…" She repeated what he'd said as she realized that he understood. From losing his dad when he had, and then his mom, he knew that nothing would ever completely fill the void that losing a parent left in one's life, in one's heart.

Emily knew that too well, and her mother hadn't been anything like sweet Jenny and loving Dale. Her mom had struggled so hard on her own. And Emily had struggled so hard after she'd lost her…

She didn't want to ever love anyone like that again and lose them. She didn't ever want to feel that alone and helpless again.

"You're tired," she said. "You should go up to bed."

"You're not coming up?" he asked.

She hesitated. She didn't want to climb

those stairs at his side, didn't want to feel like they were heading up to bed together.

Didn't want to feel like they *were* together...

Because that would never be. Emily wanted a family of her own someday, with a man she could trust to never leave her. She couldn't trust Ben Haven...even though she was beginning to believe there was more to him than she'd realized.

Much more...

CHAPTER TWELVE

LATE THE NEXT AFTERNOON, everyone gathered in the kitchen, where brightly colored balloons floated nearly to the beams of the tall ceiling. They probably would have, had Taye and Emily not tied them to little bags of candy.

Ben and the boys had helped set up for the party too. But Taye and Emily hadn't trusted any of them with the chocolate. They'd made the sign that dangled from the mantle of the fireplace: *Congrats on Getting Rid of the Cast.*

Of course, they'd started running out of room near the end of the line, so *GettingRidoftheCast* was one mashed-up word now with the letters scrawled nearly on top of each other.

The boys had been pretty much on top of Ben all day. Ian and Little Jake had accompanied him and Caleb to the barn. Fortunately, nobody had gotten hurt this time, which was nearly a miracle with as tired and distracted as Ben was.

Since Little Jake hadn't woken up screaming last night, Ben should have been rested. But that conversation in the kitchen with Emily had left him even more unsettled than his confrontation with her in the hallway had the previous evening. He knew she'd only meant that kiss on his cheek as an apology, but it had felt like so much more to Ben, like a promise of how a real kiss would feel between them. Electrifying...

Passionate.

Overwhelming...

He'd been overwhelmed with the urge to really kiss her then, but he'd held back, not wanting to ruin the moment. Not wanting to press her for more than she was willing to give him. He'd been surprised that she'd actually apologized to him, but he had no doubt that she'd been sincere.

He should have left it at the apology; he shouldn't have kept talking because then he'd upset her. The tears shimmering in her beautiful blue eyes had affected him like a fist tightly clenching his heart. When he'd reached out to comfort her, he'd been seeking comfort himself.

But it was clear that Emily hadn't wanted

anything from him. Not his comfort and definitely not his touch.

He wanted hers. He'd lain awake reliving the sensation of her lips brushing across his cheek and of her warm hands pressed against his chest; it was almost as if he was still able to feel them. As if she'd somehow branded him…

Which was crazy, because Ben had always avoided serious relationships by making it clear to his dates that he was too busy and too focused on his career to ever get married.

Maybe he was the liar that Emily probably thought he was because his career wasn't the real reason he didn't want to marry. It was his heart…

His mother had left nearly twenty years ago, but his heart hadn't healed yet. Then losing Dale and Jenny—and his mother not even returning for their funeral—had intensified the pain he still felt over her leaving.

"They're here!" Caleb yelled as he came running down the hall from the foyer to the kitchen.

This party was definitely worth the work it had taken. The minute Miller limped through the door, a smile spread across his face, lighting him up as if from within. With his sandy brown hair and those hazel eyes, the seven-year-old looked so much like his dad that Ben's heart seemed to stop beating for a moment, as he remembered his younger brother at that age.

Dale...

He'd always been so kind and funny, a lot like Caleb Morris. All heart and hard work—that had been Dale. And such a good father...

Ben was blinking hard now, having to fight against the tears that threatened to slip free. He sucked in a breath, and Emily, standing near him with Little Jake on her hip, cast him a quick glance.

"Are you okay?" she asked, and she sounded genuinely concerned.

He nodded and admitted, "It's just that Miller looks so much like Dale..." And it wasn't just the coloring of his hair and eyes. He also had the same features and—before the accident—he'd had the same sweet personality, which seemed to have returned with that big smile.

The smile slipped away now, as if Miller somehow felt guilty for having that happy reaction. Was guilt the reason he'd been so impatient and grumpy since the accident?

Ben had believed that the boy's injuries

and that heavy cast were why Miller had had no patience with his younger brothers. He'd thought then that Miller's pain was mostly physical. Now Ben wondered if Miller's suffering was mostly emotional.

"You really miss him," Emily remarked.

And he turned to find her staring intently at him. He couldn't speak—not with emotion choking him—so he just nodded.

"Miss Trent!" Miller called out to her. "Look—no cast."

She looked away from Ben then and rushed forward to greet the seven-year-old. "That's awesome, Miller. I'm so happy for you."

"I'm a little wobbly yet," he said. "But Miss Melanie says she'll help me get the leg just as strong as the other one."

Melanie stood behind the boy, her hand on his shoulder as if she was worried that he might fall without her support. She cared about her patient, just as all the women cared about the kids.

And they weren't even family…

Where was Ben's family? Only he and Sadie had attended this party.

Jake and Katie had a reason for missing it, or they would have certainly been here. But Baker hadn't made it back from the pastures to greet their nephew. And Darlene—he had no idea where his mother even was nowadays. And Dusty...

Dusty, who looked so much like the boys' father, couldn't even be bothered to act like an uncle. Anger began to simmer inside Ben, but he pushed it down and forced a grin for his nephew.

He rushed forward and picked up the boy, lifting him to his shoulders to parade him around the room. "The conquering hero has returned!" he said.

Miller laughed. "What?"

"You beat that cast and won!" Ben said.

And Miller laughed again.

The sound lifted Ben's heart, made him feel a little better about Miller's emotional well-being. But it didn't ease his anger. He hung on to it until after the party, when everyone had finished off the cookies and punch and cleaned up.

Then he slipped onto the patio outside the French doors of the kitchen. And decided to make a couple of calls. First, he called Baker.

"Where were you?"

"Working," Baker replied.

"You could have spared an hour for your nephew," Ben said, but he cringed at how much he probably sounded like Sadie, who'd tried to get them all to spend more time at the ranch and more time with the boys.

"These foremen candidates aren't going to cut it," Baker replied. "They know less about ranching than I do."

Baker knew more than he wanted to admit. Since he'd been a little kid, he'd claimed that he didn't want to be a rancher. He'd wanted to be a fireman.

He'd achieved his dream, just like Ben had achieved his of being mayor. Why weren't they happier?

Maybe careers in their chosen fields were not enough. Maybe there was more to life than work.

Ben pushed aside that thought for the moment. "I was worried about one of the kids making Jake come home early from his honeymoon. Now it sounds like you're going to call him."

"Jake's not the brother we need to call," Baker said. "There's just one person who could partially fill Dale's shoes..."

His twin.

Ben sighed. "I'll call him." He clicked off from Baker and punched in the contact for

Dusty. And he was actually surprised when the rodeo rider answered.

"Hey…" But it didn't sound like Dusty, who was usually upbeat and energetic. He sounded incredibly weary, as if he was the one who was losing sleep to screaming kids and attractive schoolteachers.

Emily probably hadn't lost any sleep last night, but she'd cost him his again. Because he couldn't stop imagining her standing before him like she had last night, when something more nearly happened between them…

"Ben, are you there?" Dusty asked. "Or did you butt-dial me?"

"No butt dial," Ben assured him. "I called to get you to come home."

"Grandma, what big teeth you have…" Dusty said, then chuckled.

"I'm not joking," Ben said. "Jake and Katie are on their honeymoon, and none of his potential ranch-foremen candidates are going to work out. You need to come home."

"To be the ranch foreman?"

"I know it's not the rodeo," Ben said. "But you could at least fill in until Jake can find someone who's actually capable of helping him like Dale did."

Dusty inhaled sharply, as if just the mention of his twin's name affected him.

"I know this all sucks," Ben said, and the enormity of their losses suddenly overwhelmed him. "Losing them like we did... like we lost Dad. But then you just took off, like Mom did, right after the funeral. You didn't even come back for Jake's wedding, man. That was cold. Jake's been handling this place all by himself since he was twenty years old—a kid himself."

"He had Dale..."

Had Dusty resented that? He and his twin had pledged since they were little to join the rodeo together. To travel all over the country... To win championships and those cash prizes... But Dale had fallen so hard for Jenny Miller that he'd refused to leave her or the ranch. He'd always helped Jake the most with it and had clearly loved it as much as Jake did.

"He doesn't have Dale anymore," Ben said, his heart heavy in his chest. "He needs you. We all need you...to come home, Dusty."

His younger brother's sigh rattled the phone. "Jake always says you're the most like Grandma..."

"I wish I was," Ben admitted, then he paraphrased Lem's warning to him. "Sadie March Haven usually gets her way."

"I can't come home right now," Dusty said. "I lost…"

"What?" Ben asked when his brother trailed off. "A competition? Who cares? We lost a lot more back here in Willow Creek. And we need you to help fill the void."

"I wasn't talking about a competition…"

"What were you talking about?" Ben asked. But before Dusty could answer, he continued, "It doesn't matter. Nothing should matter as much as your family. Not even yourself…" His face burned with embarrassment over how hypocritical he was being, since he hadn't helped out much over the past several weeks himself.

If Emily were listening now, she'd probably call him on his hypocrisy. But when he turned around, he found another woman standing on the patio behind him.

Since he hadn't heard the doors open, she must have been here when he'd stepped out, but he hadn't noticed her in the shadows of the two-story house. Melanie leaned against the cedar siding, her arms wrapped around herself.

She was probably exhausted from driving back and forth to that specialist for Miller.

He mouthed *sorry* at her; he hadn't meant to disturb her. And clearly he had, because she seemed upset, like she'd been crying or was on the verge of tears.

"You sure you should be talking?" Dusty challenged him through the speaker of his cell phone. "Were you around that much before Jake and Katie left on their honeymoon?"

Ben flinched. "I'm here now. And you should be too. Don't be like Mom, Dusty. Don't flake out when your family needs you the most." If that wouldn't convince Dusty to come home, nothing would, so he disconnected the call.

"I'm sorry about that," Ben said to Melanie. "I didn't know you were out here."

"It's okay," she said. "I was just getting some air." But as if she'd had enough, she opened the French doors and stepped back inside the house...leaving Ben outside alone with his regrets.

He shouldn't have talked to Dusty about family and responsibilities. Not when he'd been avoiding them himself.

EMILY WASN'T LOOKING for Ben. But she'd wondered where he might have gone...and she'd just wanted to make sure that he was okay.

She'd seen the tears in his eyes when it had struck him how much Miller looked like his brother. And for the first time she'd realized why Ben might not have been around that much since the accident—because he was still grieving his brother's death. And the boys obviously reminded him of their father, so much that he'd nearly cried.

But he'd blinked back the tears and poured on the charm—for the boys. He'd teased and joked around with them until they'd all been laughing and happy. She'd known then that his charm was the act she'd always suspected him of putting on… And it hadn't been to get a date or a vote, it had been to make other people happy. His nephews…

What about Ben? Was he happy? Where was he?

He hadn't been upstairs with the boys—she'd checked. Taye was there with them, and was letting the kids use her phone to Face-Time Katie and Jake.

She found herself back in the kitchen even though the party was over. It was empty.

Or she'd thought the kitchen was empty, until Melanie opened the patio doors and rushed into the room in such a hurry that she nearly knocked Emily over.

"Whoa," Emily said, and she reached out and caught Melanie's shoulders, like Ben had caught hers last night. A wave of longing passed through her that she'd stopped him from hugging her. She'd barely slept as it was, and he hadn't even held her. She probably wouldn't have slept at all if he had. And her lips had tingled all night from the contact with the stubble on his cheek. What if she'd kissed his lips?

She shook her head to clear those foolish thoughts from it and focused on Melanie, who had tears streaking down her cheeks, which were already flushed and swollen from crying.

"What's wrong?" Emily asked her. Then she glanced up when the French doors opened again, and Ben stepped inside the kitchen.

He'd been out on the patio with Melanie? She must have started crying when she'd been with him. And Emily was instantly plunged into the past, into the memories of all the tears her friends had cried over Ben—because he'd broken their hearts. She remembered Maggie Standish weeping just as recently as a couple of years ago when Ben had stopped calling her after he'd won the election. Feeling used, Maggie had been hurt and humiliated.

Her hands dropped from Melanie's shoulders and curled into fists at her sides. "What did you do to upset her?" she asked Ben.

Had he made a pass at the married woman? The woman Emily suspected was pregnant?

Fury coursed through her, and something else—something Emily refused to identify. She was *not* jealous over Ben Haven. If anything, she should have been relieved that she hadn't been wrong about him, like she'd been starting to believe, to worry...

"He didn't do anything," Melanie said, defending Ben before he'd even had a chance to defend himself. "He didn't even realize I was out on the patio."

Ben ignored Emily, his focus on Melanie. "Did my calls to my brothers upset you somehow?" he asked with concern. "I didn't mean for you to overhear any of that..."

"Of what?" Emily asked.

But now, Melanie ignored her and assured him, "Ben, *you* didn't upset me." She spared Emily a glance, a very pointed one as she added, "You did nothing wrong."

And Emily suppressed a groan. She'd done it again. She'd jumped to the wrong conclusion about Ben. He wasn't the one who'd upset Melanie. Emily didn't know what had, but she'd apparently added to her friend's discomfort when she'd accused Ben of causing it. And now she owed him *another* apology. The list kept growing…even after the one she'd made last night.

"Then why are you so upset?" Ben asked Melanie. "Did something else happen today?"

She shook her head, and her thick brown hair tumbled around her shoulders. "No. I'm fine. Just tired…" With dark circles rimming her eyes, she looked exhausted.

"Of course, after that drive you must be tired," Ben said. "You should go up to bed."

She nodded. "I will…after I see if the boys left any of Taye's cookies."

Ben glanced around the empty kitchen. "I doubt it. If there were any left, they would still be here." He turned toward Emily, but there was none of the concern or kindness on his face that he had just shown Melanie as he asked, "Where are the boys?"

Emily felt a sense of loss that he was so short with her, so obviously annoyed, and that he had every reason to be. "The boys are still on Taye's phone with Katie and Jake," she answered him.

Ben's brow furrowed. "I hope they're just catching up with them." Clearly, that was what he wanted—even though, if the kids asked the couple to come home, it would cut short his stay at the ranch.

Yes, she definitely kept getting her conclusions wrong about him. So why did she keep jumping? Why was she so determined to think the worst of him? Was she worried about him hurting the boys, or about him hurting her?

"Yes. They're telling them about the party," Emily said. "And Taye's supervising. She'll make sure they don't talk Katie into coming home early."

He nodded. But as if he didn't quite trust the cook, or maybe Emily, he headed toward the stairs.

Melanie started after him, but Emily caught her shoulders again and stopped her. "Is everything really all right?" she asked. "Did you get bad news? Is Miller going to get back the full use of his leg?"

"Miller is doing great," Melanie assured her and, with a smile, she expanded on what she'd told them all when she and Miller and first returned to the ranch, that the doctor said the little boy was doing even better than he'd hoped. "The orthopedic surgeon was thrilled with how well the bone is healing.

Miller should be done with surgeries until he gets the rod taken out next year."

Emily grimaced, thinking of that poor little boy having to have a rod in his leg for a year. "Next year? Why does it have to stay that long?"

"He's growing a lot," Melanie said. "They'll have to remove and replace it if it's still needed. Hopefully, he'll have healed so well by then, though, that it won't be necessary. Even if it is, he's used to it being in there now—it doesn't bother him anymore."

"So what's bothering you?" Emily asked.

Melanie's smile slipped away. "Nothing. I'm fine…" But her lashes fluttered as if she was fighting back more of the tears she'd clearly been crying.

"I know you and Katie are close, but she's not here. So if you need someone to talk to, know that I am always here for you, and you can trust me."

Melanie smiled again. "I know. It's just…"

Emily nodded. "I know. I find it hard to trust anyone too."

"Maybe too hard," Melanie suggested. "You certainly don't trust Ben, and I'm not sure why, when he's proved that he cares about the boys, about his family…" Her voice cracked as she trailed off.

Emily sighed. "I know. I know he does."

But it had been easier when she hadn't known that—when she'd believed that he cared only about himself. Because now she was in danger of doing what she'd seen so many other foolish women do…

She was in danger of falling for Ben Haven. But she wasn't like those women, her old friends, because she already knew what falling for Ben would get her: a broken heart.

That was why she kept making assumptions about him, why she was so determined to think the worst of him—to protect her heart.

JAKE WRAPPED HIS arm around his new bride and stared over her shoulder at the phone she held. Their son's face filled the screen, although the other boys appeared in corners of it. His heart swelled with love for her and for all of his family.

"You're really okay, sweetheart?" Katie asked Caleb. "You don't mind us being gone?"

"It's just going to be a little bit longer now," Caleb replied. "I'm a big kid. I can handle it."

Jake wondered if he would have said that

if his cousins weren't with him. If Caleb had been talking to them alone, would he have asked them to come back?

"Is everything really going okay?" Jake asked. He hadn't entirely believed Ben when he'd spoken to him the night before, even though Emily had surprisingly backed him up.

"Yeah, we just had a party for Miller with balloons and chocolate and lots of cookies."

So maybe he was on a sugar high right now.

"I'm sorry we missed that," Katie said, and he could hear the regret in her soft voice. "I'm so happy Miller's cast has come off."

"Not as happy as I am, Aunt Katie," Miller chimed in from a corner of the screen.

The boys had all piled on one bed. Jake suspected that it was probably Taye's since it was her phone they were using.

"Miss Melanie says I should be running around in no time," Miller continued.

"I'll race you," Caleb said, and the phone jiggled as if he intended to run off right now. He was definitely on a sugar high.

"Wait," Jake said. "Don't go running away just yet. I need to ask you about Midnight. Is he okay?" And why had that ornery bronco come to mean so much to Jake? He'd viewed it as an inconvenience when Dusty had first sent it to him, but he'd quickly recognized a kindred spirit in the restless animal.

"He hasn't killed Uncle Ben," Caleb said. "He lets him clean his stall and feed him. I think he likes Uncle Ben."

And maybe the horse had recognized a kindred spirit in Ben as well, which kind of surprised Jake. Ben had always seemed satisfied with his success, with becoming the mayor, like he'd always wanted.

"I don't think Miss Trent likes Uncle Ben, though," Caleb continued.

And a woman's laugh drifted out of the phone speaker. Taye wasn't visible on the screen, but she was close enough to hear what Jake's stepson had shared. Then she chimed in with, "Miss Trent hasn't killed him either." She chuckled again and added, "Yet…"

Jake laughed then, thinking about how frustrated his grandmother must be that her plan wasn't working with his brothers like it had for him.

He doubted she was going to see any successful matchmaking with them. They were all determined to remain bachelor cowboys.

CHAPTER THIRTEEN

NEARLY A WEEK had passed, a week of Ben dividing himself between the boys and the ranch. Nearly a week of trying to help Baker with feeding and tending to the calves and cattle and the horses and helping the women with the boys. And ignoring his attraction to a beautiful blonde schoolteacher...who haunted his dreams and kept him awake even when he desperately needed his sleep.

Maybe that was why just walking up the steps to the porch took so much effort. He was exhausted and not just because thoughts of Emily kept him up. He was exhausted physically and emotionally.

Being around the boys, dealing with Little Jake's sporadic nightmares and Ian's even more sporadic memory, was harder than riding a horse for hours on end. Like Baker, Ben would have preferred to stay in the saddle all day. But Jake had divided himself between their nephews and the livestock.

Neither he nor Baker were Big Jake Haven, but between the two of them, they could pull his weight. Maybe…

It was Dale's loss that Ben felt even more, though. Dale he missed the most because he knew that, unlike Jake, Dale was never coming back. He'd just opened the front door to the farmhouse foyer when his cell rang. He jerked it from his pocket and stared at the screen, hoping it was Dusty. But it wasn't.

He was going to have to face the fact that Dusty might never come back either, that he might be just as lost as Dale…or Darlene. At least Dusty had returned for the funeral, while she hadn't even sent a card. But did she know? Would it have mattered if she did? She had stopped calling and sending cards many years ago.

He pushed those thoughts from his mind and accepted his call. "Hey, Lem, sorry I haven't checked in more."

Lem chuckled. "You send emails every night. When do you sleep?"

"Sleep? What's that?" Ben asked, and he wasn't entirely joking.

"Sounds like you could use some," Lem remarked. "Almost makes me feel guilty for calling you."

"Don't," Ben urged him. "I told you to call me whenever you needed to." But his deputy mayor was so good that he must not have had any questions regarding those late-night emails Ben had sent him.

"A couple of contracts came back from Legal that need your signature. Any chance of you making a trip into Willow Creek soon?"

Ben's shoulders slumped with a sudden heaviness over the thought of driving into town. The ranch was nearly an hour away from Willow Creek's city hall. But he had responsibilities there as well as here.

"I'll see what I can do," he said. But he was worried about telling the boys, especially Caleb. The little boy was struggling with missing his mom and new stepdad, and Ben didn't want him thinking that another adult whose company he seemed to enjoy was leaving him. Maybe Ben leaving and coming back would reassure the kid that his mom and stepdad would return too.

"It'll be a quick trip, but, yes, I'll make it happen," Ben promised.

"It'll be good for people to see you around town," Lem said. "There have been some questions about where you've been." He chuckled and added, "Most of those questions have come from young women, though."

Ben furrowed his brow and asked, "What young women?" He'd not gone out with anyone since Dale and Jenny's tragic accident. And even before that, he'd only been casually dating. While his brothers teased him about being a heartbreaker like Dusty, the women he dated knew not to expect more than that.

"You know the women," Lem said. "The mail lady, the woman from the coffee shop, every female clerk in the office…"

Ben smiled at what must have been his deputy mayor's misunderstanding or exaggeration. "I'm sure they're just concerned about the boys."

"Boys?"

"My nephews."

"They weren't asking about them," Lem said. "They're interested in you."

Ben sighed. "Well, it's sweet of them to be concerned, but I'm fine. Just tired. I don't know how Jake has managed all this time," he admitted. "He definitely deserves this vacation—he and Katie both do."

"Yeah, Jake hasn't had an easy time of it," Lem agreed. "But then none of you have. How's old Sadie doing? As ornery as ever?"

As if she'd heard him mention her name, she appeared in the hallway from the kitchen, Feisty circling her feet as she walked. She narrowed her dark eyes and stared at Ben.

He chuckled and replied, "Even ornerier, Lem. She's even ornerier."

Lem laughed. "Then you can probably use the break to come to town."

"I'll let you know when I'm heading that way," Ben said. "Thanks for taking care of Willow Creek while I'm gone," he said, then ended the call.

Grandma stared even harder at him, her arms crossed over her chest. "Ornerier?"

"You don't know that comment had anything to do with you," he pointed out, since he hadn't had the call on speaker.

"You were talking to Old Man Lemmon," Grandma said, "so I know you were talking about me. And isn't he the hypocrite for calling *me* ornery?" Her voice rose as her face flushed. "He thinks I'm ornery?"

Actually, he'd just asked if she was; Ben was the one who had actually confirmed it, but he wasn't about to reveal that, not when she was getting herself so riled up already. "You're never that sweet to him," Ben said instead.

Except when Lem had been taking care of his wife; then Grandma had helped out with meals and cleaning. But she'd refused to let him thank her for it, had insisted that she wasn't doing it for him but for his wife, who'd already suffered enough having been married to him for so many years.

Grandma just snorted and asked, "What did that old fool want, anyway? Is he starting to lose it? Can't he remember how to do the job he held all those years?"

"He's about as senile as you are," Ben said.

Grandma snorted. "Then he's sharp as a tack."

She certainly was.

"If only you used your brain for good instead of evil…" Ben teased.

"Getting Katie and Jake together—that was evil? Hiring these women to help with the boys—that was evil?"

His face flushed now with embarrassment over not realizing just how much good she had done. "Okay, I'll give you all that. Katie and Jake have always belonged together. And Melanie, Taye and Miss Trent are great with the boys."

"Miss Trent?" She arched a white brow

over one of her dark eyes. "You two aren't on a first-name basis?"

He wasn't sure what basis they were on now, after she'd apologized to him only to jump to another wrong conclusion the next day, thinking he'd made Melanie cry. After that, he'd been doing his best to avoid her. They passed the kids off to each other like they were divorced parents who didn't want to be in each other's company.

He shrugged and replied to his grandmother, "The kids call her Miss Trent."

"So? You're not a kid. You're thirty years old. You should be thinking about settling down before people start thinking you're an ornery old bachelor."

He chuckled. "I'm thirty. Not eighty. People don't get married out of high school anymore like you and Grandpa Jake did."

"Dale and Jenny did too."

"And that worked for them," he said. He had no doubt that they would have stayed in love forever. "And staying single works for me." It was safer than making himself vulnerable again.

Grandma pursed her lips as if she found the idea as distasteful as sucking on a lemon. But instead of arguing with him, she suggested,

"Why don't you take Emily and the kids on a ride around the ranch? Even though Jake got Miller up on a horse a couple of times, he really hated riding with that cast on his leg. Now that it's off, I'm sure he would love to go out."

Ben grimaced with regret that he hadn't thought of it himself. That first day Ben had arrived, Miller had commented on how hard it was to ride with the cast. "I'd be happy to take Miller riding." And maybe it would be better if it was just the two of them, and Ben had a chance to really talk to the kid, to ask about that flash of guilt he'd seen cross his face the day of the party.

But Grandma was shaking her head. "You can't take just one of the boys. Caleb has been missing his riding lessons with Jake. He loves to ride."

Ben's guilt increased that he hadn't taken Caleb riding yet. The five-year-old had asked him to go, but he hadn't had the time. With the ranch's calves having just recently been separated from their mothers, it was important to make sure they were all eating well and thriving. He needed to make sure that the kids were thriving as well, though.

"Then there's Little Jake, always being left out of the riding," Grandma continued.

"After sliding off a hay bale, I don't think he's ready to start riding horses yet," Ben said.

"You could hold him on your saddle with you," Sadie suggested. "But he won't want to go unless Miss Trent goes as well."

He doubted that even Sadie Haven could say anything that would compel Emily to go riding with him. "I see what you're doing, Grandma. Your meddling is blatant now." He laughed. "But it's not going to work."

"You don't think Miss Trent is attractive?"

"Sure, she's beautiful," he said. He couldn't deny that. "But she is not a fan of mine."

"That's good," Grandma said. "You're too used to women throwing themselves at you. You need a challenge."

The challenge was finding a woman he could trust, and he would never be certain that he could trust anyone...not when he hadn't been able to trust the woman who should've loved him most. The only thing he'd been able to trust when it came to Emily was that she was always going to think the worst of him no matter what.

"I have a question for you, Grandma," he said.

She arched one of those white brows again and warily asked, "What?"

"Do you know if my mom was ever told that Dale died?" he asked. "Did anyone tell her?" He and his brothers hadn't talked about her in years, so he had no idea if anyone else was in contact with her and told her. But Grandma seemed to be aware of everything. Not that he believed Darlene would have shown up had she been notified. He just wondered if she knew, if she cared enough about the children she'd abandoned to mourn one of them dying.

Sadie shrugged. "I don't know. She never spoke to me after she left that day. I know she's written letters to some of you. Jake never opened his, so she stopped writing to him. Does she still write to you?"

He shook his head. "Not anymore…"

Not after he'd told her to stop when she'd called him for his sixteenth birthday. He'd told her to stop writing him and to stop calling— even though she'd only called a couple of times over those first few years after she'd taken off. But in those letters and during those calls, all she'd done was promise over and over again that after the next rodeo, she would come home. But she'd never come home. So when she'd called to wish him a happy sixteenth birthday, he'd told her to stop. No more letters. No more calls. No more empty promises that she had no intention of keeping…

Grandma's dark eyes filled with concern as she studied his face, and she reached out to squeeze his shoulder. "If the reason you're still a bachelor is because of your mother—"

"No!" He interrupted her with the lie, which he'd uttered with such vehemence she had to know he was lying.

Her gaze warm, she softly assured him, "Emily is nothing like your mother. Look how she's stepped up with those boys. They love her so much. So do I…"

Ben sighed. "Give it up, Grandma. I'm never going to fall in love and get married. That's not who I am." He was too smart to ever let another woman hurt him, to ever give anyone his heart.

I'M NEVER GOING to fall in love and get married. That's not who I am.

Heat rushed into Emily's face, partially because she'd realized she was becoming a shameless eavesdropper and partly because Ben had made it so clear that he was not interested in her, no matter how hard his grandmother was trying to push her onto him.

Was that because of his mother? Because

he was worried he'd end up deserted again, like she had? Like Emily's family and those foster parents had deserted her.

She'd never considered that she and Ben might have more in common than caring about the boys. She'd never even realized how much he'd cared about them until she'd seen him interacting with them with such patience and kindness.

He would make a great father someday, but clearly that was not in his future. He was determined to stay single, and the thought of that had disappointment striking her heart. It was better that she knew that for certain, though, that she had confirmation of what she'd believed—that falling for Ben would only lead to heartbreak.

Now, to avoid embarrassment over listening in on a private conversation once again, she started walking backward down the hall. She took one small step at a time, hopeful to escape before anyone noticed her.

But Feisty awoke with a start from where she'd been sleeping on Sadie's foot, and barked at Emily before jumping up to prance around her. "Traitor…" she murmured at the little dog.

When she looked up at the Havens, who'd

turned around to see whom Feisty was barking at, she realized she wasn't the only one embarrassed. Ben's face reddened too.

Then he asked, "How much of *that* did you hear?"

"Wh-what?" she asked. "I just came to find Sadie. Taye said you were looking for me."

"I was," Sadie said.

"So I'll leave you two alone," Ben said.

"No, this involves you too," his grandmother said, as if reminding him of something.

Now Emily wished she'd been eavesdropping longer on their conversation. "What involves both of us?" Besides Sadie's blatant matchmaking?

"Taking the boys for a horseback ride on the ranch," Sadie said.

Confused, Emily lifted her shoulders in a slight shrug. "What does that have to do with me?"

"You have to go with him, of course," Sadie said.

Emily laughed. "You're not going to use that on me again."

"What?" Ben asked.

Emily gave the older woman a pointed stare. "She kept making me doubt you—suggesting that you can't be trusted alone with your own nephews."

Ben narrowed his eyes in a glare at his grandmother. The older woman wasn't at all ashamed, though.

"Was I wrong?" she asked innocently. "The first time you were watching them on your own—and you only had two of them—Little Jake got hurt."

Ben sucked in a breath. "That was an accident."

"Accidents happen when you have too many things—too many kids—to watch at the same time," she said. "I know that well from raising you and your brothers."

"We never got hurt when you were watching us," Ben said…a bit begrudgingly, however.

"Not when I was," Sadie said with pride. "But your grandpa…" She shook her head. "Every time you kids came back from an outing with him, somebody had a new bruise or scrape…"

Ben's lips curved into a faint grin. "That's because he let us do fun stuff."

Emily felt a little flicker of unease at that, at the thought of Ben letting his nephews do *fun stuff*. Little Jake still had that scrape on his elbow, which probably would have healed if he would stop picking off the scab.

"Maybe a horseback ride is a bad idea," Emily suggested. At least she knew it was for her. Despite growing up in Wyoming, she'd always lived in town and had never ridden before. She didn't trust animals any more than she trusted people.

"Horseback riding!" a little boy exclaimed. "We're going riding?"

Apparently she wasn't the only eavesdropper in the house. Caleb rushed down the hall and clasped her hand in his. "Miss Trent, we're going horseback riding?"

If he'd truly been listening, he would have had to hear her say that it wasn't a good idea. But he must have tuned out that part.

"We are?" Ian asked as he joined him.

Miller limped up behind him. "I can go riding now. The doctor said I can. Please, Uncle Ben, will you take us? It's been so long."

An ache struck Emily's heart upon hearing Miller's plea. She hadn't realized how much he'd been missing it until that moment. She'd just known that he hadn't been happy, but despite being only seven years old, the kid had a lot of reasons to be unhappy.

Ben must have felt that same wrench in

his heart because he frowned before his lips curved into a smile, and he said, "Then I guess we should go for a ride."

"We want to go too!" Caleb said, speaking for Ian as he often did.

Little Jake must have toddled up behind Miller because he pushed him aside and said, "Cab... Cab..."

Was Caleb speaking for the toddler now too?

Emily closed her eyes as she felt the walls closing in around her.

"You have to go along," Sadie said. "He can't manage them all alone."

"Melanie can go."

"No, she shouldn't," Sadie quickly replied.

Emily opened her eyes and stared at the older woman's face. Was there something Sadie knew that Emily didn't? Probably a lot. The older woman always seemed to know what was going on with everyone else.

Was Emily right to think the physical therapist might be pregnant?

"Why not?" Emily asked.

Sadie shook her head. "Not for me to say..."

"That's rarely stopped you," Ben said, and he shot Emily a wink.

Which sent a powerful kick straight to her heart. Her pulse pounded hard and fast now.

Sadie narrowed her eyes at her grandson. "I can be trusted, and I'm not the only one…" She looked at Emily now.

She could be trusted, yes. Apparently she could also be manipulated because she found herself agreeing—when the boys continued to plead—to go along on this ride on the ranch.

What was the worst that could happen?

She could fall off the horse.

But she couldn't fall for Ben.

CHAPTER FOURTEEN

BEN STARED AT EMILY, her blue eyes wide with apprehension, as she looked at the horse. He'd saddled all the smaller mounts for Miller, Caleb and Ian. So that had left Buck, one of the gentle horses, for her to ride. The buckskin quarter horse was Jake's, and Jake, being *Big Jake* now, also had to have a big horse to ride.

Ben had adjusted the saddle and stirrups for Emily. But she stood there in the barn as if frozen in place. Along with the apprehension, there was a vulnerability about her that touched something in Ben. He refused to consider that it might have been his heart. He barely knew Emily, so no matter what Grandma claimed, he had no reason to trust her.

She obviously didn't trust him either, but he assured her again, "Buck is super gentle."

"I don't care how gentle he is," she replied. "He's *huge*."

Probably especially to her—she was so petite. The boots she wore added nothing to her height but made her legs look longer in her slim-fitting jeans. She had on a white blouse with the jeans, and she'd bound her long blond hair back in a loose braid. She was gorgeous.

Buck's size didn't seem to be her only issue with the horse. She'd looked at the other—smaller—ones with nearly the same apprehension.

"Have you ever ridden before?" he asked.

Her teeth sinking into her bottom lip, she shook her head.

No wonder she hadn't wanted to come along with them, but Grandma and the boys had been relentless with their pleading. "You don't have to," he told her.

"Yes, you do!" Caleb interjected in protest. "You have to go with us."

Miller added, "We can catch bugs again, if you want." And he cast a mischievous glance at Ian.

Ian clutched the reins of his horse tighter, as if the horse would protect him from the insects or his brother's teasing. "We can't carry any more stuff with us," Ian pointed out.

They had already divided the picnic dinner Taye had packed them between the saddlebags on Ben's horse.

"It's easy, Miss Trent," Caleb insisted. "You just pull which rein you want to go in the direction of, and you say 'giddyap' and pat them a little bit to go faster." And as he did that, his horse surged forward—toward Emily—and she gasped. Ben reached out to steady her with his hand on her shoulder, and she gasped again.

Maybe he'd just startled her. Or maybe she'd felt that same little zing he felt every time he touched her. That zing that made him feel about as apprehensive as she seemed about riding the horse.

"It's okay. Peanut won't run you over," the little boy assured her. He pulled back on the reins and said, "Whoa," and the horse stopped.

A little breath escaped Emily's lips in a shaky sigh.

"It really is that easy," Ben said, before he went over some of the rules with her. "Do you think you got all that?"

She jerked her head up and down in a nod.

"You're not going to forget, Miss Trent?" Ian asked.

Ben's lips twitched in amusement at the thought of the little boy with the concussion doubting his teacher's memory. Emily's lips curved too, even as the uneasiness stayed in her eyes and in the tension of her body.

"No, I'm not going to forget," she assured her student. Yet she hesitated.

"You gotta pick her up," Caleb said.

And now the tension gripped Ben's body. "What?"

"Mommy's short like Miss Trent, so Daddy Jake has to lift her into the saddle. You need to do that with Miss Trent. Pick her up."

Despite the weird fluttery sensation in his own stomach, Ben chuckled. "You heard the little man," he told her as he placed his hands around her waist. And, again, at the contact with her warmth, that feeling traveled from his palms up to his heart.

She jumped and pulled away from him as if he'd scalded her. "I—I can do it." But when she tried to lift her foot to the stirrup, her boot pushed against Buck's side well below the leather strap. The horse shifted away from her, and if Ben hadn't caught her, she probably would have fallen.

"He's too big for you—" Ben said.

"I know!"

"—for you to get into the saddle without help," he said, finishing his thought. "You just need a boost."

She stared up at him. "Let me stand on your thigh like you did with the boys."

He'd kneeled next to each horse for them so that they had been able to reach the stirrup... except for Little Jake, who'd been patiently waiting for him. But the now bored toddler started wandering away in the barn, toward Midnight's stall.

"Hey!" he called out to him. "We're riding Spot," he told Little Jake and pointed toward the Appaloosa Ben always rode when he came out to the ranch. "Come back here." He nearly cringed as the little boy walked back, too close to the horses the older boys were seated on.

Getting impatient himself, Ben murmured, "We don't have time for this." And he encircled her small waist again and lifted her up to Buck's saddle. She was light but lifting her—holding her—brought a heaviness over Ben that settled deep within him.

She reached out and clutched at the saddle horn before swinging her leg over the horse. Then she released a shaky breath and murmured, "Hey..."

It must have been in protest of Ben's action because Buck didn't move, as if he knew she was nervous, and he held perfectly still for her. "He's a good horse," Ben told her. "Jake trained him, so he's a lot like him and takes care of others. He won't let you get hurt."

"He's just a horse," Emily murmured, as if she doubted his ability to keep her safe. Or maybe she was worried that she was going to get hurt some other way than riding.

Ben was beginning to worry about that himself.

EMILY'S HANDS ACHED from gripping the reins and the saddle horn so tightly. Not that she was using them to steer the horse. Buck just seemed to know what to do on his own and ambled along after the boys, which was good since she kept glancing over her shoulder to check on Ben and Little Jake.

He easily held the toddler in front of him on his saddle, and Emily felt a pang of envy. She wished she was the one riding with Ben, leaning sleepily back against him like Little Jake was, his small body totally relaxed probably because he felt safe.

She wouldn't have felt safe being that close to Ben, though. She wouldn't have been able to relax with his body touching hers. Even now she could feel the warmth and strength of his hands wrapped around her waist, and she shivered at the thought of how easily he'd lifted her into the saddle, nearly as easily as he'd lifted Little Jake onto the horse with him.

The toddler had loved riding so much that he'd actually made a lot of noises—little giggles and sounds—before the movement of the horse had started rocking him to sleep. Her lips curved into a smile as she thought of it.

Maybe Sadie's idea hadn't been all bad. Maybe it hadn't been just a manipulation to throw Emily and Ben together, especially since they had four little chaperones along on the ride. She was glad she wasn't alone with Ben, and she was glad that she wasn't alone with the boys.

Ben had to keep calling out to them to come back as they rode off ahead, urging their horses faster and faster.

"Boys!" Ben called out again.

Emily turned her head and noticed that they were quite a distance in front of her, galloping through a puddle that sprayed muddy water everywhere. No. It was more than a puddle; it looked like a pond stretched across the trail. And the boys were making the most of it.

Droplets spattered the white hats they'd rarely removed since the wedding. Emily grimaced at the thought of trying to clean them later.

"Come on, guys!" she called out too, and her voice must have startled Buck. Or he'd just decided he wanted to join the boys because he shot forward…into that muddy water.

When she'd been turned around, watching Little Jake and Ben, she must have loosened her grasp on the reins because they slipped through her hands and she fell off the saddle, landing with a big splash in the middle of that huge mud puddle. The water was warm, but the sudden submersion in it had her gasping in shock.

It was deeper than she'd realized, so deep that the water covered her to her waist, then the mud seemed to suck her deeper yet. Was it quicksand?

She let out a shriek of alarm. And Ben was there.

"Are you okay?" he asked as he dismounted his horse on the edge of the puddle, Little Jake clasped against his chest. The toddler wriggled in his grasp, reaching out either toward Emily or toward the mud.

The other boys were still in it with their horses, their movements spattering more mud onto Emily's face and hair.

"Miss Trent!" Caleb called out. "Are you all right?" He started to slide off his saddle, but Ben called out again.

"Don't get down, boys. Get your horses out of the water, and I will rescue Miss Trent."

"No!" she protested. She was not some damsel in distress who needed help getting out of a puddle—no matter how big and deep it was. "We don't all need to get dirty. I can get out." But when she tried, she found it wasn't easy—not easy at all.

The mud had her stuck, like a suction cup against a glass windowpane. She had to use both hands, sinking them deep into the water to push against the ground and lever herself up. But when she tried to stand, her boots slipped from beneath her and she went into the muddy water…facedown.

The water rushed into her nose and mouth, making her choke. She whipped her head up, sending water shooting off her wet bangs and braid, which slapped across her face and back.

"Emily! Are you all right?" Ben asked, his voice gruff with concern.

She nodded even though tears stung her eyes.

"Miller, can you take Little Jake?" he asked, as he held the toddler out toward the boy's oldest brother. "I'll help Miss Trent."

"I can help her!" Caleb offered.

But Emily was already crawling out of the puddle on her hands and knees. Before either of the heroic males could help her, she was clear of the water, but mud clung to her clothes and skin and hair.

She could even feel the grittiness of the dirt in her mouth, on her tongue and teeth. She grimaced.

And Little Jake giggled.

Then the other boys started to giggle, all of them laughing at how ridiculous she must have looked. She might have laughed too, had she not been so close to tears of frustration, had she not been brought back to all those kids staring at her in school, feeling sorry for the poor little orphan nobody had wanted.

That was how Ben looked at her now—with concern and probably pity. "I've got a blanket in the saddlebag," he said, and he was already pulling it out. He wrapped the plaid flannel blanket around her.

The mid-June day was warm, but the mud and water had chilled her skin. She was grateful for the blanket, but she'd clenched her jaw too tightly to thank him. She'd clenched it to hold back the little sob that threatened to slip free.

"Can you ride back?" he asked.

She nodded.

"Are you sure?" he asked with more of

that concern and probably some skepticism as well.

She bristled with wounded pride. "I won't fall again."

"I meant that you're going to be so wet and uncomfortable," he said. "Do you want to wait here and I'll ride back with the boys then come and get you with a truck?"

She glanced at the horse standing just outside the puddle of water. Buck seemed to be ignoring her now. Maybe he was embarrassed that he hadn't taken care of her like Ben had promised he would.

She glared at the horse. "I should ride him back and get him as muddy as he got me."

"You were supposed to hang on, Miss Trent," Caleb admonished her. "Not slide off the saddle like Little Jake did."

Heat rushed to her face now. She wasn't sure how to defend herself. But she didn't need to. Ben did. "Buck was startled because of you guys messing around in that puddle. Now apologize to Miss Trent for getting her all muddy."

"Sorry," each of them mumbled.

"You're really muddy, Miss Trent," Ian observed. "What happened?"

Miller groaned. "How can you forget that already?" he asked. "She's still wet."

And despite the warm sunshine, she was beginning to shiver—maybe more in reaction to falling off the horse than from being cold.

"Wait here," Ben told her. "I'll bring the boys to the barn, get a truck and come back for you."

Tears stung her eyes again, but now it was because of his kindness…and some regret too. She should have been holding on instead of mooning over him; then she wouldn't have fallen and ruined their ride. So really it was *his* fault—for being as handsome as he was, for being sweet with Little Jake…

For being sweet to her now…

She tried to summon some irritation with him. But she couldn't. After fighting to free herself from the puddle, she had no energy left. So she dropped onto a dry area of ground. "I'll wait here," she said.

"Daddy Jake says that you're supposed to get back on the horse you falled off of," Caleb said.

"These are extenuating circumstances," Ben answered for her. "Now come on, guys." He reached for Little Jake, taking him from Miller's arms. "Let's hurry back to the ranch."

It wasn't until they'd ridden off with Buck following behind them that Emily remembered she had her phone on her. In the front pocket of her once white blouse. The snap on the pocket had kept the phone from falling out, but it wouldn't have kept the water from seeping in. She pulled it out of her pocket and noticed that the screen was still lit up.

The waterproof case really was as good as the online reviews had claimed it was. At least she had that...

She quickly punched in Taye's contact and told her what had happened. Before the cook could reply, Emily warned her, "Don't laugh—the boys did enough of that..." Which had brought her back to her embarrassing childhood. On the top of that big horse, she'd felt as small and helpless as she had as a child, as helpless as she was beginning to feel over fighting her attraction to Ben.

"Are you okay?" Melanie asked. Taye must have had the phone on speaker. "Are you hurt?"

"I'm fine," she said. "I just need someone to pick me up. Ben's riding back now with the boys to get a truck. But I'm wet and miserable."

"I'm on my way," Taye said. "I'll come get you."

"You're sure you're okay?" Melanie asked.

"I'll be better once I get back to the house and get cleaned up." She wasn't really okay. She was entirely too attracted to Ben. And she didn't want to be the fool that her high-school friends who'd fallen for him had been, especially because she knew—by his own admission—that he was never going to fall in love.

She'd always thought she never would either, but she'd already begun to fall for the little Haven boys. When she hung up her call with Taye, she noticed she'd missed a call from the principal.

She swiped her mud-crusted finger across the screen until she played his message. "Summer planning sessions are starting in a few weeks, Emily. I need to know what your plans are for the upcoming school year. I need to make sure that you're coming back..."

Mr. Kellerman didn't say anything else, just ended the call there, but she knew what he'd left unsaid. If she wasn't coming back, he was going to have to replace her.

She was going to lose her job, the teaching position she'd wanted since she'd moved into her first stable home with her former third-grade teacher. She owed Mrs. Rademacher for her kindness, which was why she'd become a teacher and why she'd agreed to care for the Haven kids.

She'd wanted to repay the kindness Mrs. Rademacher had shown her. The Haven boys wouldn't need her forever and then where would she go? She couldn't lose her job at the school.

But she wasn't ready to leave the ranch yet. Her heart ached at the thought of saying goodbye to them. And it wasn't just their sweet faces that flashed into her mind, but Ben's as well.

He had been caring toward her; he had shown her compassion when she'd fallen, when she'd expected him to laugh like the kids had, like she probably would have laughed at him had the roles been reversed and he'd landed in the mud. She was glad she'd called the women to come get her.

She didn't want to see him now, while she was wet and muddy and vulnerable. She didn't want to risk falling again—not into the mud, but into love with a man who wanted nothing to do with love. She couldn't get up her hopes like she had so many times in her past only to be disappointed again when someone didn't love her enough to keep her.

CHAPTER FIFTEEN

SHE HADN'T WAITED for him. She hadn't wanted his help. Ben and the boys hadn't been anywhere close to the barn when Taye and Melanie had driven past in Taye's truck. He'd been surprised her phone had worked to call them, and he'd wondered why he hadn't thought to use his own phone to make the call.

But maybe he hadn't thought of it because he'd wanted to be the one to come to her rescue. He hadn't been able to rescue her from the puddle because she'd scrambled out on her own before he'd had the chance.

He wouldn't have been able to put down the toddler without him winding up in that puddle too, which had been surprisingly deep. The little guy might have gotten hurt while Ben had been trying to play hero to a woman who was making it very clear that she didn't need one.

Emily Trent could take care of herself.

So he'd taken care of the boys and the horses, which hadn't been easy on his own with Little Jake running off anytime he let go of him. And the other boys hadn't been much help, since they'd been more focused on Midnight than they were taking care of the horses they'd ridden. He'd had to make sure they didn't open that stall door and release the restless bronco.

Where was Dusty...?

As MIA as their mother...

He'd had to force thoughts of both of them from his mind to finish up with the horses. So it was no surprise that Emily and Taye and Melanie had beaten them back to the house. Once Ben shepherded the boys out of the barn, he saw Taye's truck parked near the front porch.

Chunks of mud littered the steps but stopped next to the boots, socks and jeans Emily must have discarded before entering the house. His pulse quickened at the thought of her running through the house in just her underwear and that mud-covered white blouse.

But then he remembered she'd had a blanket too—his blanket...

There was no trace of it among the other muddy things. Looking at the boys, who'd not escaped the muddy water unscathed either, he ordered them to shuck their boots and jeans.

So they ran into the house wearing only their cartoon-character underwear, shirts and hats.

He only had to take off his boots. Then he followed the boys into the kitchen, where they found Taye at the sink, washing her hands, while Melanie sat atop one of the stools at the long island.

"How come you didn't take off your jeans too?" Taye asked him, her lips curving into a broad grin.

"Uncle Ben didn't fall in the mud like Miss Trent," Caleb answered for him.

"How did Miss Trent fall in the first place?" Melanie asked them.

All the boys, even Little Jake, looked down at the floor with some guilt. And Ben felt a twinge of regret for admonishing them earlier.

"We were galloping our horses through the ginormous mud puddle and spooked Buck. When he ran, Miss Trent fell off," Caleb replied, taking responsibility. He wasn't Jake's son biologically, but he sure acted like him. He was a good kid; they all were, and clearly they felt badly now for causing Miss Trent to fall.

"It was an accident, guys," he assured the little boys.

"But then we laughed at her," Caleb reminded him. "And she looked so upset, it was like when the kids laughed at me for not knowing about cowboys and ranches when I first came to Willow Creek."

His new nephew's admission had sympathy and remorse filling Ben's heart. Poor kid…

Ben should have been there for him and Katie when they'd first returned to Willow Creek. That was one of the things he loved most about the town he served—everyone looked after everyone else. Maybe that was why he hadn't figured he needed to because there had always been other people to help out. Just like Grandma and Grandpa Haven had stepped up to raise him and his brothers, and how Jake and Dale had stepped up after Grandpa died.

He had to do that now. "I'm sure Miss Trent didn't mind," he told Caleb. But he wasn't so sure; he'd seen her face when they'd done that, and she had looked so hurt. "And you can apologize to her once you've gotten cleaned up too. You all need to do that now—head upstairs to the bathroom." He gestured toward the stairs, which they all dutifully began to climb, even Little Jake.

Ben would have to help him wash up, but before following them up, he asked Emily's friends, "Is she okay?"

Melanie nodded. "I think so. She wouldn't let me check her over until she got cleaned up."

"I don't think she's physically hurt," Taye said. "But Caleb might have been right about emotionally…"

Ben nodded. "I'll get the boys cleaned up and apologize to her."

"Did you laugh too?" Taye asked, and she sounded horrified that he might have.

He shook his head. He'd been too concerned to laugh. Watching her fall from that horse and being unable to reach her in time…

He'd felt helpless, like he had too many other times in his life. Like when his father had died, and his mom left and…

He shook his head again, unwilling to wallow in any more of the Haven family tragedies.

"Then you have no reason to apologize," Taye assured him.

But a half hour later, after cleaning up the boys and then changing out of his soap-sudsy clothes, he found himself outside her door, his hand raised to knock. But he hesitated, wondering if she wanted to see him.

She'd called Taye to come and get her before he'd had a chance to even get back to the barn. And while he'd been dealing with the boys, she hadn't stepped in to help as she usually did.

Maybe she hadn't been able to...

Maybe she was hurt.

His pulse quickening with concern, he knocked and called out, "Emily? Are you okay?"

A long moment of silence followed his knock. Pressing his ear to the door, he listened for the sound of her footsteps, or maybe a call for help. Perhaps she wasn't inside at all but had gone downstairs to join the others in the kitchen.

Before he could step back from the door, it opened, and he nearly stumbled inside her room. He grasped the doorframe, stopping himself from falling into her. His weight would have knocked her down even harder than she'd fallen from the horse. She was so petite.

She stood beside the door, a robe wrapped tightly around her, her hair damp around her flushed face. "What are you doing?" she asked, her blue eyes wide with surprise.

"Checking to make sure you're all right," he said. "And when you didn't answer my knock, I was worried that you were hurt."

"I'm fine," she said. "My pride probably took more of a hit than my body."

"The boys feel bad for laughing at you," he said. "They're going to apologize."

Her lips curved into a slight smile. "You already made them do that," she reminded him. "Back at the puddle…"

"It was more than a puddle," he said. "You could have been seriously hurt."

"I was probably lucky it was so deep," she said. "I didn't hit the ground too hard." Yet she flinched as she shifted her weight from one bare foot to the other.

"You are hurt," he said, alarmed again. "I'll go get Melanie or Baker—" But when he turned to go, she grasped his arm and stopped him.

Her hand was on his bare skin, her fingers warm and soft. That heat spread up his arm to his heart, and for a moment it felt like it stopped. But then it resumed beating at a frantic pace, and fear gripped him. Not fear that she was hurt but fear that he was about to get hurt.

WHEN BEN TURNED back around to face her, Emily noticed the look on his face. It was almost as if he was afraid.

"I'm fine," she assured him. "I don't need medical attention."

He blinked, and for the first time she noticed how long and thick his lashes were, like Little Jake's. "What?" he murmured, and now he seemed more similar to Ian and couldn't remember what was going on.

"You said you were going to get Baker or Melanie," she reminded him. "But I'm probably just sore from riding. I've never been on a horse before."

"Will you go riding again?" he asked.

She shook her head.

"Remember what Daddy Jake told Caleb," Ben said, his lips curving into a grin, "you gotta get back on the horse you falled off of." He shook his head and murmured, "Too bad that kid doesn't have a better teacher..."

Instead of being offended, like she probably would have been in the past, Emily laughed and playfully swatted at his shoulder. It was so broad; he was so strong, but he stumbled back as if her light swat had unbalanced him. And she laughed again.

Instead of laughing with her, his breath shuddered out in a ragged sigh. "That's better," he murmured. "You're smiling again..."

Regret tugged at her. "I haven't smiled at you that often," she admitted.

He shrugged. "I know. But… I just needed to make sure you were okay. When you took that fall…" His breath quivered again as if someone had struck him hard, hard enough to knock the air out of him. "I was worried that you were hurt. And when the boys laughed at you…"

Her smile slipped away then, and she wrapped her arms around herself, feeling exposed and vulnerable. That moment, their staring at her and laughing, had sent her spiraling back to her past. To how she'd often been pointed at in school, how people had whispered about her. They hadn't laughed; it probably would have been better if they had. Instead, they'd pitied her.

"That's what happened," he said. "That look… Caleb compared it to how he felt when kids made fun of him for not knowing about ranches and cowboys when he first moved here from the city."

She sighed. "I know they gave him a tough time—but for Ian. Ian was his champion then, just like Caleb is his now."

"Was that what it was like for you in school?" Ben asked. "Were you picked on?"

She shrugged, but the past weighed heavily on her yet. She'd never quite been able to shake it off, shake off the disappointment and distrust she'd felt so many times in her childhood. "I wasn't so much picked on as pitied."

His brow furrowed. "I wish I remembered you. I'm sorry that I don't…"

"I should be glad that you don't," she admitted. "Most people from school remember me as the little girl nobody wanted so she had to live with a teacher."

He gasped. "I don't understand…what happened?"

She shrugged again. "My mother died, and none of her family wanted me. And I bounced around some foster homes for a while until Mrs. Rademacher talked Social Services into letting me live with her. She was my champion." Tears stung her eyes as she thought again of the teacher's kindness.

Ben groaned and reached out, his arms sliding around her to offer the comforting hug he'd tried to give her the other night.

This time Emily didn't hold back. She slid her arms around him and held him too. He felt so good, so solid and strong. She pressed her head against his chest, where his heart beat hard and fast beneath her ear.

"I'm so sorry, Emily..." Ben murmured.

She lifted her head and stared up at him. "Why?" she asked. "Because you don't remember me? We weren't in the same grade. We had no classes together. I shouldn't have expected you to know who I was back then."

"I remember hearing about you now."

"Don't feel sorry for me," she said, and she felt herself stiffen in his embrace. "I was lucky. Mrs. Rademacher was so sweet and kind to me. She even helped me pay for college and sold me her house in town."

"She's why you became a teacher."

It wasn't a question, but she answered like it was. "Yes. But I think I would have even if she hadn't taken me in. I really love teaching."

He nodded as if he understood that kind of love.

"Is that how you feel about being mayor?" she asked as she pulled away from him to study his face. She'd once believed he'd just wanted the position for power and fame, but now she wondered if she'd misjudged everything about him.

He nodded again. "I love it. My grandma always told me stories about her father, about the things he'd done for the town, about how much he'd cared about it. He died before I was born, but he still inspired me to go into politics, to use that position to improve life for the townspeople."

He was a better man than she'd given him credit for being. "You love the town," she said, "like I love kids…"

"They love you," he said. "So much that they're going to be devastated when you leave."

She closed her eyes and sighed at the thought of having to leave them, of breaking their hearts like hers had been broken so many times. Leaving them would make it break once again.

He tipped up her chin with his thumb underneath it. "What's wrong?"

"I missed a call earlier," she said. "From Mr. Kellerman…"

"The principal?"

She nodded, and his hand dropped away from her face.

"What did he want? You to come back to work?"

She shrugged. "I don't know. I haven't called him back yet." She didn't want to call him back; she didn't want to have to make a choice now. Not between the boys and her job…not when she loved them both.

Ben stepped back then, pulling farther away from her physically, and maybe emotionally as well. She'd gotten vulnerable with him, when she'd shared parts of her life with him, but he'd also been vulnerable. Maybe too vulnerable for his comfort. "I should let you call him," he said.

Once again, when he turned to leave, she reached out to stop him. She couldn't let him go yet. "I'm sorry," she said.

He couldn't seem to meet her gaze. "So you are leaving?"

"No, I—I don't know," she admitted. "I'm apologizing to you—belatedly—over jumping to the conclusion that you upset Melanie that night after Miller's party."

He turned back toward her then, his brow furrowed as if he'd forgotten what she was talking about.

"I thought you made her cry," she reminded him.

"Why?" he asked.

She sighed. "Because I've seen you make other girls cry."

His dark eyes widened with shock. "Who? Who did I make cry?"

She shook her head. "I can't break confidences…" Especially since the women had moved on since high school. Even Maggie Standish had started dating someone else after Ben had broken her heart.

Emily realized now that she was the one who hadn't moved on, who wouldn't let herself forget how Ben had hurt her friends. She wished that was just out of loyalty to them, but she knew there was more to it, just as there was more to Ben than she'd realized. She didn't want to forget that he'd hurt all those who'd fallen for him…because she didn't want to fall for him and get hurt.

"I'm sorry," he said. "I don't know who you're talking about, but I certainly never purposely made anyone cry. So I was definitely *not* the reason Melanie was crying."

"I know," she assured him. "That's why I'm apologizing."

He leaned down and turned his cheek to her. "Last time you apologized, you kissed me," he reminded her.

She rose up on tiptoe then, but when she moved to press her lips to his cheek, he turned his head. And his mouth brushed across hers. Her breath caught, trapped in her lungs, as her pulse quickened then raced. And just like when she'd toppled off the horse earlier, Emily could feel herself falling…

"How dare he..." Sadie murmured to Feisty, who'd settled onto her lap for them to watch their shows in the sitting area of the master suite. Feisty barely lifted an ear at Sadie's comment. She was not concerned.

But Sadie was still not over Old Man Lemmon calling her ornery. He was one to talk. He was always short with her. She chuckled. He was just short. Maybe that was his issue with her—that he barely came to her shoulder.

He'd been ticked off ever since she'd passed his height in the fifth grade. That was something he'd never been able to beat her at, like they'd competed for grades and in playground races. "Old fool..."

"Talking to yourself?" a deep voice asked, and she glanced up to find her grandson standing just inside the door to the hall. Ben's face was flushed, and he looked disheveled.

She narrowed her eyes. "What's up with you?" she asked. "Everything okay?"

"No," he said, and he sounded angry—with her. "It's not okay. You need to stop doing this..."

"Doing what?" she asked when he trailed off.

"Manipulating," he said. "Meddling..."

268   THE COWBOY'S UNLIKELY MATCH

She widened her eyes, feigning innocence. "I don't know what you're talking about."

"Throwing me and Emily together over and over again like you think something's going to happen between us," he said.

And she began to suspect that something had.

"It's all pointless, anyway," he said. "She's not staying."

Sadie tensed. "What are you talking about?"

"The principal called her. She's going to have to go back to her job at the school."

Sadie held her breath for a moment, so that she didn't curse Kellerman aloud. What was he thinking? She'd thought they had an agreement. He was supposed to give Emily as long a leave as she needed, as long as they needed her.

"The boys are going to be devastated," Ben continued.

She suspected they weren't the only ones. She shrugged as if she was unconcerned when she was anything but. "Miss Trent only agreed to teach the boys through the end of the school year. She probably will have to return to her job if she wants to keep it."

"Didn't you hear me?" Ben asked, and his voice shook a bit with anger...or desperation.

"The boys are going to be devastated. They are so attached to her, and they can't lose someone else they love. You're going to have to get her to stay."

She quirked a brow. "You just told me that I have to stop," she reminded him. "That I shouldn't manipulate or meddle anymore."

He pushed one of his hands through his already tousled hair. "You shouldn't, but it's too late now."

Her pulse quickened with excitement. Had her plan worked for Ben?

"You already brought her here," Ben said. "You've already got the boys devoted to her, so you can't let her leave."

"I can't hold her hostage," Sadie pointed out. "So how am I going to keep her here?"

"I don't know…"

"I know how we might get her to stay," Sadie mused.

Now Ben tensed. "I'm probably going to regret this," he murmured. "But how?"

"You could marry her…"

CHAPTER SIXTEEN

AFTER THAT CONVERSATION with his grand-mother, Ben had no choice. He had to leave.

He waited until the next morning—until he and Caleb tended to Midnight. Then, after returning him and Little Jake and Miller to the house and into Taye's care, Ben hopped into his SUV and drove back to Willow Creek.

The boys would probably just think he was off with Baker, helping on the ranch. And he probably should have been. But he'd needed to make a trip to town.

Less than an hour later he pulled into his space at city hall. Mayor Haven. That was what the sign fastened to the building in front of his parking spot said.

Mayor Haven…

He'd wanted that title, this role, for so many years. He couldn't remember a time he hadn't wanted it, probably like Dusty couldn't remember a time he hadn't wanted to be a rodeo rider. He heaved a heavy sigh of disappointment for how he'd spoken to his brother the last time they'd talked; he'd been unnecessarily hard on Dusty, especially when he was the one who should have understood him most.

Understood how much a person could want something...

Like a job.

Like a woman...

His heart thudded hard in his chest as he let his mind slip back to last night, to that kiss. Emily's lips had been so silky, her breath so warm, her mouth so sweet...

He'd never wanted that kiss to end. But then he'd remembered that nothing lasted forever. Not a kiss. Not love. And he'd pulled back and hurried out of her room.

And Emily hadn't tried to stop him from leaving again. She'd probably been happy to see him go. He hadn't seen her this morning. She'd already started her lesson with Ian when he'd brought the other boys out to the barn, and when he'd returned, she must have still been working with the forgetful little boy.

But all Ben had to do was close his eyes to see her face, to see how flushed her skin had been, how dark her eyes had gone, with the pupils dilated so much that they'd eclipsed nearly all of the blue. That kiss had affected her too. But he doubted that—or he—could make her stay at the ranch.

He snorted at his grandmother's suggestion. *Marry her...*

He shook his head at her ridiculous comment. And then he jumped when someone tapped on his window. He turned to find Lem standing outside his SUV. Ben drew in a deep breath before opening his door and stepping into the parking lot.

"I didn't know you were coming," Lem said. "You said you were going to call first."

Ben grimaced and nodded. "I know, I just..." He'd had to get away. From Grandma...

From the ranch...

And, most of all, from Emily.

Lem chuckled. "Sadie getting to you?" he asked.

"She's not just ornery," Ben told his deputy mayor. "She's out of control."

Lem chuckled. "More like she wants all the control..."

"You don't have to tell me that," Ben said. He'd experienced it firsthand during their last conversation.

Before he'd been able to remind her that he never intended to get married, she'd shaken her head and remarked, "No. You can't marry her. To keep the little boys happy, she needs to stay here at the ranch all the time, and you keep claiming that you have to live in town."

"I do…" he'd responded. So even if he'd changed his mind about getting married, he couldn't marry Emily. He couldn't take her away from his nephews. Little Jake needed her all the time right now, but most especially at night, to comfort him when the nightmares woke him up. And Ian needed her extra tutoring so that he didn't fall far behind in school. And Caleb loved her too much to lose her like he had his dad. No. Ben couldn't be that selfish. Not that Ben ever intended to get married…to anyone.

He couldn't risk his heart on someone who might leave him, like his mother had, like Emily would probably leave the boys. But if Emily left them, he didn't want it to be because of him—because he'd put his own needs before theirs, like his mother had when she'd deserted him and his brothers. She'd put her love for the rodeo over her love for them, if she'd ever really loved them at all…

And thinking of all those birthdays she'd missed and holidays…all those promises she'd made to come back and hadn't kept…

Leaving him sitting on the porch, expecting her to come for his twelfth birthday and then his thirteenth and fourteenth and fifteenth…

That was why he'd told her not to bother anymore, not to contact him again. It had hurt too much to be let down over and over again, to never see the person you loved most.

He didn't want the boys to have to go through that again, not after losing both their parents.

"You okay?" Lem asked.

Ben nodded. "Yeah, I'm sorry I didn't call you first. Were you on your way to a meeting or something?"

Lem shook his head. "I was actually thinking about coming out to the ranch, bringing you those contracts to sign, so that you wouldn't have to make the trip to town with everything you have going on right now."

"Thank you," Ben said. "I really appreciate that."

"You helped me so much when my wife was sick," Lem said. "I'm happy to repay the favor however I can."

Hmmm…

An idea began to form in Ben's mind. A plan. A scheme…just like his grandmother's.

Maybe he was the most like her, just like his brothers claimed. A grin tugged at his mouth.

"But it's probably a good idea you came to town," Lem said. "It'll be good for the voters to see you at city hall."

As if on cue, a horn tooted as someone drove past them. Without even looking, Ben raised his hand to wave. "I'll be back to work next week," Ben said. "When Jake and Katie return…"

"That's good," Lem said.

No. It wasn't. That didn't give him much time to work on his plan. He was going to need some help. "Why don't you come out to the ranch tomorrow for dinner?" Ben asked. "You've been missing Taye's cooking at the diner."

Lem nodded. "That's an offer I can't refuse," he said. "But will Sadie be okay that you invited me?"

No. She wouldn't be okay at all—especially when she realized Ben was borrowing a page from her matchmaking playbook. "Probably not," he admitted.

And Lem chuckled. "That makes the offer even more appealing then," he admitted.

Lem Lemmon was a match for Sadie Haven; he was strong enough to handle her.

Stronger than even Jake had been, since he'd fallen into her trap so easily. Ben was not going to fall for it...

But then his mind flashed back to that kiss, that kiss he'd never wanted to end. But it had.

Just as Jake and Katie's honeymoon would end and Ben would return to town. Would Emily come back too? To Willow Creek and her job?

Or would she stay with his nephews?

Either way, Ben knew that she would never be with him. He couldn't live at the ranch, and once Jake and Katie returned, he wouldn't be needed full-time. He'd be able to visit more often than he had...and keep his job in town. But for Emily, he didn't see how she could keep hers without breaking the boys' hearts. They needed her so much more than they even needed Jake and Katie, since she'd been there for them the most since the accident and they were the most dependent on her for comfort. As he acknowledged the hopelessness of the situation, his heart broke a little.

HE WAS GOING to break their hearts—just like Emily had been afraid he would. But then he'd been so sweet with the boys—with her—that she'd made the mistake of beginning to think he cared. Instead of paying any attention to the movie Emily had started on the TV in the playroom, they kept asking where Uncle Ben was.

She'd been asking that herself. She hadn't seen him all day. "I'm sure Uncle Ben is just out in the pastures helping Uncle Baker." But she doubted that was where he really was… unless he'd driven his SUV there. And given that it was a luxury vehicle, she doubted that he'd be out in the fields with it. He'd gone somewhere else with it. Town? Just for the night, or had he left for good? Had that kiss they'd shared scared him as badly as it had her? Even now, thinking of it, had her trembling a bit in reaction to all the feelings that had overwhelmed her. The attraction, the desire, the fear…

"But it's late," Caleb pointed out. "Usually Uncle Ben is in the house by now. Usually he eats dinner with us."

He had missed it despite Taye holding the meal for a while for him. Even Sadie hadn't known where he was, and she'd probably tried calling him. Wasn't he answering his phone?

Emily hadn't tried calling; she didn't have his number. Not that she would have called, anyway. That might have made him think that she cared, that that kiss had affected her… which it had.

"You guys watch the movie," she said. "I'll go downstairs and get the popcorn."

"I don't want popcorn," Caleb said. "I want Uncle Ben."

She swallowed the groan of frustration and anger burning the back of her throat. Why hadn't he told anyone where he was going? Because he was used to being single and un-attached…like he'd vowed he always would be. That was why she had to forget about that kiss. But forgetting about Ben…

That wasn't possible for his nephews.

"I'll see if he's back," she said. "You— watch…" She gestured toward the TV, where the animated movie played out even though none of the boys was watching it. They were all watching her.

"I'll be right back," she promised, and she hurriedly slipped out of the room and down the backstairs to the kitchen, which was filled with the scent of popcorn. Melanie sat at the island while Taye drizzled melted butter over the bowl.

"It's almost ready," she said.

"They don't want it," Emily told her. "They

want Uncle Ben." And she was worried that they weren't the only ones who wanted him.

She had…last night. The way he kissed…

It was no wonder that women had cried over him. She'd nearly cried when he'd stopped, when he'd walked away from her. But it was for the best. He'd made it clear—at least to his grandmother—that he had no intention of ever getting married. And she wasn't going to fall for a man who couldn't commit to a future with her, to a family with her. She'd been hurt too badly in the past when her own family hadn't been able to commit to caring about her, to ensuring that she had a future. She had to make sure that when she finally gave her heart to someone that it was to someone she could trust with it.

Taye glanced at her wristwatch. "He should be back soon."

"You know where he is?" Emily asked with a pang of something she refused to identify.

Taye nodded. "Yeah, he called to ask me—"

The sound of a door opening cut off Taye's reply. Before she could finish, he was there, carrying in a few bags of groceries. He set them on the island next to Taye. "Make sure I got everything you need," he told the cook, who was already pulling a carton of blueberries from one of the bags.

"If he likes those muffins, he'll love my blueberry cobbler," Taye said.

"Who? What's going on?" Emily asked. And why did Ben look so good? He was wearing his black cowboy hat and boots with a suit and tie, as if he'd had some formal event.

"Were you gone all this time shopping?" Heat flushed her face as she heard how she sounded—like a suspicious wife. No wonder Ben had vowed to remain single forever.

He shook his head. "No. I had to go into town to sign some contracts and then I made a couple of appearances around town."

She'd assumed politicians' public appearances were fundraisers and ribbon-cutting events, so she incredulously asked, "At the grocery store?"

"Farmer's market," Taye answered for him. "That's where I get the fresh blueberries. Thanks for making the trip."

"Thank you for agreeing to help me."

Emily narrowed her eyes and studied the two of them. "What are you up to?"

"You'll love this," Melanie assured her.

"You know too?" Had she been the only

one left out of whatever he and Taye were planning?

Melanie nodded. "Tell her, Ben," she urged him.

His mouth curved into a grin, but he wasn't looking directly at Emily, like he couldn't quite meet her gaze. She couldn't meet his either after that kiss…

They'd never talked about it. He'd just walked away, and then today when she hadn't seen him…she'd wondered if he'd left because of that, because of her.

"We're going to give Sadie a little of her own medicine," he said.

Thoroughly confused, Emily asked, "Blueberries?"

Ben chuckled. "Lem…"

"What?"

"We're going to meddle with Sadie's love life," he said. "We're going to set her up with my deputy mayor."

"Old Man Lemmon?" Emily asked with shock.

"They're the same age," Ben said as he helped Taye unload the grocery bags. "They went to school together."

"And they hate each other," Emily said. She'd heard enough disparaging remarks from both of them about the other over the years to know that.

"Or do they?" Taye asked, and her pale blue eyes twinkled. "Sometimes people act like they don't like someone because they're actually really attracted to them."

While Ben ignored Taye's comment, Melanie chuckled. And more heat rushed to Emily's face. Was that what she'd been doing? Why she'd been so quick to think the worst of Ben, because of how attracted she was to him?

She shook her head. "I'm not so sure about that. What is this plan?"

"Lem's coming to dinner tomorrow," Ben said. "So Taye agreed to make all his favorite foods."

Emily chuckled. "Is that how you're getting him to come to dinner?"

Ben shrugged. "Maybe...but he always asks about Grandma. I think he could be romantically interested in her."

"It's a good idea," Taye assured him. "Sadie deserves some happiness too."

"She's only going to be happy when she marries off all her grandsons," Emily said. "To one of us." She glanced at Melanie. "You're the only one who's safe."

The color rushed out of Melanie's face then.

"Are you okay?" Ben asked the brunette.

She nodded. "Yes, I'm just getting a little tired." The sudden paleness of her face accentuated the dark circles around her eyes. She slid off the stool then and headed toward the stairs.

"I'll go up with you," Taye said, "and bring the boys their popcorn." She carried up the bowl behind Melanie, leaving Emily and Ben alone in the kitchen.

"Is she okay?" Ben asked. "She was crying that night on the patio, and she's been looking so exhausted."

After a sleepless night herself, Emily probably looked exhausted too. "I've tried to get her to talk, but Katie's the only one she's likely to open up to..."

"She'll be back soon."

Emily felt a flash of panic at that. Not because her friend was returning, but because that meant someone else would be leaving. "The boys are upset," she told him. "They missed you today at dinner."

He grimaced. "I'm sorry. I really didn't intend to be gone so long. But when it occurred to me to mess with Grandma like she's been messing with all of us, I had to lay some groundwork."

While she'd lain sleepless last night after that kiss, she'd had a few uncharitable thoughts of her own about Sadie's interference in her love life. It reminded her too much of the teachers and parents who'd urged kids to befriend the "poor little orphan" so that she'd never known if they had genuinely liked her. Even though Ben had kissed her, she wasn't sure he genuinely liked her. She really hadn't given him any reason to like her. But she liked his idea. She gestured at the counter. "Blueberries are your groundwork?"

He sighed. "If that was all I had to do..."

"What?" she asked, suddenly intrigued at what lengths he'd gone to and where he'd gone that day. The boys weren't the only ones who'd missed him.

"I took Lem shopping," he admitted. "And to the barber..."

"Oh, I can't wait for dinner tomorrow night," Emily said.

"I can't wait for this," Ben murmured, and suddenly he lowered his head to hers, his lips brushing across her mouth.

She gasped and pulled back in shock. Last

night hadn't been an aberration. And it hadn't been all her doing…

"I'm sorry," he said. "I just…couldn't resist."

They needed to talk about that kiss, about why it happened, about why it shouldn't happen again. But at the moment Emily didn't care.

She only knew that she had to kiss him again. So she reached up, knocked off his hat and pulled his head back toward hers. Then she kissed him back like she had the night before, moving her mouth across his, deepening the kiss.

A low moan emanated from his throat as he pulled her closer, flush against his tall body. But that wasn't the only sound Emily heard.

Someone gasped and cried out, "No!"

She pulled back from Ben and whirled toward the stairs, where Caleb was standing, his blue eyes wide with surprise, his small body shaking with it.

"No!" he repeated before bursting out in tears and turning to run back up the stairs.

Emily pressed a hand against her madly pounding heart as she repeated the same thing. "No…"

No. She shouldn't have been kissing Ben.

And not just because she'd hurt his nephew, but because she was about to get hurt too.

She started to follow Caleb, but as she'd stopped Ben so many times, he stopped her with a hand on her arm.

"Let's let him settle down a bit," he suggested. "And then I'll go up to talk to him. I'll assure him I'm not stealing his girl."

She had a bad feeling it might have been too late. That no matter how hard she'd tried not to, she was starting to fall for Ben Haven...

CHAPTER SEVENTEEN

JAKE HAD NEVER seen anything as beautiful…
as his bride. Katie sat on the balcony of their
Hawaiian beach house, her face bathed in the
pinkish glow of the setting sun. "I have never
been so happy," he admitted.

But he was worried that she wasn't the
same, that she was missing their son too
much. He missed Caleb too, and his nephews and the ranch and even that dang horse
Dusty had sent him. Katie turned her head
and smiled at him. "I love you," she said.

And he had no doubt that she did, that she
loved him as much and as deeply as he loved
her. He twined his fingers with hers on the
top of the patio table. Next to their joined
hands, Jake's cell phone began to ring.

"Taye," Katie said, and she grabbed the
phone to accept the call.

A shaky voice emanated from the phone.
"Daddy Jake…"

And Jake's heart ached with the pain in that little voice.

"Caleb!" Katie exclaimed. "What's wrong? Why are you crying?"

"I wanna talk to Daddy Jake," he murmured.

"I'm here, son," Jake assured him. "What's wrong? What happened?"

"Is Mommy listening?"

"Uh, don't you want her to hear this?" Jake asked.

"I wanna talk to just you," Caleb said. "Man to man…"

A smile tugged at Jake's lips and at Katie's too. She stood up. "I'll leave you two alone to talk," she told her son as she slipped back through the patio doors and into the cottage.

"Is she gone?" Caleb asked.

With a sigh of regret, Jake said, "Yes." But then he focused on his son, who was clearly upset. "What's going on? What's wrong?"

"Uncle Ben is kissing Miss Trent!" he exclaimed, and now he sounded even angrier than he did upset.

Jake had to bite his lip to hold back a laugh. He cleared it from his throat, then replied, "Are you sure?" He could have sworn Emily wanted nothing to do with his brother.

"Yeah, they were kissing in the kitchen," Caleb said. "I saw them."

"I'm sorry, son," Jake said, seriously. He knew how big a crush the boy had on his pretty teacher. "I know this is hard to hear, but Miss Trent is a lot older than you—"

"I know," Caleb said, and he sounded so frustrated. "It's just…"

"I know," Jake said. "Do you want me and Mommy to come home?" And get Uncle Ben away from his girl?

"No," Caleb said. "Miss Taye showed me on the calendar on her phone. You're coming home soon, anyway. I'll be okay."

"I'm sorry," Jake said again, his heart aching for the little boy's pain. "But if you change your mind and want us there, we'll come back."

"I'm okay, Daddy Jake," he insisted, and he emitted a little growl of frustration now. "I'm just mad at Uncle Ben."

"I don't blame you," Jake said. He was a little mad at his brother too, for hurting his son. But he was also amused. Another phase of Sadie's plan was playing out just as the old woman had plotted.

"I gotta go brush my teeth now," Caleb said. "Tell Mommy I love her." Then he clicked off the cell.

Katie must have been watching through the glass because she stepped back onto the patio. "What's wrong?" she asked anxiously. "Does he want us to come home?"

Jake shook his head. "I hope you didn't start packing. He's not missing us."

"Then why was he so upset?" Katie asked. "You know he hardly ever cries…"

"He's upset because my brother is stealing his girl."

Katie's green eyes widened with shock. "Baker and Emily?"

"Uncle Ben."

Katie shook her head. "No. Emily can't stand him."

Jake shrugged. "I don't know what's going on, just that Caleb saw them kissing in the kitchen."

Katie giggled, then shook her head. "Our poor son. His heart must have been broken."

Jake sighed. "I don't know what's worse. Caleb getting his heart broken or how insufferable my grandmother will be if she marries off another one of us."

BEN PASSED TAYE on his way to Caleb's room. She had just closed the boy's door. Lowering his voice to a whisper, he asked, "Is he okay?"

"Are you?" Taye asked, and she touched his chin, tipping his face from side to side.

His skin flushed with embarrassment. "What? What are you doing?"

"I'm looking for the slap mark," she said.

A chuckle slipped out of his lips. "So you heard…"

"She didn't hit you hard enough for us to hear," Taye said as she released his face. "Doesn't look like she slapped you at all."

"It was…"

"What?" she asked.

He couldn't call it a mistake, not when it felt so right, not when he felt so much. He shrugged. "I don't know…"

She jerked her thumb toward the closed door, saying gently, "He thinks it's a betrayal."

Ben smarted with that knowledge. "I know. I'm going to try to talk to him."

"Good luck," she said before she headed down the hall toward the stairs to the kitchen and Emily. Ben almost felt sorry for her and the teasing she was bound to face, but he was saving all his sympathy for Caleb right now.

He lifted his hand and knocked on the boy's door. "It's Uncle Ben," he said. "May I come in?"

Caleb didn't answer, but since he hadn't said no, Ben turned the knob and opened the door. Caleb was in bed, the covers pulled over his head as if he couldn't even bear to look at Ben right now.

"I'm sorry, buddy," Ben said. "I know how you feel about Miss Trent—"

"I love her!" Caleb called out from beneath the covers.

Ben stepped inside and closed the door. When he approached the bed, Caleb tugged off his blanket and glared at him. "Do you love her, Uncle Ben?" he asked.

Ben sucked in a breath as a panic gripped his heart for a moment. But, no…

It wasn't possible. He'd decided long ago to never fall in love. That it was foolish to trust anyone with his heart after his mother had so mercilessly broken it.

"We're just friends," Ben said.

"I love my friends," Caleb said.

Ben couldn't say it—couldn't say that he loved Emily too.

"I don't kiss my friends, though," Caleb continued. "And why were you kissing Miss Trent? She doesn't even like you."

Ben flinched.

"She's not your friend," Caleb insisted.

Ben sighed and settled on the edge of the mattress next to his nephew. Maybe by explaining it to Caleb, he would be able to understand it himself. "We both care very much about you and about Ian and Miller and Little Jake, so we have become friends—because of all of you."

"You kissed her because of me?" Caleb asked, his blue eyes narrowed in skepticism.

The kid was too smart. A far better debater than any political opponent Ben had ever faced.

"Uh, I kissed her because..." Because he hadn't been able to stop himself, because his attraction to her had overwhelmed him...

"Because she's pretty?" Caleb asked.

"She is pretty," Ben admitted. "And now that she isn't mad at me anymore, we are becoming friends."

"Are you going to marry her?" Caleb asked.

Ben's whole body tensed. This kid hit below the belt; he was very much Sadie Haven's great-grandson.

"We're just friends," Ben said.

But Caleb looked disbelieving. "So Miss Trent likes you now?"

Ben shrugged. "I think so..." She still didn't trust him completely, but he suspected she was a lot like him in that she couldn't trust anyone completely.

"What if she wants to marry you?" Caleb asked.

"Miss Trent and I aren't talking about getting married," Ben assured him. "So don't worry about that…"

"I'm not worried," Caleb said, and he flopped back onto his pillows with a sigh. "I know that I'm just a kid, and by the time I'm old enough to marry her, she'll be old."

Ben bit his lip to hold back a laugh. "Well, you might not want to share that with her…"

"I know she'll be married and have kids before then," Caleb said. And suddenly he sounded very old.

And Ben felt very old and weary, his shoulders bowing with the weight of the reality that Caleb was forcing him to accept.

Emily was too good with kids to not want to have some of her own someday. To not want to get married and have the family she'd never really had. The family she deserved to have.

His heart ached at the thought of her marrying someone else. But he'd vowed long ago that he was never going to make that commitment himself. Changing his mind now…

He just couldn't do it. He couldn't risk his

heart, not even on Emily. Maybe most especially not on Emily. Even if she liked him now—and he wasn't sure that she did—he couldn't disrupt their current situation now or probably anytime soon. The boys needed Emily too much for her and Ben to take unnecessary risks on dating. What if it didn't work out? That would surely change things between Emily and his nephews. And even if things did go well, he was always in town, always working, when she needed to be here. The boys depended on her too much for her to spend much, or any, time away from them. But eventually she was going to leave.

And Caleb would get his heart broken all over again. Ben put his arms around the little boy and eased him into a hug. Caleb was stiff at first, but then he sighed and threw his arms around Ben's neck.

"I'm sorry, buddy," Ben said again.

"It's okay," Caleb told him. "I still love you, Uncle Ben."

Tears stung Ben's eyes—tears of relief and of emotion. These kids, his nephews, were all so special. "I love you too," Ben told him.

EMILY HAD TO make sure Caleb was okay. She'd been so worried about the little boy that she'd had to make sure that he was all right, that he wasn't too upset over witnessing that kiss.

So when she came to his door and saw it open just a crack, just enough that she could hear Ben and see when he hugged his nephew, something squeezed her heart so very hard that she nearly gasped at the sudden pain. Her hand shaking, she pulled the door shut all the way and stumbled back into the hall.

"Are you okay?" Melanie asked.

Emily couldn't reply; she could only shake her head.

Melanie guided her down the hall and into her room. "What's wrong?" she asked. "You look like you're about to pass out."

Emily must have gone as pale as Melanie had earlier. "I'll tell you if you tell me what's going on with you," Emily challenged her.

She expected Melanie to shut her down as she had every other time Emily had pressed her to share what was going on with her. But this time Melanie smiled and said, "Okay…"

And Emily held herself still. "You'll talk to me?"

Melanie nodded. "I can trust you," she said. "I know I can. I just haven't been ready to tell anyone yet."

"Not even Katie?" Emily asked.

"I didn't tell Katie," Melanie said. "But she did figure it out."

"You're pregnant," Emily said.

The brunette dropped onto the edge of her bed and nodded. "Yes."

"I thought you had the flu…" She should have realized it then; that must have been when Katie had. But Katie had been pregnant before—Emily hadn't even been in a serious relationship. She could never quite bring herself to trust someone enough to let them get that close to her. "So how far along are you?"

"Almost four months," she said. "I saw a doctor when I brought Miller to Sheridan. An ultrasound confirmed it."

"Oh, Melanie…" Emily didn't know what to say; she couldn't tell if the other woman was happy or not. "How do you feel about it?" she asked.

"Overwhelmed," Melanie admitted. "I'm having twins. There are two of them in here." She pressed her hands to the slight swelling of her belly.

"No wonder you're so tired."

Melanie nodded.

"Can I ask…?" She trailed off before she did, not wanting to upset the pregnant woman or overwhelm her more.

"About my husband?" Melanie asked.

Emily nodded. "Does he know? Where is he?"

Melanie shook her head. "He doesn't know, and I have no idea. He left me over two months ago. I haven't talked to him since…" Then her body began to shake as sobs racked her.

Emily settled onto the bed with her, like Ben had with Caleb, and she wrapped her arms around the other woman, holding her while she wept.

She couldn't imagine how scared Melanie was, being abandoned to raise her children alone. Twins…

No. Emily could imagine how scared she was. She'd often been that scared herself—when she'd had no one to rely on and nowhere to go. When her mother had died, and her grandparents had promised they just needed a break and had passed her onto her aunt, who'd passed her onto one of her cousins…

And that cousin had called Social Services…and the fear and helplessness had continued for Emily, until she'd finally found someone she could trust in Mrs. Rademacher. But Emily had vowed to never be that vulnerable and helpless again. And she intended to keep that promise.

CHAPTER EIGHTEEN

BY THE NEXT MORNING, Caleb had totally forgiven Ben. Maybe it had helped that Ben had spent the night in Caleb's room, cramped in that little bed with him. Ben's neck and back were sore from the uncomfortable position in which he'd spent most of the night, half-falling off the mattress.

But when the little boy smiled at him as they walked out to the barn, the heaviness lifted from Ben's heart, and he knew it had been worth it. He didn't want Caleb or his other nephews to be hurt ever again.

Instead of kissing Emily last night, he should have talked to her about her teaching position…at the school. He should have found out if she'd talked to the principal—if she had to go back. And he had to figure out how she could get more time off for the boys. They were not ready for her to leave the ranch yet, if they ever would be.

Right now she was having another of her

one-on-one lessons with Ian. Melanie was working with Miller and Little Jake was helping Taye bake cookies. And Caleb—sweet, forgiving Caleb—was helping him.

"You missed a spot in that corner," Caleb directed from where he was leaning over the top of the stall. He'd just fed Midnight his carrots.

Ben spared him a glance to make sure the little boy still had all his fingers, but as Caleb had assured him, the horse was gentle with the child. They truly had bonded.

But when he glanced back, Midnight was in Ben's face. He butted Ben's back with his big head, as if nudging him to get back to work. "Hey, he's telling me I missed that spot too," Ben said. "You two stop ganging up on me."

Caleb giggled.

And Midnight nickered, as if sharing the laugh with the little boy. Then he nudged Ben again, and when Ben looked at him, the horse's big eyes were warm. "You are a good boy," he murmured to the animal.

"I told you," Caleb said. "He's not mean like most people think he is. He's my friend."

The horse tossed his head then and backed up, pawing at the ground and making that weird guttural noise. Ben, trapped in the corner of the stall with him, was a little uneasy, but the horse didn't lash out at him. Instead his focus was on the open door to his stall, where Baker stood.

"I don't understand why you get in there that with thing," Baker said, shaking his head. "I'd move him out while I cleaned the stall."

Ben shrugged. "He's fine with me." But he eased past Midnight with his full shovel and dumped it inside the wheelbarrow just outside the door.

"He's Uncle Ben's friend now too," Caleb said, backing him up.

Baker groaned. "Then what's his issue with me? I'm in this barn all the time," Baker remarked. "You'd think he would be getting used to me by now."

"He probably feels threatened by you," Ben said. "He knows you're trying to be the top stud around here."

Baker laughed. "You're never going to let me live down that calendar thing."

"Nope," Ben admitted. "When's the shoot for next year's?"

Baker shrugged. "I don't know and don't care."

"You're not going to do it?"

Even in the shadow of the brim of his hat, it was apparent Baker's face had flushed with embarrassment. "I want to say no, but it benefits a good cause."

"Yeah, your love life," Ben teased.

"I don't have a love life," Baker said.

"Uncle Ben does," Caleb said. "He was kissing Miss Trent last night in the kitchen."

Baker's mouth fell open and a roar—of laughter—spilled out of him. The horse, already nervous, reared up then. And Baker swung that door shut before turning back toward Ben to laugh some more. "Oh, how the mighty have fallen," he said.

Ben shook his head. "I—I haven't fallen."

"They're just friends," Caleb helpfully added.

"Friends?" Baker scoffed. "I didn't think she even liked you."

Caleb nodded. "Me neither, but she was kissing him back like Mommy kisses Daddy Jake."

Ben spared the little boy a brief glance. "You and I have to have a little talk about kissing and telling…"

"I'm not kissing anybody," Caleb said with a grimace of disgust.

Baker laughed some more, and despite

Ben's irritation over being teased, he smiled as warmth filled his heart. It was good to hear his little brother's laugh again; it had been a while since he'd heard it last. A while since Baker had probably had anything to laugh about...

If the firefighter spent some time with the kids, he would have definitely found something to laugh about, but Baker blatantly avoided the house. Ben wasn't sure if he did that to avoid Grandma and her matchmaking trap, or if he did it to avoid the kids.

"I thought you weren't going to fall into Sadie's meddling," Baker teased him. "I thought you were too smart to be manipulated like that."

Ben shook his head. "I haven't fallen..." His voice trailed off, though, as he wondered...

But, no. He couldn't fall for Emily for so many reasons. One of them being that, like Baker, he wasn't sure she even liked him.

"Grandma's scheme isn't working on me," Ben said. "And, in fact, I'm turning it around on her."

Baker pushed back his hat and narrowed his eyes. "How? What are you talking about?"

"Come to dinner tonight," Ben urged him. "And you'll see sparks fly."

"Between you and Miss Trent?" Baker asked, and he snickered like the horse had at him earlier.

"Between Grandma and her date," Ben said.

Baker snorted. "Grandma has a date? Since when has Grandma been dating?"

"Since dinner tonight," Ben said.

"You're setting her up without her knowing it," Baker mused. "Who's the guy?"

"Lem."

"Old Man Lemmon?" Baker asked, and then he laughed again. "What? Are you trying to kill off your deputy mayor?"

For the first time since he'd concocted his plan, a little frisson of uneasiness skittered through Ben. Was he making a mistake? Was this going to backfire horribly on him? Was Grandma going to hurt Lem, or worse yet, would she get hurt?

He shook his head. "No. I'm sure they'll be fine."

Baker sniffed. "Yeah, right. The two of them are not friends." He narrowed his eyes. "But then I didn't think you and Miss Trent were either, and apparently you've been kissing in the kitchen." He glanced down at Caleb, who nodded in confirmation.

"Yup, they were."

Baker sighed. "Oh, Grandma is going to be unbearable after this…"

"Her date?" Ben asked.

"Your date."

But he and Emily hadn't even been on a date—not technically, and not one that hadn't included four little male chaperones. And nothing good had happened during those outings but bugs and a fall in the mud.

He wasn't going to date her, and he wasn't in love. No matter what Baker thought.

Ben was still single and always would be. Always.

He remembered.

Emily stared down at the test paper on the table she'd converted to her desk in the boys' playroom. Ian had gotten more of the questions right than wrong, but these were things she'd taught him since the accident. Things that he should not have remembered…if he was still struggling with the aftereffects of his concussion.

She glanced across her desk at the little boy who was playing now with some Legos. He still asked about his parents, though—still asked at least once a day where they were.

How had he remembered all this math and spelling but forgotten that?

Or had he not forgotten? Maybe he just didn't want to remember what had happened.

Miller had been to a specialist to have his cast removed. But she couldn't remember when Ian had seen a doctor last.

And maybe it wasn't just a medical doctor that he needed to see.

The little boy began to blur before her eyes as tears filled them. She had to blink furiously to clear her vision, and when she did, she found him staring at her.

"Are you okay, Miss Trent?" he asked with concern.

He was such a sweet boy. They all were.

She couldn't imagine leaving them, which was maybe why she hadn't called Mr. Kellerman back yet. She knew he would want her answer about the upcoming school year, and she couldn't give him one. Not yet...

But as she glanced down at Ian's test again, it stared back at her with proof that he was doing better than she'd realized, better than he'd revealed. He could pass into first grade.

He didn't need a private tutor anymore.

"What are you looking at, Miss Trent?" Ian asked.

"Your test," she said. "You did very well on it."

"What test?" he asked, so automatically that she almost wondered if that had become his standard response, his first instinct to repeat what had been said to him as a question.

But Emily was a kindergarten teacher, not a psychologist. She felt like Ian needed to see a psychologist. Maybe all of the boys did.

She couldn't make an appointment, though; she had to share her concerns with one of the boys' guardians so they could make that call. Ben…

His was the face—the unfairly good-looking face—that popped into her mind. He would listen to her; he would care. She knew that now.

But ultimately the decision would probably be Sadie's or Jake's to make. Jake would be home very soon. Emily could wait to talk to him. Or she could seek out Sadie now.

Maybe she needed to do that, anyway—talk to her about the situation at the school, about how she didn't want to lose her job and how she might not be needed here as much as she'd been when Sadie had first hired her.

While she might not be needed as much, she wasn't sure she was ready to leave the boys…or Ben. He wasn't the man she'd thought he was. He wasn't self-involved or superficial. He cared about his family, about his job, about the town. He cared so much about the town that when Jake and Katie returned, Ben would be leaving. He would go back to the city limits of Willow Creek and his job and his life there—a life that he was determined to live out single.

Without a wife…

Without a family…

It was good that Emily had overheard him make that declaration to his grandmother, that she knew he was never going to let himself fall in love. Then maybe she could stop her feelings for him from going any deeper—because she didn't want to get her hopes up. She didn't want to get attached only to be rejected. She didn't want to start envisioning a future she could never have: a future with Ben Haven.

THE DOORBELL STARTLED Sadie and Feisty, making one of them jump up from their afternoon nap to start yapping and running around the sitting area. Sadie eased out of her chair and opened the door of her suite. Then, following a little more slowly than Feisty, she headed down the hall to the foyer. Nobody rang the bell around here.

All the kids just ran in and out of the unlocked doors. And the ranch hands only ever went to the business office or called up to the house.

And Sadie didn't have an appointment with anyone. Still, she opened the door, and then shook her head as she saw who the visitor was. "What the Sam Hill are you doing here?"

"My name's Lemar Lemmon, not Sam Hill," the old man said. "Is your grandson right? Are you starting to slip?"

"The only thing that's going to slip is my hold on this door, and I'm going to slam it in your wrinkly old face," she snapped at her old nemesis.

"You're looking quite your age too, Sadie," he chided her.

She sucked in a breath at the insult and glared down at the short man standing before her. "And you look ridiculous. What happened to you?"

His white beard and mustache were closely trimmed—for once—and he was wearing jeans and a button-down shirt with his boots. The bright blue of the shirt matched his eyes, and the buttons were a shiny silver, like the tips of his boots. She'd never seen him not in a wrinkled, oversize suit, not even when she'd helped out around his house for a bit with his dear, sweet wife.

Lem stared down at himself as if bemused too. "Your grandson took me shopping and to the barber."

And Sadie snorted. "'Bout time someone did." Then she laughed as she realized what Ben was up to. She wasn't supposed to have favorites. She knew that—it had gotten her in trouble in the past with her own kids. Ben's dad wasn't the only son she had. But even her grandsons didn't know that—because their dad was the only son she talked about...

The only one who'd talked to her.

No. She wasn't supposed to have favorites, but there was a reason Ben had been named after her father: he was so much like him. So much like her...

That didn't always make him her favorite, though. Especially not now, when it was so clear he was trying to turn the tables on her. "Come on," she said to Lem, and she grabbed his arm.

She'd expected it to be skinny and brittle since he was so old. But there was actually some muscle beneath that blue shirt, and he moved quickly too, as she tugged him along behind her toward her suite.

She waited until he and Feisty had stepped inside and she'd closed the door before she said, "You know what he's up to, right?"

"Giving you a taste of your own meddling medicine," Lem replied.

And she laughed. "Maybe you're not the fool I've always thought you were…"

He laughed too. "Just old…"

She nodded and sighed. "We both are. Why'd you agree to be part of my grandson's silly stunt?"

He shrugged. "Nothing better to do, and I owe him. He's a good man. He was there for me when I needed him most." He curved his lips into a slight smile. "So were you, Sadie."

"I was there for Mary," Sadie said. "She was a good woman."

"The best," he said, as his blue eyes glistened with unshed tears.

Sadie hadn't realized she was still holding his arm, but she squeezed it now.

"And Big Jake…" Lem sighed. "He was a giant of man—a true hero."

Sadie blinked furiously now as she nodded in agreement. He'd been her hero. "We were lucky we had them," she said. "Lucky to have had that love."

Lem nodded. "Sure were…"

"That's all I want for my grandsons," she said. "True love."

"But is it true if *you* orchestrated it?" Lem wondered aloud.

And Sadie felt a pang of alarm. "My grandsons are an awful lot like me and Big Jake," she said. "They're not going to willingly fall, but they won't be able to resist when they find the real thing."

"They didn't find it, though," Lem pointed out. "You did."

She grinned. "Yes, I did. I found their great loves. They just don't know it yet but for Jake and Katie."

They would be home soon from their honeymoon, so time was running out for Sadie's scheme because of that and because of what Ben had said about the principal calling Miss Trent. She needed to get Ben married off to Emily. But, because Ben was so much like her, Sadie needed help—even if that help came from this ornery old cuss, Lemar Lemmon. She swallowed hard, choking down the lump of pride in the back of her throat, then she murmured, "I need your help…"

Lemar leaned closer to her. "I must be so old that I'm getting hard of hearing. I couldn't quite make out what you just said there, Sadie…"

She grimaced, then repeated, "I need your help."

He chuckled. "That's something I never figured you'd say to me."

"Me neither," she admitted.

"So this must have something to do with your family," he surmised. "They're all you care about."

"They're all I have," she murmured.

He nodded. "Sure, what do you need?"

She narrowed her eyes and asked him, "Is it true Ben would do better with voters in the next election if he was married?"

Lemmon chuckled again. "Probably just the opposite. It would be more likely that he'd lose some of the female voters. I think they're really happy that he's single and available."

Sadie wasn't. And she wasn't paying any mind to his claim that he intended to stay that way. She hoped that if Emily had overheard it that she hadn't believed it. "Not for much longer," she murmured.

"Not if you have your way," Lem surmised. "I already warned the boy about you."

She glared at him. "You warned my own grandson about me? What did you say?"

"That whatever Sadie March Haven wants, Sadie March Haven gets..."

She wished that was true. She really wished it was...

CHAPTER NINETEEN

OF COURSE, he would have been early. Lem always was. So when Ben walked up from the barn, he wasn't surprised to see the deputy mayor's vintage white Cadillac parked near the porch. As he passed it, he glanced inside to see if Lem was in it. If Grandma had already tossed him out of the house...

But the vehicle was empty. Ben hurried up the porch steps and pushed open the front door. He glanced quickly into the formal living room that nobody ever really used. That was probably where Grandma would have left Lem, yet the room was also empty. She wouldn't have invited him back into the kitchen...

He hurried down the hall, though, just in case. Taye glanced up from the stove, and Emily, who was sitting at the island, hopped down from a stool and approached him, her face lit up with excitement.

"I think your plan might be working," she told him.

Ben glanced around the big room. "How do you know?"

"I saw her let him into the house," she said.

That was more than he'd actually expected Grandma to do. He'd figured she would probably send him straight home, if Ben didn't stop her in time. "If she let him in, where are they?" he asked.

"After they talked for a bit in the foyer, she dragged him down the hall to her private suite!" Emily exclaimed, her eyes bright excitement.

Ben's breath caught in his lungs for a moment as her beauty struck him. Her skin glowed as she seemed to radiate that beauty and optimism and happiness.

Taye chuckled. "What?" she asked. "You think she's having her way with him already?"

Ben groaned at the thought. "No. She probably brought him in there to kill him where there would be no witnesses but Feisty."

Taye chuckled again. "Because we all know how loyal Feisty is to her. She'd never talk. She'd probably even help Sadie dispose of the body."

Emily laughed now. "You're terrible."

Ben shook his head. "This might have been a terrible idea. I need to find Lem."

"Here I am, Ben," the older man replied as he strolled into the kitchen, with Sadie holding on to his arm.

She grinned at Ben, like she was thrilled he'd invited her nemesis to dinner. Or like she'd already figured out what he was up to and had outsmarted him.

That frisson of unease raced down his spine again. Trying to turn the tables on his grandmother definitely hadn't been a good idea.

"Something smells wonderful," Lem remarked.

"Hello, Mr. Lemmon," Taye greeted the older man, leaning down to press a kiss against his wrinkled cheek.

He patted her shoulder. "I certainly miss you at the café, honey, and I know Mrs. Campbell especially misses you."

Sadie snorted. "Then she should have paid her more."

Taye shook her head. "I don't cook for money."

Ben suspected his grandmother was paying her well, but that clearly wasn't why the young woman had moved out to the ranch. She cooked for love. To express it and to share it…

He felt a gaze on his face and turned to

see Emily staring at him. He shared a look with her, and without a word spoken between them, he knew they'd come to the same realization. Taye cooked for love, which was the same reason that Emily taught. Because she loved teaching and she loved the kids. Just like he loved the town and being the mayor.

He didn't want Emily to give up the job she loved, but he was so torn because he knew how much the boys adored her. And losing her right now, so soon after their other devastating losses...

He didn't want them to go through that, through what his mother had put him and his brothers through—that abandonment. Darlene leaving had been worse than his dad dying; it had hurt so much more. Their dad's death had been a terrible accident. While bailing hay in one of the fields, he had somehow fallen off the tractor and it had run over him. Then right after his funeral, their mother had run off.

Emily wasn't the boys' mother, but with their mother gone, they gravitated toward the young teacher for the maternal nurturing she gave them. If she left the ranch and moved back to town, she wouldn't be available to comfort Little Jake after his nightmares. And with the boys no longer in the grade level she taught, she would barely see them at school.

Did she love the boys too much to leave them?

He hoped so.

Just then his nephews burst into the room like lightning, following the thunder of their footsteps on the stairwell as they'd raced down to the kitchen.

"Are you all cleaned up for dinner?" Emily asked them. And four little heads bobbed up and down in reply. "Then let's greet our dinner guest, Mr. Lemmon."

"You don't look like Santa Claus in a suit anymore," Caleb remarked with his usual candor.

Instead of being offended, Lem laughed. He enjoyed kids. That was why they all thought he was Santa. He played the role every year during the holiday season, starting with the Thanksgiving Day parade, and continued to greet kids in the town square—which was decorated annually to look like the North Pole—until Christmas Day.

Most of the kids in Willow Creek had climbed on to his lap at least once to recite their Christmas list. Ben felt a flash of pain as he imagined what his nephews would ask Lem for: their parents back.

If only that was a wish Lem could grant...

While his beard and mustache were trimmed now, Lem must have looked enough like Santa yet that the kids monopolized him all during dinner. He was good with the four boys, so good that Ben caught even Sadie smiling at him as he talked with the children.

Maybe Ben's plan wasn't as doomed as he was worried that it was. Maybe he might be able to make a match between Grandma and his deputy mayor.

The evening passed quickly, so quickly that Ben hadn't even realized it had ended until he was walking Lem back out to his car. "Thanks for coming," he told him.

"Thanks for having me," Lem replied. "Dinner was delightful. And those boys..." His voice cracked as it trailed off. Then he cleared his throat and added, "Are something special."

Ben nodded. "Yes, they are." And he would do anything for them, even ignore his attraction to Emily so he wouldn't be tempted to pursue a relationship with her—one that might take her away from the ranch and the boys. Ignoring that attraction hadn't been easy, though. All through dinner, he'd kept glancing at her to share a smile over something that the kids did or that Lem said... and every time their gazes met, they'd held a little longer.

And Ben had held his breath, not wanting to break that contact—that connection—with her. It was as if they'd shared the same thoughts all evening, had found the same enjoyment in the conversation and the dinner.

He'd never felt as connected to anyone else as he had her. He released that breath he hadn't realized he'd been holding.

"Just shows you how resilient kids really are," Lem remarked. "Like that Emily Trent..."

Ben tensed. "What about her?"

"You must know her story," Lem said. "She was about six when her mama died. And she was passed from grandparents to aunts to cousins until her case manager put her in foster care." He sighed. "She didn't fare any better there. Too old for anyone to want to adopt. If it hadn't been for Mrs. Rademacher..." He pulled his mouth into a smile that shifted his mustache. "But look at the wonderful person she became, how loving and patient she is with those children. Just an amazing soul..."

Tears stung Ben's eyes as he realized just how tough Emily's childhood had been. No wonder she'd been so willing to help out with his nephews. She'd known all too well how much they'd been suffering and how scared and helpless they must have felt.

At least he'd always had his grandparents. They'd always been there for him, and he'd known they always would be. He'd never had to worry about where he was going to sleep and what he would eat.

Sadie had made certain of that.

"It seemed like my grandmother was really enjoying your company this evening," Ben said.

Below his mustache, Lem's lips curved into a slight smile. "Of course she did," he said with a chuckle. "Why wouldn't she? Sadie and I go way back."

Despite the warmth of the early summer evening, Ben felt that faint chill again. "Yes, it's a shame you two don't spend more time together," he said. "You'll have to make a point of having her out for dinner next."

"With Miss Cooper cooking in her kitchen, Sadie has no reason to eat anywhere but the ranch," Lem pointed out.

Ben nodded at the truth of that. There was

no better chef or baker in Willow Creek. Poor Mrs. Campbell...

"Well, then we'll have to make a habit of having you out here to eat with us," Ben said.

Lem's expression went blank. "You're not moving back to Willow Creek?" he asked.

Ben jerked his head in a nod. "Of course I am. The minute Jake and Katie get back, I'll pack up and return to my condo." Why did the industrial space seem uninviting to him now? "But I'll be making more visits out here than I did before," he said. He couldn't let his responsibilities to his family slide like he had for those six weeks after the funeral. He couldn't let down those little boys like so many people had let down Emily Trent.

She really was something special.

"We need to get started on your campaign soon," Lem said.

Ben's brow furrowed. "We do? The next election is over a year away."

"Best time to start some polling," Lem said. "See what your approval rating is. See what you need to improve. Then you have time to fix what needs fixing."

Ben nodded. "Makes sense."

"I ordered them earlier," Lem said. "The

pollster can meet with you later this week, go over the data."

Ben stiffened with a sudden suspicion. "Who ordered them?" he asked. "You or my grandmother?"

"Me," Lemmon replied. "I don't want you to lose, Ben. You've been good for Willow Creek. The town needed your fresh, young blood and bright ideas running it. That's why I supported you in the last election and why I want to make sure you win the next one."

That was all Ben cared about too. Being mayor, carrying on his great-grandfather's legacy and carrying out all of their dreams for the town.

Or so he'd thought. Now there were more things—more people—he cared about. One of them being a certain beautiful blonde he might care about a little too much.

EMILY FELT LIKE she was back at college, living with her sorority sisters, as she and Taye and Melanie giggled together in the kitchen. Nobody at college had known the sad story of her upbringing, so she had been able to just be herself. Like she was with Melanie and Taye. And it seemed like neither of them knew the sad story of the kiss she'd shared with Ben. Or if they knew, neither of them had mentioned it to her yet.

"Ben did good," Taye said.

"With his deputy-mayor makeover?" Emily asked.

"Mr. Lemmon looked really cute," Taye said. "I saw that Sadie kept sneaking looks at him, like she was seeing him for the first time."

Melanie put away the plate she'd dried. "Did you notice that when she came back from using the restroom, she had put on lipstick?"

"No!" Emily exclaimed. "How did I miss it?"

"I saw that too," Taye said. "And she'd brushed her hair."

"Too bad she didn't walk Mr. Lemmon out to his car instead of Ben," Emily said, surprised that Ben hadn't insisted that Sadie did. But then she doubted he could have forced his grandma to do something she didn't want, and the older woman had claimed she'd needed to walk Feisty after dinner. "Mr. Lemmon might have asked her for a date."

"He is braver than I realized," Taye said.

"He seems like a nice man," Melanie said. She was the only one who didn't know the deputy mayor, since she wasn't from Willow Creek. "The kids love him almost as much as they love you, Emily."

"That's because he plays Santa Claus every year," Taye said. "I'm surprised I didn't crush him the last few times I sat on his lap, and that was over a dozen years ago."

Even as a kid, Taye had probably been tall because she was nearly six feet now, like Sadie. Sadie was much taller than Mr. Lemmon. The two of them coming down the hall to the kitchen had looked a little like Feisty walking alongside that bronco.

Melanie bringing up the kids reminded Emily of what she'd intended to ask her friends earlier. "Are you two all right watching the boys without me on Friday night?" she asked. "I have plans in town."

"Is Sadie not the only one in this house with a gentleman suitor?" Taye teased.

"Is it Ben?" Melanie asked.

So they must have heard about the kiss, even if they hadn't brought it up. Heat rushed to Emily's face, but she shook her head. "No, it's not Ben."

"Oh, so you have a date on a Friday night with someone else?" Taye asked, her pale blue eyes wide with surprise.

It wasn't a date, but before Emily could clarify that she was meeting friends—fellow schoolteachers—she noticed a shadow on the kitchen floor. She peered past Taye to see Ben standing in the doorway to the hall.

His mouth was pulled into a frown for once, and his dark eyes were cold, so cold that Emily shivered a little. She was used to seeing Ben with that grin on his face, with his eyes lit up, even though she now knew that he sometimes forced that look, that it was just a handsome mask to cover up his real emotions. Like his grief over losing his brother and sister-in-law.

"Why don't we go upstairs?" Taye suggested to Melanie. "Make sure that the boys aren't wrestling so hard that someone gets hurts."

Melanie headed toward the stairs behind Taye, but she murmured, "Somebody always gets hurt."

And Emily shivered again. Was Melanie talking about the boys or...

"What's wrong?" Emily asked. "Didn't your blind date go well?"

"It wasn't my blind date," Ben said. "It was Lem's and Sadie's. I'm not the one dating. Apparently you are. Friday night?"

A smile tugged at her lips, but she fought it in order to tease him. "Are you jealous?" she asked.

"You act like I'm a player," he said. "What

about you? First you're two-timing Caleb with me. And now you're two-timing me with some guy on Friday night?"

She laughed. "With some friends," she said. "I'm meeting friends for dinner, probably a few of those friends whose hearts you broke in high school or later…"

She'd expected him to smile—with relief that she wasn't playing him—but that frown remained on his mouth. Maybe she shouldn't have teased him, but she hadn't wanted to tell him the truth and bring up the possibility of her having to leave the ranch. She was unwilling to admit that she was actually meeting up with some coworkers. She doubted that he'd dated any of them since she was the youngest one on staff.

"I really didn't mean to hurt anyone," he said. "I feel bad that I did. I'm always very clear when I'm dating that I'm not looking to fall in love or get married."

"Because of your mother?" she asked. "Because you don't trust anyone?"

He shrugged. "Maybe. Maybe it's just that all I ever cared about was being mayor. What about you? How easily do you trust people after everyone except Mrs. Rademacher let you down?"

She felt her whole body go rigid as she admitted, "Not easily..."

He closed the distance between them and eased his arms around her shoulders as if he expected her to reject his comfort.

She could accept his comfort, just not his pity. "I'm fine, you know," she said.

"You're amazing," he said. "Strong, smart, beautiful..."

She laughed. "That's your problem, Haven. That's why you break so many hearts. You're just so effortlessly charming..."

No. That wasn't his problem. It was *hers*. Because she was falling for him...

For a moment she felt dizzy, light-headed, and she reached out, her fingers brushing across his chest. He was so muscular, so warm, so solid...

But instead of feeling steadier, touching him unsettled her even more. Before she could do something stupid, like kiss him, she turned for the stairs. "I better check on the boys..." Yet she couldn't make herself move, and when his hand cupped her shoulder and turned her back toward him, she reached for him again and pulled his head down for her kiss.

CHAPTER TWENTY

"So when's the wedding?" Baker asked the next morning when Ben stepped out of Midnight's clean stall. Fortunately, Caleb wasn't there to overhear this conversation. He'd stayed in the house to do some craft activity Emily had come up with for the boys.

Ben's heart skipped a beat at the thought of her, and he glared at his younger brother. "Very funny…"

It should have been—the thought of him getting married should have made him laugh. But instead…

"So you're not as good a matchmaker as Grandma?" Baker asked. "Your evening didn't go as planned?"

Ben arched a brow. "You'd know if you'd showed up. You missed a great dinner." He laughed then and added, "It really was fun. Lem fit in surprisingly well at the ranch and with the kids."

Instead of being happy, Baker sighed. "Too

bad neither of Jake's ranch foreman candidates fit in. They've both packed up their stuff and left."

Ben groaned. "Jake's coming home Sunday."

"I know, it's just a few days away," Baker said. "So we can handle the ranch until then."

"But what does Jake do when he gets back?" Ben asked. "He can't kill himself trying to do everything alone. He has a wife now. A family. We have to figure out a way to help him more."

Instead of arguing with him, Baker nodded. "I know. I'll try to work my shifts at the firehouse so I have more days off in a row and can come out and work the ranch then."

Ben shook his head. "That's when you need to rest from those long shifts. Not work so hard."

"If only Dusty…" Baker murmured. "But that's a lost cause."

"He won't return my calls," Ben said with a pang of regret. That was probably because of how their last conversation had gone, over Ben comparing Dusty to their mother. If his brother had done the same to him, he wouldn't have wanted to talk to him for a while either.

Baker sighed. "Here," he said. "Let's see if he'll take mine." He pulled out his cell and punched in their brother's contact.

"Hey, Baker." Dusty's voice emanated from the speaker on Baker's phone.

And Ben grimaced. "So it's just my calls you're not taking?"

"Yours and Grandma's," Dusty replied. "You both keep saying the same thing. That I need to come back."

"Just because they're pains in the butt doesn't mean they're wrong," Baker remarked.

"I can't yet," Dusty said. "I'm still looking for something…"

"What?" Ben asked. He'd intended to apologize to Dusty for how he'd spoken to him last time they'd talked, but his brother's comment frustrated him. "What are you looking for? Fame, fortune? Titles? Championships? Records? You've accomplished all of that. What else is there?"

"*Who* else," Dusty said, his voice gruff with emotion.

"Are you looking for Mom?" Ben asked, his breath catching. Baker's hand holding the phone began to shake a little. "Is that why you keep going from rodeo to rodeo? You think she's still riding? She'd be too old."

"Mom left the rodeo circuit a while ago," Dusty said. "I'm not looking for her."

Baker cleared his throat then asked, "So you know where Mom is?"

"Yes," Dusty replied.

Ben had to ask then what he'd asked his grandmother, what had had all his old resentment of Darlene twisting in his stomach since the accident. "Do you know if she knows about Dale and Jenny?"

"Yeah, I told her…"

"So she knew, but she didn't come for the funeral." Ben staggered back a step and leaned against the door of Midnight's stall. As if the horse sensed his pain, or maybe he just recognized Dusty's voice, he arched his neck over the door and nudged Ben's hat with his head. "She didn't reach out to her grandsons or to any of us…" His voice trailed off as that sense of abandonment crashed down hard on him just as it had all those years ago when his mother had deserted them.

And the cell shook a little bit more in Baker's unsteady hand.

"I'm sorry," Dusty said.

Resigned, Ben sighed. "No. I know better. I know that she's never going to change. People don't change."

"Do you really believe that?" Dusty asked. "That you are what you are? That you can never change?"

At the moment, Ben wasn't feeling like he could ever trust anyone, nor could he trust himself to let anyone in. Not after his own mother couldn't stick around, couldn't help raise her children, couldn't even come around to help her grieving grandchildren. "I need you to change," Ben said. "I need you to come home. To help out at the ranch. You're the only one who can take Dale's place."

"Nobody can take Dale's place," Dusty said, and he clicked off the cell.

Baker let out a sigh. "He's not going to take my calls now either."

"Probably not."

"He's right, though," Baker said. "Nobody can take Dale's place."

Overwhelmed with emotion, Ben could only nod, and he had to close his eyes against the threat of tears.

"Oh," Baker remarked. "Emily. I didn't see you there."

With his eyes closed, Ben couldn't see her now. He kept them closed, even as he heard Baker walk away, his boots clomping against the concrete. He didn't hear her walk away, but she was so graceful that she could have. She could have left him, just as his mother had all those years ago.

But then slender arms wrapped around him, holding him tight, and she pressed her head against his heart.

EMILY HAD COME out to the barn to talk to Ben about setting up an appointment with a psychologist for the boys. That was why she'd brought up the craft for them to do this morning—the one that Taye and Melanie were able to manage without her. But as she approached the barn door, she'd heard the brothers talking…and she couldn't bring herself to walk away.

Now she listened to Ben's heart, and it was almost as if she could hear it breaking. Hers was breaking for him because she knew how it felt, how painful it was to be rejected by family.

That was what his mother had done, when she'd left them, when she hadn't come to the funeral, and it was what Dusty was doing now too, when he kept refusing to come home.

"I'm sorry," she murmured.

His arms slid around her, and he held her close for a moment as if he was accepting her comfort. But then his hands cupped her shoulders and eased her back. She tipped her head up, waiting for his kiss…needing his kiss.

He cleared his throat. "You brought your entourage…"

She stepped back and whirled around to find that the kids, Taye and Melanie had followed her out to the barn. Heat rushed into her face, and she regretted that she hadn't shared with the women the reason why she'd needed to seek Ben out alone.

She'd worried that they would think what they were obviously thinking now as they grinned at her.

Caleb sighed. "So they're not just kissing in the kitchen anymore…"

Melanie laughed. "I didn't know they were kissing in the kitchen."

Emily cleared the humiliation from her throat and asked, "What happened? I thought you were all making decorations for Jake and Katie's welcome-home party on Sunday."

"The decorations are done," Melanie replied, "and the boys wanted to show you and Uncle Ben."

"And I wanted to bring Midnight his carrots since Uncle Ben forgot," Caleb said.

"Why don't you and I feed Midnight while

everybody else shows Emily the new decorations," Ben suggested.

Maybe he wanted to get rid of her. Or maybe he just needed a moment to compose himself. She wished she had a moment, but she had no escape from the others as they walked back to the house.

"So you're kissing Uncle Ben now," Taye murmured.

"In the kitchen and the barn," Melanie added with a little giggle.

A smile twitched at Emily's lips, but she suppressed it. These women felt like the sisters she'd never had, the family she'd always wanted. So she had to be honest with them. "Just the kitchen..." Well, partially honest, she didn't add that they'd kissed first in her bedroom. That sounded much more intimate than it had been.

"So what did we just interrupt?" Taye asked.

Emily sighed and slowed her walking until Miller and Ian were far enough ahead of them not to overhear. Little Jake, with his shorter legs, trailed behind them, but whatever he overheard he wouldn't repeat.

Unlike Emily.

She shared with them the conversation

she'd overheard, her voice cracking as she remembered the pained faces of both the brothers.

"That sucks," Taye said.

Emily nodded. "Yeah…"

"Sorry that you know that," Taye said. "That you've been through that too."

Emily sighed. "I know what it feels like to have family not be there for you, to abandon you when you need them most."

Tears pooled in Melanie's dark eyes. Maybe she was emotional because she was pregnant, or maybe she was thinking of how her husband had abandoned her when she obviously needed him most.

Emily slid her arm around the other woman's expanding waist and gave her a side hug. "We're here for you," she said. "We're your family."

Melanie nodded, and one of her tears slipped free of her thick lashes to trail down her cheek.

Taye drew in what sounded like a shaky breath of her own and said, "Sometimes it's better if they leave you alone than if they try to do something they don't want to do. Then they just resent you."

For the first time, Emily wondered about

Taye's background. The cook was always so happy and upbeat that Emily figured she'd had an idyllic childhood. But now she knew that some people were just very good at hiding the depths of their feelings...like Ben.

She couldn't believe now that she'd once thought him shallow and incapable of caring about anyone else. She suspected now that he cared too much.

And that she was beginning to care too much about him...

Melanie wiped away that errant tear and squared her shoulders. "That's true," she said. "That's why they should stop trying to get Dusty to come home. If they force him, he'll only resent them for it—if they make him give up something he loves."

Now Emily wondered about her other friend. How was it that Melanie, who'd never been to Willow Creek until she'd been hired as Miller's physical therapist, knew Dusty so well?

Dusty had already been gone when she'd arrived, so they'd never met.

Unless...

She shook her head. No. It wasn't possible. Surely, Melanie would have said something by now. Dusty couldn't be Melanie's mysterious husband. From how she remembered him from high school, Dusty Haven had been even more unlikely to ever get married than Ben was.

Or maybe not…

He had obviously forgiven their mother's abandonment enough to seek her out and have a relationship with her. Ben hadn't even known where she was.

He clearly wanted nothing to do with her. And was it because of her that he wanted nothing to do with marriage? That he was unable to trust any other woman with his heart?

Emily understood not being able to trust anyone. She'd had too many people let her down to easily trust anyone with her own heart. She didn't want to fall in love or get attached and not have her feelings reciprocated. But how much longer could she fight the feelings she was developing for him?

Could she last until Sunday, when Jake and Katie returned from their honeymoon?

BEN WASN'T WORRIED about staying at the ranch—not anymore. He'd rediscovered his love for it, and his love for both the land and the boys was helping him overcome some of the grief he'd felt over losing Dale and Jenny.

He wasn't worried about lasting at the ranch. He was worried about protecting his heart…from Emily. Instead of being disappointed that his nephews, Melanie and Taye had interrupted them moments ago, he'd been relieved.

After that call with Dusty, he was feeling vulnerable—more vulnerable than he could remember feeling in a long while. And Emily had been there, comforting him, understanding him…

Like at dinner the night before, he'd felt so connected to her, as if they hadn't even had to talk to know what the other was thinking and feeling.

Did she know that he was beginning to fall for her?

Caleb obviously did because the minute the others left the barn, he asked, "When are you going to marry Miss Trent?"

Ben felt like Midnight had kicked him as he stammered, "Why—why would you ask that?"

Caleb stopped at Midnight's door and turned to look at Ben—kind of like he was an idiot. That opinion was in his voice when he replied, "You keep kissing, like Daddy Jake kept kissing Mommy, so you have to get married like they're married now."

If Ben had married every woman he'd kissed...

He would have been married too many times. Maybe Emily was right. Maybe he hadn't been as careful with the hearts of the women he'd dated as he thought. Even though he'd told them that he wasn't interested in anything long-term, maybe he'd unintentionally misled them. He felt a twinge of regret over that.

"So when are you going to propose to her?" Caleb persisted.

Ben peered down at the kid holding that bunch of carrots that felt like the proverbial shotgun to Ben, like the kid was trying to force him to the altar. "Are you working for Sadie?" he asked.

"Sadie?" Caleb's brow furrowed beneath that lock of blond hair that always fell into his eyes, but then he nodded. "Yeah, I'm working for Grandma."

Ben tensed at the kid's honesty. He'd just been joking. "You are?"

Caleb nodded. "Yeah, she pays me in cookies for walking Feisty for her."

Ben released a shaky breath. "Oh..."

"You should wait until Mommy and Daddy Jake get back from their honeymoon to get married," Caleb said. "They will want to be there. Can I be your best man too?"

Ben's head was whirling. "Slow down," he murmured.

"And when you marry Miss Trent, you can both stay at the ranch like Mommy and I are going to, now that she married Daddy Jake."

So that's what this is all about.

Now at least Ben understood where the boy was coming from, why he wanted him to marry Emily. And now, he had to tell him. "I can't move out to the ranch, Caleb. My job is in town." His job was the town. But it wasn't his whole life anymore—he couldn't let it be. "But I'll come out to visit a lot," he promised. "I'll still take you riding and play video games with you. We'll even have sleepovers. I'll stay at the ranch sometimes, and you and the boys can come stay at my condo sometimes."

Maybe then it wouldn't feel as sterile as it had begun to seem to Ben. Maybe then, with kids in it, it would feel like a home.

"Sleepovers will be fun," Caleb said. "But Miss Trent needs to live here at the ranch, to teach us and take care of Little Jake. She can't leave. So you can't marry her."

He should have been relieved that the little boy had stopped pressuring marriage. But instead, Ben felt a flash of disappointment. Not that he wanted to get married…

He was too busy with all the projects he wanted to accomplish in Willow Creek to even think about dating let alone getting married. And if he and Emily dated and it didn't work out… He couldn't do anything that would risk Emily's relationship with the boys. He didn't want them to feel like he'd felt when his mother had left, like he'd done something wrong or that he was unlovable. He felt that way again now, after learning that his mother knew about Dale's death and hadn't come back, hadn't cared enough about any of them to pay her respects and offer comfort. And he hadn't thought she could even hurt him anymore.

He'd thought only Emily, and his growing feelings for her, could hurt him. And he didn't want to let her close enough to do that. It was bad enough that she could hurt the boys.

And yet she had a job and a life in Willow Creek that she'd overcome some tough circumstances to build. Would she give that up for his nephews? Or would she break their hearts like his mother had broken his and his brothers' hearts when she'd returned to the life she'd loved: the rodeo?

Ben had to help Caleb see reality. "What if Miss Trent has to go back to her job in town?"

Caleb sucked in a breath like Midnight had kicked him in the stomach. "What? She can't!" Tears pooled in his bright blue eyes. "She can't leave!"

Ben heard the panic and reached out to squeeze the little boy's shoulder. "I'm not saying that she is…" But he couldn't promise that she was staying, though he knew beyond a doubt that Ben couldn't be the reason she left. He didn't want his nephews to resent him…like he resented his mother. "But… you're moving on to the next grade. Won't you need a new teacher?"

He shook his head. "No, she taught Miller too and he's two grades ahead of me. She can keep teaching me and Ian here at the ranch and taking care of Little Jake…as long as she stays. So you better stop kissing Miss Trent," Caleb told him sternly.

Ben sighed. "You're right. I better stop." But he suspected it was already too late for him. He'd already fallen for her.

CHAPTER TWENTY-ONE

EMILY FOUND IT hard to leave the ranch on Friday night, and not just because Little Jake kept clinging to her. Taye and Melanie distracted the boys with cookies and the promise of a video-game marathon, and Taye peeled Little Jake off her so she could leave.

Still, she hesitated before walking out to her car and driving away from Ranch Haven. Maybe it would have been easier if Ben had been there, if he'd been part of the video-game marathon. But he'd left earlier that afternoon to attend to some business at city hall.

Maybe he'd given up on the idea of getting his grandmother together with Old Man Lemmon. Emily hadn't had a chance to talk to him since that day—a couple of days before—when she'd overheard his and Baker's conversation with Dusty. She hadn't had a chance to bring up her concerns about Ian and the other boys with him. Maybe Ben had been embarrassed that she'd seen his pain and vulnerability, because she'd seen very little of him since that day. He'd been spending more time out in the fields and pastures with Baker…but then the ranch-foremen candidates had left, leaving more work than Baker probably could've handled without help.

She would wait to talk to Jake and Katie about the boys. The newlyweds were returning in just a couple days. A couple days before Ben would move back to town… She couldn't even consider doing that herself yet, but she might have to…depending on what she learned during her dinner with her co-workers.

Tears stung her eyes, but she blinked them away to focus on the road in front of her. It was good that she had, because she noticed a car speeding toward her, swerving slightly over the double yellow lines. She jerked the wheel and tooted her horn, and the vehicle pulled back in its lane. As she passed it, she recognized the deputy mayor's Cadillac.

Why was he in such a hurry? And where was he headed?

Toward the ranch?

To Sadie?

Maybe Ben's plan was working after all.

Ben…

Every thought she had seemed to lead back to him. She wasn't ready yet to acknowledge her feelings for him. Because every time she started to admit to them, she heard his voice in his head telling his grandmother how he was never going to fall in love and marry. After learning more about his mother, she understood why.

No. It was better to focus on the boys than Ben. One of the people she was meeting up with tonight was the school psychologist. Beth Lancaster might have some insight into how Emily could help the boys even more. She'd been at the school a long time and had counseled many troubled kids. Emily knew because she'd once been one of them.

Maybe Ben should have talked to Mrs. Lancaster too, all those years ago, about his father's death and his mother's abandonment. As Emily neared town, she was surprised to find it so busy. More businesses had opened up.

A brewery.

More boutiques.

An art gallery…

She should have been coming to town more often; it might have made it easier for the boys when she eventually left the ranch. And she would have to leave eventually. She'd asked this group of friends to meet her because they all worked at the school with her. They all knew if Mr. Kellerman would be willing to give her just a little more time off before replacing her. That was really all she felt like she needed.

Miller's leg was recovering well. He would be able to come back to school in September. And Ian and Caleb would both be advancing to first grade. So Little Jake was really the only one who still needed her.

Nobody else did. Certainly not Ben. But she was beginning to worry that she needed him. She shook her head to clear him from her mind and focused on finding a spot to park. As busy as downtown was now, she couldn't find one anywhere near the café. So she parked two streets over and had to hurry back to Main Street.

She was late, so her friends were already seated. When she pushed open the door to the café, George, the fourth-grade teacher, stood up and waved wildly at her from a table in the back of the long space. She smiled at him and waved back before winding around the people waiting to be seated. As she walked through the crowded restaurant, she noticed a couple in one of the dimly lit booths.

The man wore a dark suit that looked tailor-made for him as it clung to his broad shoulders and molded against his long, lean torso. He'd taken off his black cowboy hat; it sat next to him on the vinyl seat of the booth.

The woman was smiling widely at him, clearly charmed by whatever he was saying. But then Emily knew how charming he could be.

She ducked her head down and hurried past the booth where Ben was sitting with Maggie Standish.

He was already mayor. So what was his reason for meeting with the beautiful political advisor? The last time she'd talked to Maggie, the woman had been dating someone else—someone who could commit to a relationship. Unlike Ben, whom she used to date…

Ben, by his own admission, was never going to fall in love. But despite knowing that about him, Emily had fallen for him, and she felt now as if the wind had been knocked out of her. She arrived at the table in the back with her lungs burning, feeling like she'd run a marathon, feeling like she was about to pass out from the pain gripping her.

Even though she'd known better…

Even though she'd known it would lead to nothing but pain…

She had fallen hopelessly in love with Ben Haven.

BEN HAD WANTED to meet with the political advisor alone, so that he could have her add questions to the poll that he didn't want Lem to know. Like how the voters might feel if he conducted some of the city business remotely, from the ranch.

Suspecting, especially after today, that Lem was working for his grandmother, he'd asked Maggie Standish to have dinner with him. Lem had tried to invite himself along, but Ben had pulled him aside and insinuated that he was romantically interested in the political advisor and wanted to be alone with her.

Let Lem share that with Sadie…

From the look on Lem's face when Ben had said that, it was clear that the deputy mayor hadn't noticed the big ring Maggie was wearing on her left hand. He chuckled at the thought of his grandmother's panic over her plan falling apart. Unfortunately, he suspected that Sadie would have the last laugh on him.

"Congratulations on your engagement," Ben said again. "I'm so happy for you."

"I am very happy *now*," Maggie said.

Something about her tone made Ben lean a little closer. "Now?"

Maggie's pretty face flushed, and she sighed. "I probably wouldn't be telling you this if I hadn't just seen Emily Trent rushing through here…"

He tensed. "Emily?"

How had he missed her? This must be where she was meeting her friends for dinner.

He would have looked around for her, but it was clear that Maggie was upset and deserved his full attention.

"Yes, poor Emily," Maggie said.

Ben flinched and murmured, "She hates that…" She was too proud to be pitied and too successful as well.

"Oh, I don't mean like that…" Maggie said. "Not like how kids treated her in school, like she was a charity case."

He felt a tightening in his chest and considered cutting the meeting short. Maybe he didn't need those polls. Maybe he didn't need to get elected again. Maybe he just needed

Emily. "She's the one being charitable now," he said. "She's been helping out with my nephews at the ranch."

Maggie smiled and nodded. "Did she tell you?"

"Tell me what?" he asked.

"How I cried all over her after we broke up?"

Maggie seemed to be aiming for light self-deprecation, but Ben flinched again... for another reason. "Broke up?" he asked. He couldn't remember them ever really being together. "We went out a few times to talk about the election..."

Had there been more? Something he'd forgotten?

"Oh, this is embarrassing," Maggie said, and she pressed her hand to her face, which was undoubtedly hot from how red it was. "I really shouldn't have brought it up."

Ben shook his head. "No, I'm glad you did. I know Emily has this opinion of me as being some kind of heartbreaker, but I really never intended to hurt anyone. I'm sorry if I hurt you..."

Maggie nodded with what looked genuine appreciation, though a touch of embarrassment lingered. "I know you made it clear in the beginning that you were going to stay single. That the voters had to know that about you…"

That had been his intention, but now it sounded like an empty life.

"I guess I took that as some kind of challenge," Maggie said. "Just like the girls back in high school did."

Now Ben's face burned with embarrassment. "A challenge?"

"Yeah, your brother Jake was in love with Katie, and Dale was in love with Jenny. So everybody thought you would surely fall in love too—like your brothers."

"Dusty and Baker weren't in love."

"They didn't seem as mature as you three," Maggie said good-naturedly.

He smiled. "They still aren't." And they weren't teenagers anymore. Neither was he. "I really wasn't that mature back then," he admitted. "I was pretty self-involved."

"You were focused," Maggie said. "You knew even then that you wanted to be the mayor. And nobody doubted that you would be. You won student council positions every year in high school." She sighed again. "I guess we should have all realized then that you were going to stick to your other goal too, that one to stay single."

He'd always been vocal about that as well. "I was surprised when Emily told me that I broke hearts in high school."

She smiled. "You really didn't know?"

He shook his head. "Like I told you, I was self-involved." Emily had pointed out that to him. She'd taught him so much about himself. She'd opened up his heart.

"Where is Emily?" he asked.

"She headed toward a table in the back. Looks like all teachers. They've probably started planning for the new school year. When I once told Emily I was jealous about her having summers off, she laughed and assured me that they actually work quite a bit over the summer."

Was that what she was doing? Working?

She hadn't told him she'd called Mr. Kellerman back.

But then he'd been avoiding her since she'd witnessed his emotional reaction to learning that his mother knew about Dale and Jenny's deaths and still hadn't come back to Willow Creek—not even for their funeral.

That knowledge had affected him so much the last few days. Had his mind racing with thoughts about Emily now. But assuming that Emily had decided to return to school was as unfair as when she'd kept thinking the worst of him. And yet, with Darlene on his mind so much, he couldn't get over this feeling that he was about to be betrayed, that he and the boys would be left behind.

No. Emily wasn't family to the boys. She hadn't agreed to anything beyond finishing out the last school year with them. So even if she had decided to go back to her job and her life, she wasn't betraying anyone. Still, he felt like someone had plunged a knife into his heart. And he realized why he was reacting this way—because despite all his proclamations that he was never going to fall in love, he had.

THE DOORBELL WASN'T just ringing now—it was incessantly buzzing like someone had stuck their finger on it and couldn't get it off. Through the racket, Feisty kept yapping and running around…

Everyone was upstairs in the playroom, so they were spared. Sadie was not. She swallowed a curse as she headed through the foyer and jerked open the door. "What do you want?"

"You!" Lem said, his face flushed as he pointed a finger up at her.

Her heart slammed against her ribs. "What are you—"

"You screwed up," he said, using that pointing finger, which was slightly bent, to punctuate his statement. Maybe he had arthritis, as she did, or maybe it was all twisted up because he'd been pressing it so hard against the doorbell just now. He was wearing a suit again, but this one didn't look like he'd slept in it. Maybe Ben had taken Lem to his tailor when he'd taken the deputy shopping. "All your talk about polls," Lem continued, "about making Ben think that he needed to be married to get reelected…"

She smiled over the genius of her plan. She knew how much being mayor meant to Ben, how much he'd always wanted it.

"He took the polling girl out on a date," Lem continued.

And Sadie's breath caught. "What? He's on a date?"

Lem nodded. "Yes, woman. You screwed up."

Had she? No. No. She could fix this. "Where did they go?" she asked.

"The café."

Someone gasped, and Sadie whirled around to see Taye, Melanie and the kids standing behind her. They must have heard that ringing doorbell and the barking Chihuahua after all.

"Look what you did now," she murmured to Lem.

"Emily is meeting her friends at the café," Melanie said. "If she sees Ben on a date, she's going to be heartbroken."

Sadie pressed a hand against her chest. Emily wasn't the only one who was going to be heartbroken. "I can't believe he's done this," she said. But she should have known that he would make it the hardest for her since he was the most like her.

"Uncle Ben said he can't marry Miss Trent," Caleb said. "He said he has to live in town, and we don't want Miss Trent to leave the ranch."

No. *She* had done this…

Her grand plan was falling apart now because she hadn't made her intentions clear from the start. She'd wanted to manipulate her grandsons, but in doing so, she risked breaking the hearts of her great-grandsons.

"Miss Trent can't stay at the ranch forever," she told Caleb. Like she should have weeks ago…

She'd just been hoping that the women she'd hired would fall in love with the ranch and with her grandsons.

"She's a teacher," she said. "She'll probably want to go back to the school to teach."

"She can keep teaching us here," Caleb said. "Like she's been teaching Miller even though he's grades ahead of me and Ian."

"*I* want go back to school," Miller said. "I want to see my friends. I don't want to hang out in that playroom all day every day."

"School is fun," Ian said. "We have the big playground with the tall slide and the merry-go-round and the swings. And even if it's raining, we can play in the gym."

"Yeah, school is fun…" Caleb nodded, as if he was considering this for the first time. "So I guess Uncle Ben can be with Miss Trent after all."

But was it too late? Had he already blown it by taking another woman out on a date?

Emily already hadn't trusted him because of his reputation—one Sadie hadn't thought he'd earned. But now she wondered…

Was her grandson a heartbreaker?

Was he breaking Emily's heart right now?

CHAPTER TWENTY-TWO

EMILY'S HEART WAS BREAKING. The pain was so intense that she couldn't focus on her friends. She couldn't ask Beth Lancaster about the boys. She couldn't even think about food with the way her stomach was churning. It wasn't with jealousy—she wasn't jealous. She didn't think Ben was actually on a date. What had her so upset was the realization that she wanted him to be on a date...with *her*. She loved him. She loved him like she'd loved her mother. And like she'd loved her family—all those people who'd let her down. And she was so scared that he was going to let her down, that he was going to hurt her.

"Excuse me," she said, and she jumped up from the table to rush into the bathroom. Fortunately, she was alone. So she grabbed some folded paper towels and ran cold water over them before pressing them to her hot face.

The door creaked open, and a woman

asked, "If those are cold, can you spare one? I just made a fool of myself."

Maggie Standish…

Emily emitted a soft groan and lowered the paper towel from her face. "Hey, Maggie…"

"Hi, Emily," the woman greeted her. "I saw you walk past the booth I was at with Ben. I wish you would have stopped. You might have saved me from embarrassing myself."

Emily hadn't been envious, but now it nagged at her a bit. "I thought you were seeing someone," she said. And that Ben was interested in Emily…

"We're not on a date," Maggie assured her. "We're just talking about polls."

"But the election is over."

"He wanted to ask some questions to start getting ready for the next one, but he didn't get the chance before I made that stupid confession to him."

"What confession?" Emily asked.

Maggie sighed. "You're going to laugh. I admitted to crying all over you about how I misinterpreted the couple of dates we'd been on as a relationship. Then I made it even worse when I told him how much of a challenge he was to all us girls in high school. How his saying he was never going to fall in love just made us more determined. We wanted to make him fall for us like his brother Jake fell for Katie and Dale for Jenny…"

"What?" Emily asked.

Maggie nodded. "That's right. You weren't interested in him. You didn't chase after him like the rest of us did."

"No…"

"You were always the smart one," Maggie said. "He stayed true to his word. He never fell in love." She lifted her left hand then and nearly shoved it in Emily's face. "Look. I did. I'm engaged."

Emily's mind was reeling so much that she couldn't even congratulate the woman. "What…?"

"I haven't seen you in forever," Maggie said, beaming, "or I would have told you. But I know you've been busy out at the ranch taking care of Dale and Jenny's kids."

Emily nodded.

"They're probably going to be pretty devastated that you're going back to school soon."

"What?" Emily asked.

Maggie's brow creased. "That's what Ben and I figured when we saw you with all the other teachers, that you've started planning for the next school year."

"Ben thought that?" she asked, anxiety forming a knot in her stomach.

Maggie nodded. "Yeah, I don't think he was too happy about it. He cut our meeting short."

"He left?" Emily asked. A wave of panic swept through her that he would think she'd just desert the boys without any notice.

"He was waiting for the waiter to bring the check first, but yeah, he's probably gone now."

Emily shoved past the other woman and pulled open the restroom door. The booth where Ben had been sitting with Maggie was empty but for a wad of cash and the dirty dishes.

He must have just gotten up, though, because Emily caught a glimpse of his broad back as he walked out the front door. Then she did what she'd sworn she would never do.

She chased after Ben Haven.

BEN NEEDED AIR. The realization of how hard he'd fallen for Emily had taken the breath from his lungs. He'd suddenly felt so hot and panicky that he'd needed to get out of the café. He'd needed a minute to compose himself and to think…

Once the waiter had finally brought the check, Ben had tossed down a wad of money and hurried outside. He was just crossing the street when somebody yelled, "Ben!"

And he froze at the sound of Emily's voice. He wasn't sure if he could face her right now and not declare his love for her. But that wouldn't be fair to her, not when he had no idea how they could make a relationship work. He was needed in town, and he didn't want to be the one to take her away from his nephews and the ranch...if she even returned his feelings at all. She'd been so determined to not trust him. And maybe she shouldn't. He was still screwed up over his mother abandoning them—the last few days proved that. He loved Emily, but what if the only heart he had to offer her was a broken one? She deserved more. She deserved every happiness.

"Ben!" Emily yelled louder, with more urgency. And then her small hands gripped his arm and pulled him back...just as a vehicle swerved around him.

He started shaking now—over nearly being struck—and with the emotions that overwhelmed him. He might not have been the only one who would have been hit. "Emily, what are you doing?"

"What are *you* doing, running out into the street?" she asked.

Panic pressed on his lungs, on his heart, as he thought back to that time when his mother had taken off, leaving only a note behind to explain why she'd had to go. "Are you meeting with those other teachers because you're going back to school? Weren't you going to talk to us about it first? Or were you going to do what my mother did and just take off?"

She inhaled sharply, clearly offended. "I would hope you know me well enough to know I wouldn't do that…"

Lights blinded him for a moment as another vehicle headed toward them. He grabbed her arm and pulled her out of the street and onto the sidewalk. He shook his head. "I'm sorry. I know I'm not being fair…"

She sighed. "Did you just jump to conclusions like I used to about you?"

"Used to?" he asked. "You didn't when you saw me with Maggie?"

She shook her head, and when she met his gaze, he saw only concern in them, not accusation. "Not this time. I know now how wrong I was to always think the worst of you."

He shrugged. "I don't know if you're wrong. I was self-involved, and I am selfish."

"Ben," she said. "Stop being so hard on yourself. You've been wonderful with the boys."

He stared down at her then, at her beautiful face aglow in the streetlamp. "I want to be selfish," he admitted. "I want to ask you to take a chance on me."

She gasped. "What are you talking about?"

"It doesn't matter," he said. "It wouldn't be fair." He looked away from her as he asked, "Have you decided to go back to school?"

She hesitated for a long moment before she sighed again. "I haven't made a decision yet." She gestured back at the diner. "That wasn't just dinner with friends, though."

He groaned. "So you are considering it?"

"I haven't talked to Mr. Kellerman yet," she admitted. "I don't want to get an ultimatum. I don't want to be forced to decide between my job and the boys."

"What would you choose?" he asked. Because he needed to know…

"If the boys still need me, I would choose them every time," she assured him. "I won't do what your mother did to you and your brothers. I would never leave without saying goodbye. I would never hurt them like she hurt you." She stepped closer to him and slid her arms around his waist. "I would never hurt you…"

His breath shuddered out in a ragged sigh. "Oh, Emily…that's why I love you so much."

She stepped back then and stared up at him, surprise shimmering in her eyes along with tears. "You said you were never going to fall in love," she reminded him. "That you were never going to get married."

He snorted over what a fool he'd been. Over how he thought he could fight love…

Or his grandmother.

Sadie Haven really did know best. Maybe because she'd had such a great love of her own.

"I didn't know you when I made that claim," he said softly. "I didn't know how amazing you are. How special, how trust-worthy…"

She snorted. "I sound like Feisty now."

"You are," he agreed. "Fiercely loyal and loving."

She smiled.

And he had to tease her. "And a little bit yappy sometimes."

Instead of being offended, she laughed. "Like when I'm yelling at you for something you didn't do…like making Melanie cry or letting the boys get hurt." Her lips twisted into a grimace. "I've been terrible to you. How could you love me?"

"I don't know when it happened…" he admitted. "Maybe it was when you were yelling at me about those things I didn't do or taking me to task for the things I did do…" He sighed. "You make me a better person." The truth of that hit him. He never wanted to let her go… But he had to.

"You were always a good person, Ben," she said. "I just wouldn't let myself see it."

"I always saw how good you are, how patient you are with Ian's memory lapses, how loving you are with all of them, how you even tackled your nerves over riding to protect them that day we rode around the ranch," he said. "And I'm as crazy about you as my nephews are." And he wasn't sure how he was going to manage without her. "And if it was possible, I would marry you tomorrow. But it's not possible. And I can't hurt them either. And I don't want to hurt you, so I'm not going to ask you to choose."

The tears spilled out of her eyes now and streamed down her face. "And that's why I love you," she said.

CHAPTER TWENTY-THREE

HE LOVED HER. Ben Haven had told her he loved her, but then he'd refused to take a chance on them. And after declaring their love for each other, they'd gotten into their separate vehicles and driven separately back to the ranch.

She'd once accused Ben of being a heartbreaker, but she knew now that he had never intended to hurt anyone. And because he didn't want to hurt anyone now, he wouldn't propose to her. So Emily waited until they'd both parked in the driveway and walked up the porch steps before she dropped to her knees in front of him.

"Emily!" he exclaimed, his hands gripping her shoulders. "Are you all right?"

And she heard it all his voice—the concern, the love. "I've never been better," she realized.

"What are you doing?" he asked.

"I'm doing what you're afraid to do," she said. "I'm asking you to marry me."

"What?" he asked as all the color drained from his face.

"I love you," she said.

He hesitated. "Are you sure?" he asked, his voice gruff with emotion. "My own mother didn't..."

"I felt like nobody loved me either," she reminded him. "I had no idea that you were going through the same things I was, that you'd lost so much, including your ability to trust anyone."

"How can you trust me now?" he wondered.

"I've seen how big your heart is, how much you love your family," she said. "And I want to be part of that family. I want to be your wife."

"I want that too," he said. "But you deserve more, Emily. You deserve someone who can put you first always, like your family should have all those years ago. I'm all wrapped up in town, with my job, and you're here—at the ranch."

"And you care enough about me to put my well-being over yours. To put the boys' needs over yours too," she said. "That's why I want to make a life with you—either here on the ranch or in town or maybe both places. I don't care where we are just as long as we're together."

Ben dropped to his knees then and cupped her face in his hands—hands that trembled against her skin. "I love that after everything you've been through, you're still brave enough to open up your heart, to trust again. And because of you, I can be that brave too. We can do this…" he murmured. "We can figure it out. I can drive back or forth. It doesn't have to be all or nothing."

She shook her head. "It does. It's everything. When we're together, we have everything. Love. Family. Trust. With you, I've found everything I've always wanted. And I'm not letting it go. I'm not letting *you* go."

"I'm not going anywhere," he assured her. "I'm right where I want to be…with the woman I love, the woman I'm going to make my wife."

Her breath escaped in a ragged sigh of relief. "Oh, Ben…" Tears of happiness stung her eyes, followed by a bit of a panic. "We may have to wait a bit and make sure that the boys are going to be okay with more changes in their lives." She would talk to him about counseling for them later.

Tears glistened in Ben's eyes now. "That's why I love you so much," he said. "You are so loving and thoughtful. And I don't care how long it takes for us to figure everything out, I know we're both committed to each other. Forever."

He leaned forward and pressed his mouth against hers, sealing their proposal with a kiss.

HE COULD HAVE kissed her forever—right there on the porch, with both of them on their knees. But then he heard a little voice… "What are they doing?"

"Kissing on the porch," Caleb replied with a sigh.

"Did he say yes?" That voice wasn't little. It was Lem's.

Ben had been so upset from his confrontation in the street with Emily that he'd barely made note of the deputy mayor's Cadillac parked in the driveway. "I said yes," Ben announced loudly. Then he whispered to Emily, "They were spying on us."

She laughed. "I can't say anything about that. I've been doing more than my share of eavesdropping lately."

Ben stood up then and lifted Emily to her

feet, and then into his arms. When the door opened, he carried her over the threshold of the ranch house.

"You're not supposed to do that until after you're married," Caleb said. "That's what Daddy Jake did."

"We are going to get married as soon as we figure out some logistics," Ben promised him. "Are you guys going to be okay with that—with sharing Miss Trent with me?"

Four little heads bobbed yes.

And Caleb giggled. "She'll be Mrs. Haven, though."

Ben gazed down at the woman in his arms, his heart full of love for her. For his whole family. Instead of letting his mother's desertion hurt him, he felt only pity for her now, pity for all she was missing. All this love... "Yes, Miss Trent will be Mrs. Haven." Unlike Jake and Katie, they would probably have to wait more than a couple days. They would have to wait until the boys were truly emotionally ready to share Emily.

"What are logistics?" Caleb asked.

"Details," Ben explained.

"Well, I've already figured out the cake," Taye said.

"And we've got the dresses," Melanie said.

"Can we wait until Mommy and Daddy Jake get home?" Caleb asked.

Ben nodded. "Yes, we'll wait for them and to figure out some other things…" Like where they were going to live and when Emily was going to go back to work…

He knew now that they would be making their decisions together—for the future they were going to share. But they both knew they had more than just the two of them to consider. The boys didn't seem concerned about themselves, though. They seemed excited.

"We'll go call them now, and tell them to come home early," Caleb offered.

Ben closed his eyes as he imagined how that call would go. Lips pressed against his cheek that he knew weren't Emily's silky ones. He lifted his lids to give his grandmother the side-eye.

"You're welcome," she told him with a smug smile.

Lem grinned. "Told you, son. What Sadie March Haven wants…"

"It's what I want too," Ben acknowledged. He'd been afraid of it, afraid to love as hard as Sadie had loved the original Big Jake Haven. But now that he'd found the woman he loved, the woman he could trust with his heart, it wasn't scary at all. It was right.

It was fate.

"YOU HAVE TO come home now!" Caleb said when Jake answered his cell. He felt a flash of alarm.

And Katie pressed a hand to her heart. "What happened? Did someone get hurt?"

"Someone got engaged!" Taye announced. The boys must have been using her cell again, but Jake could see only Caleb's face on the screen.

Jake laughed. "Sadie got Ben to propose?"

"No," Melanie chimed in. "Emily proposed to him."

Katie laughed now. "No way."

"That's why you gotta come home," Caleb said. "Uncle Ben and Miss Trent are going to get married when you get back."

"Oh…" Katie murmured.

"You don't have to hurry," Taye said. "They're not getting married right away."

Jake was shocked that his brother was even engaged, but that hadn't been his only recent shock.

Katie pressed a hand to her stomach.

And Jake's heart flipped even though she'd

already told him that morning, after she'd taken the test. He'd been surprised it would work so soon, but it had come back positive. They were going to have a baby.

"We'll be back on Sunday," Jake reminded Caleb. "That's less than two days away…"

"We'll see you soon," Katie promised.

"Okay, guys," Taye said. "Let them enjoy the last of their honeymoon."

Once the phone screen went black, Jake turned to his glowing bride. She was shaking her head. "Wow…"

Jake nodded. "Baker better go into hiding. Sadie's going to be unstoppable now."

"What about Dusty?" Katie asked.

Jake grinned. "He might be what stops the meddler. He's always sworn he was never getting married. So he could be her Mount Everest."

"We'll see how things turn out soon enough," Katie replied. "We'll be home soon."

Jake had loved his honeymoon, but he was ready to go home. To the ranch and to his growing family…

He'd once worried about having too many responsibilities. But now, he knew he could handle anything with Katie and the rest of his family.

And they were all family. His nephews, his stepson, Sadie, his brothers and the women Grandma had hired to help with the boys.

He had no doubt that by the time his grandmother was through, every one of them would officially be family.

* * * * *

If you enjoyed
The Cowboy's Unlikely Match,
then be sure to check out

A Rancher's Promise,

the first book in the Bachelor Cowboys series by Lisa Childs.

Available now from Harlequin Heartwarming!

Get 4 FREE REWARDS!

We'll send you 2 FREE Books plus <u>2 FREE Mystery Gifts</u>.

The Charming Checklist — HEATHERLY BELL

A Rancher's Touch — ALLISON LEIGH

FREE Value Over **$20**

The Wrong Cowboy

Both the **Harlequin® Special Edition** and **Harlequin® Heartwarming™** series feature compelling novels filled with stories of love and strength where the bonds of friendship, family and community unite.

COUNTRY LEGACY COLLECTION

Get 4 FREE REWARDS!

We'll send you 2 FREE Books plus 2 FREE Mystery Gifts.

FREE
Value Over
$20

Both the **Romance** and **Suspense** collections feature compelling novels written by many of today's bestselling authors.

#419 RECLAIMING THE RANCHER'S SON
Jade Valley, Wyoming • by Trish Milburn

Rancher Evan Olsen lost everything, including his son, in his divorce. Now he wants to be left alone. But when a snowstorm traps him with cheerful Maya Pine, he might discover she's just what he needs.

#420 HILL COUNTRY PROMISE
Truly Texas • by Kit Hawthorne

Eliana Ramirez is optimistic but unlucky in love. So is her best friend, Luke Mahan. Single and turning twenty-seven, they follow through on a marriage pact. Could their friendship be the perfect foundation for true love?

#421 THE MAYOR'S BABY SURPRISE
Butterfly Harbor Stories • by Anna J. Stewart

Mayor Gil Hamilton gets the surprise of his life...twice. When a baby is left at his door and when his political opponent, Leah Ellis, jumps in to help! Can a man driven by duty learn to value family above all?

#422 HER VETERINARIAN HERO
Little Lake Roseley • by Elizabeth Mowers

Veterinarian Tyler Elderman has all the companionship he needs in his German shepherd, Ranger. But when he meets widow Olivia Howard and her son, Micah, this closed-off vet might discover room in his heart for family.

HWCNM0322